ALSO BY KIMBERLY MULLINS:

Notebook Mysteries ~ Emma (Book 1)

Notebook Mysteries ~ Decisions and Possibilities (Book 2)

Notebook Mysteries ~ Changes and Challenges (Book 3)

Notebook Mysteries ~ Unexpected Outcomes (Book 4)

Notebook Mysteries ~ Haunted Christmas (a novella)

Notebook Mysteries ~ Suspicions (Book 5)

Notebook Mysteries ~ Parisian Intrigue (Book 6)

Notebook Mysteries ~ A Party to Remember (a Novella)

Notebook Mysteries ~ Art of Deception (Book 7)

Stand alones:

Divided Lives (K.R. Mullins)

1897-A Mark Sutherland Adventure

Notebook Mysteries

Notebook Mysteries

Art of
Deception

KIMBERLY MULLINS

NOTEBOOK MYSTERIES ~ ART OF DECEPTION

Notebook Mysteries Series

Copyright © JKJ books, LLC 2024

First edition: August 2024

All rights reserved.

No part of this book may be reproduced in any form or by any electronic or mechanical means, including information storage and retrieval systems, without written permission from the author, except for the use of brief quotations in a book review.

Mailing address for JKJ books, LLC; 17350 State Highway 249, STE 220 #3515 Houston, Texas 77064

Library of Congress Control Number: 2024911040

ISBN (paperback): 979-8-218-43144–0

ISBN (hardback): 979-8-9886080-9-7

ISBN (ebook): 979-8-988608-0-8-0

This is a work of fiction. It is based on historical events within Chicago during the time period of the 1880-90's.

Edited by Kaitlyn Johnson, Strictly Textual

Cover Art by Miblart

To Jonathan who brings humor into everything. To Joshua who helps me with his ever reaching knowledge. And to Claudia, who is a long way away but who I always feel is close by.

PROLOGUE

Ahhhh!

The man's arms flailed about as he tried to grasp the air around him. It was no use; he plummeted more than 200 feet into the rushing water.

The other man stepped back and closed the door of the still moving train.

One down, he thought.

CHAPTER 1

eggy and Tony Marella, at their home

"Peggy, you need to rest," Tony said as he watched his heavily pregnant wife move back and forth in front of the fireplace.

"No, I can't! Where is he?" She stopped and put her hand on her belly to rub the active baby.

He continued to keep his voice low and calm. "You saw his apartment. It's vacated; he's gone."

"But why? He was finally settled here. Are you sure we were in the right place?" she asked, grasping at straws.

"Yes," he said firmly. "We've been there before."

"What if someone took him?" Peggy asked as she started to pace again.

"With all of his things?" murmured Tony.

She ignored that comment and stopped suddenly. "Emma!"

"What about her?" asked Tony with a frown.

"She's an investigator; she can find him."

Tony was an off and on again member of an investigation

team that Emma Evans led. "I'm not sure…" He hesitated. Emma would help, there was no question, but he didn't want to drag her into this potentially complicated mess. Peggy's brother had just come back into their lives. He could tell when he met the man that there was something about him that he didn't trust. Tony hadn't mentioned these worries to Peggy. She'd been so excited when her brother had suddenly appeared back in their lives.

"I am," she said firmly. "Please contact her." She moved to sit beside him. Taking his hand, she pulled it to her belly and said, "For me? For us?"

He felt the baby under their clasped hands. He'd do anything to help calm her nerves. "Fine. I'll go see her in the morning."

"Good," she said and laid her head on his shoulder.

This time, the adventure will start with us, thought Tony.

CHAPTER 2

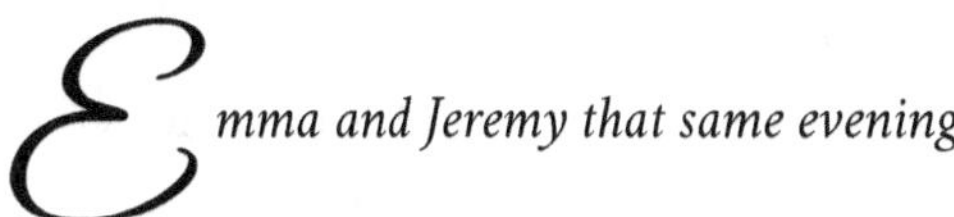

mma and Jeremy that same evening

Emma sat next to Jeremy on the settee in the sitting room, reading. It was late and the other family members had retired to their beds.

They heard a knock at the door.

"Who could that be?" asked Jeremy as he started to stand.

Emma shrugged. "Let's find out." She stood and walked to the door with Jeremy coming up close behind her.

Emma opened the door and blinked when she saw who stood there. "Tony! What're you doing here? Is Peggy okay?"

"Emma, give the man a minute," Jeremy said and waved to Tony. "Come in."

"Thanks," Tony said gratefully as he stepped into the foyer and pulled the door shut behind him. "Can we go to the sitting room?" he asked.

They nodded and the three made their way there. Jeremy

and Emma sat back in the settee. Tony moved and sat in a seat across from them.

"Peggy's the reason I'm here," Tony began. He saw their faces mirror concern and hastened to assure them. "The baby's fine and Peggy's fine, too. Well, physically anyway. I'd planned to come by tomorrow morning, but I received a note." He reached into his pocket and pulled out an envelope.

"May we read it?" Emma asked.

He nodded and handed it to her. Jeremy moved closer to read it over her shoulder.

"Theodore, Peggy calls... called him Teddy. He is... was Peggy's brother," explained Tony.

"He's dead," Jeremy stated as he looked up from the telegram.

"Trains," murmured Emma.

"Guess he didn't tuck and roll," Jeremy said drolly. He referenced Emma's past experiences fleeing from bad guys by jumping off various trains.

"Hmm," said Emma.

"Emma," called a child's voice from the stairway.

Tony turned toward the stairway and saw a girl about thirteen years old standing there. Emma put down the telegram and ran over to her. With a hand placed on her head, she asked the girl, "Hen, what is it baby? Did something wake you up?"

Henrietta put her arms around Emma's waist, burying her face, and replied in a muffled voice, "Bad dream."

Emma hugged her close and leaned down to kiss her head. "Would it help if I went back up with you?"

"That and maybe a story?" Hen negotiated.

Emma smiled. "I can work that out." She turned to Jeremy and Tony. "I'll be back," she said to Jeremy. She missed Tony's frown.

Jeremy nodded. "We'll still be here. I hope your dreams are nicer, Hen."

"Me, too!"

Emma took Hen by the hand and headed upstairs with her.

Jeremy sat back down and looked at Tony, who was still staring at the doorway, the frown still in place. "Something you want to talk about, pal?"

Tony pulled his gaze from the doorway and refocused on Jeremy. "No, no. Who was that?"

"Hen? She's our ward."

"Ward?"

"Hen needed help and we, Emma and I, took her in."

"But..." Tony looked up at the stairs where Hen and Emma had gone. "She'd said... I thought..."

Jeremy watched him but didn't comment. He could see his friend was conflicted.

Tony finally shook himself and said, "No, that isn't why I'm here. Will Emma be down soon?"

Jeremy sat back with his arms crossed over his chest. "It shouldn't be long. Hen has the occasional nightmare."

They sat in silence, with Tony glancing frequently at the entrance. Finally, shoes sounded on the stairs and Emma appeared.

"I'm sorry, Tony. We want to hear your story." She took the seat next to Jeremy.

"Hen okay?" Jeremy asked.

"Yes, she fell asleep as soon as I started to read."

Tony stared at Emma until Jeremy prompted him. "Tony. You were saying?"

Emma raised her eyebrow and Jeremy subtly shook his head. That topic could be discussed later. She started again, hoping to get her friend talking, "I didn't know Peggy had family in town." Peggy had been a widow when they met. Tony seemed to be her only family since they were married.

"Teddy moved back recently. We were getting to know him," Tony said as he tried to concentrate on Peggy.

"How long was he here?" inquired Jeremy.

"Maybe six months."

"Teddy has a home here?" Emma asked as she pulled out her notebook and pencil. As she turned to a blank page, she saw that it was filled up from previous cases and she'd need to get a new one. She moved to the desk on the far side of the room and started to pull out notebooks. Each one was full of their prior cases. She dug until she finally found an empty one.

"Yes, we were there earlier tonight."

"Why?" asked Jeremy.

"Dinner."

"Prearranged?" asked Emma and moved back to sit down.

"Yes. We have a standing dinner, the same day each week, since Teddy arrived."

"You didn't receive any notification that he wasn't there?"

"No, we had no idea until we got there."

"What did you find at his apartment?"

"Nothing," Tony replied.

"You weren't able to get in?" Jeremy asked.

"No," he corrected him. "The door was ajar, and we went in. There was nothing left. His art, furniture, clothes, everything. It was all gone. The only thing left were wires that had been used to hang art."

Emma knew that sometimes the clues could be in something minor. "We should go there."

"Agreed," Jeremy said.

"When?" asked Tony, thinking of Peggy.

Emma pursed her lips and glanced toward the stairs. "I don't want to be away if Henrietta needs me tonight."

Tony let out a sigh of relief. "I'm glad you said that. Peggy will want to be there and tomorrow would be easier."

"Does she know about Teddy?" Jeremy asked, holding up the telegram.

"Not yet. She was resting when it arrived. The stress of him disappearing had gotten to her." He dropped his head in his hands. He looked up, his face showing strain. "And now this, I'm not sure how much more she can handle."

Emma thought about her previous interactions with Peggy and spoke up, "Tony, I think she's stronger than you give her credit for."

Her friend nodded but didn't say anything. He stood slowly and moved toward the door. At the entrance to the sitting room, he turned to them. "If she gets some rest tonight, she should be able to meet in the morning."

"We'll meet you at your house in the morning," Emma promised.

"Thank you," he said and looked at her again, then up the stairs. He shook his head and went to the door.

They followed him out. "Tomorrow?" he asked again.

"We'll be there," Jeremy said firmly.

Emma closed the door softly and they heard his feet on the steps outside. Emma turned slowly to Jeremy and said, "What was that about?"

"The murder? Well, I don't know yet. Isn't that why we're investigating?"

"Jeremy…" Her tone held a note of warning.

"Whoa now. I know what you're asking about. Tony didn't know about Hen and us being her guardians."

She frowned. "Why does that matter?"

He shook his head and took her hand in his. "Babe, you know why. You told him you never wanted this type of life. It was the reason you gave for breaking up with him."

"But that was years ago, and we were so young." Emma gripped his hand tightly and asked, "He doesn't regret marrying Peggy?" *And the baby?* she thought to herself.

Jeremy shook his head. "No, I don't think so. I think you were his boyhood dream."

"Should I talk to him?" She glanced at the door, worried for Tony.

"No, I think it's best that we let it go by."

She nodded and walked back into the sitting room to sit on the settee. "This case is a strange one," she commented, drumming her fingers on her lips.

"You said it. Teddy, Peggy's brother who had just moved back to town, goes missing and now has turned up dead."

"Hmm, and apparently died from falling from a train. Other than that?"

"We know almost nothing."

"Except someone out there wanted him dead."

"And did they get what they wanted by killing him?"

"We won't be able to figure that out tonight."

Jeremy looked at his watch and said, "Bed. We have an early morning."

"Yes," she said with a yawn. He stood and offered her his hand. She took it and accompanied him upstairs.

CHAPTER 3

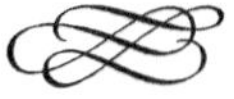

he next morning

Emma pulled on one of her boots and called to Jeremy through the open doorway connecting their rooms. "I need to tell Ethan I won't be in this morning."

"Will he or Mr. Pennington have any issue with you being out?" he asked as he walked back into her room.

"I don't think so. Our current trial is ongoing, and they will be busy with that."

"No other investigations?"

"Not for now. What about you?"

"I'm between cases currently."

"Good."

"Ready?" he asked as he pulled on his jacket.

She pulled on her other boot and quickly fastened it. She stood and grabbed her jacket. "Ready."

"See you on the other side." Jeremy departed and pulled closed the secret door hidden by a bookshelf.

Emma waited a moment inside her room so they both wouldn't exit at the same time. Henrietta had noticed how they seemed to do this simultaneously. Emma and Jeremy wanted to keep their room arrangement a secret from her a little longer. They weren't sure how she might react knowing that they slept together at night and were unmarried.

A knock sounded on her door; she walked toward it and pulled it open. Jeremy was waiting on the other side. He smiled at her and offered his arm. She closed the door behind her and took his arm to accompany him downstairs.

"Morning, Emma, Jeremy," Henrietta said as she hurried past them on the stairs.

"That used to be you," commented Jeremy as they watched the girl bound down the stairs.

"Still is on occasion. I'm not that old."

He laughed as they stepped down into the foyer.

Hen stuck her head out of the dining room. "Well, come on. I'm hungry."

"You're always hungry," Emma stated as she walked over and put her arm around the girl's shoulders.

"I can't help it. I'm a growing girl."

"Did you have any more bad dreams last night?"

"No, it was just the one."

"Good. You can always come to me or Jeremy if you need us."

"I know," Hen said confidently. She'd lived with them for a while now, having joined them around Christmas the previous year.

The trio walked into the dining room. Henrietta walked over to the baby Lottie to kiss her on the head and waved toward Patrick. "Hey," she said as she took her seat and waited for breakfast to begin.

"Hey, Hen," said Patrick. He was a year younger than the 12-year-old Hen and was like her brother.

Emma and Jeremy said good morning to everyone at the table as they sat. Dora and Tim were already at the table with Lottie and Patrick. Ethan was also there talking to Jake. His wife Savannah was still in bed from a late night working at the theatre. Their family home was a boarding house that Dora managed. Though most everyone who lived with them were now considered family and were active members of their investigative team.

The door to the kitchen swung open and Amy and Ethyl entered with trays of breakfast food. Emma and Jeremy moved to the kitchen to retrieve the pitchers and the pastry tray.

The pitcher was set on the table and, as Emma took her seat, she turned to Ethan. "I'll need to be out today." He ran the calendar for the office.

Ethan looked up from his breakfast. "I think that should be fine. I'll notify you if Mr. Pennington has any concerns in court."

"Thanks," Emma said as she reached for biscuits and added two to her plate to start her breakfast.

"Do you have a new case?" asked Dora.

"Maybe." Emma picked up a biscuit and started to add jam and butter to it. "Tony was by last night and his brother-in-law appears to have been murdered."

The group at the table had heard worse and Dora asked, "Did he ask you to investigate the murder?"

"He wants us to look into it," Emma confirmed and bit into her biscuit.

"What'll you do first?" Tim asked.

"Probably go to the brother's apartment," Jeremy added and picked up a piece of bacon.

"Why there? Was he found there?" Dora asked as she broke up a biscuit for Lottie to eat.

"No, it looks like he left the train. Before his stop," Emma said drolly.

Hen was listening closely and spoke up. "Someone threw him off a train?"

Emma smiled slightly and winked at her. "It appears so." Hen picked up clues as fast as Emma.

"Why the apartment?" asked Tim. "What do you expect to find?"

"Funny you should say that. We don't expect to find anything," Jeremy said.

Tim and Dora frowned. "Why?" Tim asked for them.

"Tony said he and Peggy went over and found that he'd disappeared, and all of his belongings were gone."

"Everything?" Dora asked.

"That's what Tony said."

"Then why go?" asked Hen as she put a large forkful of eggs in her mouth.

"Mouth closed, please," Jeremy admonished.

Hen nodded and continued to eat. Emma answered her. "Sometimes, we find clues in the smallest things left behind. I also want to see where he lived and maybe what kind of man he was."

Dora was thinking about Peggy and looked at Tim. "We should take some food over to Peggy and Tony."

"Of course. Once you get organized, we can go over," Tim said.

"Can you hold off on that for a bit?" Emma asked.

"Why?" asked Dora, puzzled. "We always take food to families who have a loss."

"I know. And I still want you to, but let me check a few things out first. I don't want to call any attention to Peggy right now. Especially with her this close to having the baby."

"I guess that makes sense. Let me know when I can go over. I don't want Peggy to think we don't care."

"I will," Emma promised.

Jeremy had finished breakfast and picked up his plate. "Hen, you might go get your things for school," he suggested.

"I will," she said and shoved several pieces of bacon into her mouth. She jumped up to leave and Emma called, "Plate first, please." Hen grinned as she continued to chew and grabbed her plate to take it to the kitchen. Emma and Jeremy followed her with their plates.

Ethyl took the offered plates and Hen ran to the door and said over her shoulder, "I'll meet you downstairs."

"Of course," Jeremy murmured to the closed door.

They heard running feet and followed her through the dining room. Tim called out to the girl, "Slow down, no reason to run." Her pounding feet could be heard as she raced up the stairs.

"Didn't slow her down much," stated Emma as they moved back to the dining room.

"Too much like her guardian," teased Dora as she wiped Lottie's face and lifted her out of her chair to the floor. She maintained a hand on her arm to keep the squirming girl close to her.

"Ha ha," Emma replied, smiling at her sister as she and Jeremy went upstairs to gather their things for the day. They met back downstairs and were putting on their hats while they waited for Hen to appear. She hurried down the stairs toward them. Jeremy asked her the same question he asked her every day. "You got everything?"

She looked down at her bag. "I have everything."

Jeremy turned to Emma. "You got everything?"

Emma looked panicked, turned and ran up the stairs toward her room.

"Slow down, no reason to run," Tim called after her. Hen giggled at this.

They could hear rummaging around upstairs and, after a few

minutes, she came walking back down. "I needed the notebook I started last night," she said at Jeremy's questioning glance.

"Of course, you did."

"What? The last one was filled with notes on the case of The Girl who Knew Too Much and The Vanishing Woman. I had to squeeze in the Christmas Caper in the last two pages."

"I didn't say anything," Jeremy said.

"All right, smart guy. Do you have everything?"

"Yeah, Jeremy. Do you have everything?" Hen asked mockingly.

Jeremy looked panicked and started patting himself down as Hen and Emma giggled at him. He stopped and smiled. "I have everything. Let's go." He held his hand to Hen, and she handed her bag for him to carry. The three of them walked outside.

Now that it was spring, they could escort Hen to school via the trolley and then walk the additional blocks. Transportation had been arranged to move the girl from school to her job at the charity that Emma stewarded. Her safety was important to them; children left alone could be in danger. They could be snatched by anyone. And had been in their previous cases.

Once at the school, Emma kissed her on the cheek. Jeremy leaned down and kissed her, too, and handed her the book bag. "We'll pick you up this evening," he said.

Hen started through the door and turned back to them. "Let me know if you find out who murdered Peggy's brother."

"We will," Emma told her.

"Hold on," Jeremy called to Hen. "Ah, you probably shouldn't mention this to anyone." He didn't want her put into any unnecessary danger.

Hen looked conflicted. Emma walked over to her. "This is something that we'd say is a 'family only' thing. Does that make it better?"

The girl tilted her head and studied Emma. "A family thing? I like that. Okay, I won't mention it." She turned and headed inside.

"Good catch there," Jeremy said to Emma.

"You know, she'll be exposed to our cases and, as intelligent as she is, she'll want to know what we're involved in and probably help as well."

"You're right." He nodded and held out his hand to her. "Ready to start our day?"

"Definitely." She took the offered hand, and they moved toward the road. Jeremy waved for a carriage. "Let's go see Peggy."

"All right." The carriage pulled up and Jeremy helped Emma into it. He gave the driver Tony's address and they headed to Peggy and Tony's home.

"Do you think Tony told her yet?" Emma asked.

"I hope so. I would not like to be there for that conversation."

The carriage moved into an affluent area, where the buildings were made of stacked stone and had tall white columns.

The carriage stopped and the two of them descended to the sidewalk. Jeremy paid the driver and they headed to the front door. Jeremy reached up and knocked on it.

The butler answered the door. "Hello, Mr. Tilden, Miss Evans."

"Carmichael, good to see you," said Jeremy.

He nodded to them formally and stated, "Come in, the family is in the morning room. Follow me, please."

"We need to get one of those," murmured Emma, watching the man.

Jeremy raised an eyebrow. "And what would you do with him?"

She smiled innocently.

Jeremy shook his head. "After you, my dear."

Emma went first as they followed the butler's lead. The morning room was across the foyer through a grand entry;

windows brought bright light into the room. There, they found Peggy and Tony at the table eating breakfast. Tony stood immediately and went to them. "Thank you for coming over so quickly this morning."

"Yes, thank you." Peggy said as she struggled to stand. The baby prevented her from moving quickly.

Tony rushed back over to her. "No darling, stay. There's no need to get up."

She nodded and stopped trying to get to her feet. Instead, she rubbed her cheek on the hand he placed on her shoulder. Emma walked over to Peggy and kissed her on the cheek.

"Please, sit," said Peggy. Emma and Jeremy moved to sit across from them. Tony stayed by Peggy's side.

"Would you like something?" asked Peggy.

"No, thank you, we ate before we left. We're sorry for your loss, Peggy," said Emma and Jeremy nodded.

Tears welled in Peggy's eyes. She picked up her napkin and touched it to her face.

Tony's hand on her shoulder tightened and he suggested, "Why don't we move into the sitting room?" He helped Peggy to her feet and walked with her toward the room, Jeremy and Emma following.

Tony and Peggy sat together on the settee; Jeremy and Emma took two chairs facing them.

Peggy sighed and laid her head onto her husband's shoulder. Emma and Jeremy waited silently while she gathered her composure. Once she calmed down, she looked over at Emma. "Thank you for helping us."

Emma nodded. "Of course."

"Would you be okay with going to Teddy's apartment this morning?" ask Jeremy.

Peggy took a deep breath and sat straighter. "I want to accompany you."

"You're sure?" Tony asked her.

"Yes, I need to do this."

Emma nodded. "Good. May I ask a few questions before we go?"

"Yes."

Emma pulled out her notebook. "What business was Teddy in?"

"I don't know."

Emma frowned. Tony spoke up. "Whenever we asked, he changed the subject to something else."

"Was he successful?" asked Jeremy.

"He appeared to be," Tony replied. "Since he moved back, he lived in a nice place with nice things."

"He always paid for dinner when we were out together," said Peggy.

"You mentioned you haven't been in contact for some time?" Emma asked.

"Not for years, six months ago, he showed up at our door," said Peggy.

"You didn't expect him? "

"I haven't had any letters or any other communication for many years."

"What was your relationship like now?" asked Jeremy.

"It was like he was never gone," Peggy said faintly. "He'd stay after dinner, and we'd be up for hours talking."

Jeremy leaned over to Emma and said, "We should head to his home."

Emma nodded. "I agree." She looked at Peggy and Tony. "Peggy, shall we go?"

The other woman nodded and kept her hand in Tony's as he helped her up. They moved into the foyer to put on their hats in preparation to leave.

Tony motioned to Carmichael. "Is the carriage ready?"

"Yes, sir, it is waiting for you."

"Thank you," Peggy murmured.

They headed out and Emma and Jeremy waited patiently as Tony helped Peggy into the covered carriage. Once she was settled, they joined her. The driver had the address and they started on their way. The location was in the same area as Tony and Peggy's home. The carriage pulled to a stop in front of the Manhattan Building on South Dearborn street. Emma and Jeremy observed the location; the building had been in place since 1888. *Teddy must have had money*, thought Emma.

Peggy confirmed their thoughts when she said, "He owns a floor in this building."

"Owns? Not rents?" asked Emma. *An apartment in that building would've been extravagant, but a whole floor?*

"Owns," Peggy confirmed.

"Well," Tony quantified, "we think he did." He looked at Emma and Jeremy. "We were led to believe he owned it."

Emma continued to study the building's intricate architecture as they got out of the carriage and approached the door. The doorman stood in the entrance and opened the door for them. "Mister and Miss Latimer, I didn't expect you this morning."

Tony said, "We would like to go up to Mr. Latimer's apartment." They started toward the elevator.

He stopped them with a stutter. "Sir, you can't go up, I will need to get the manager's permission."

"Why is that?" asked Peggy with a frown. "We were here last night."

"Yeah, well," he said, putting his hand up to rub his neck, "last night the apartment still belonged to Mr. Latimer."

"And today?" asked Emma.

"Today, a man from out of town, a Mr. Capps, took ownership."

"Who is that?" ask Peggy, bewildered by yet another change.

Tony walked over to the man. "Tom, we just want to see the space, nothing else."

"I don't know," said Tom with a frown.

"Tom, Mr. Latimer died last night, and these are investigators," he said and motioned toward Emma and Jeremy.

His eyes widened and he swallowed. "I am sorry."

Peggy put a handkerchief to her eyes and nodded.

He looked around. "The manager's out, so you have to be quick."

"We will be," promised Tony.

"Go on up," he said and went to call the elevator for them. Once it arrived, the operator let them on. Tom gave him the number and the operator started to protest. He had received the same instructions as Tom: the new owner would be arriving in a few days and no one other than cleaners were allowed up.

"Mr. Latimer passed away," explained Tom.

The operator looked at Peggy and back at Tom and stepped back to allow them in.

"Thank you," said Peggy to Tom and the operator.

They moved onto the elevator and rode silently to the floor.

Once it started up, Peggy spoke. "Oh! We should go back and ask for a key."

"Would you like me to take you back down?" the operator asked.

Jeremy laughed.

Tony smiled. "Don't worry, we have one with us." Peggy frowned but didn't say anything.

They exited the elevator and approached the door. Tony tried it first and found it locked.

"I thought you had a key," Peggy said.

"He meant me," Emma commented. She moved to the door, knelt, and pulled out her lockpick kit. Peggy watched fascinated as Emma inserted a lockpick into the lock and moved it around. After a few seconds, they heard a click and Emma pushed the door open for them.

As she stood, Peggy asked, "How do you know how to do that?"

"A couple of sweet little old ladies showed me that one afternoon while we were having tea," Emma said simply.

"Oh," Peggy said and followed her into the apartment.

Tony and Peggy weren't surprised by the size of it or the missing furniture. Nothing had changed since the night before. Jeremy and Emma took in the expanse. The walls were paneled with wonderful carved details. Wires, where paintings had hung, were still dangling from the walls. There was packing paper debris strewn throughout. Built-in cabinets and doors stood open. Emma and Jeremy walked from one end to the other while Tony and Peggy watched them. They didn't move from their position near the entrance.

"What was the space like before this?" Emma asked, peering into the open cabinets.

Tony looked around the space and said, "The walls were covered with original works of art and beautiful furniture filled every room."

Peggy commented. "The cabinets were filled with rare books and glassware that he'd found all over the world."

Jeremy and Emma continued their review and entered the two bedrooms and saw all the personal items had been removed.

"No clothes," observed Emma.

"No bedding even," Jeremy said.

"No bed either," said Emma wryly.

They moved back out to the main living areas where Peggy and Tony stood.

"Nothing left anywhere," Jeremy observed.

Tony opened his mouth to mention something when Cole Tilden, Head of the Chicago Pinkerton Detective Agency, came into the apartment. He was accompanied by another man. Jeremy was the first to react.

"Pops! What're you doing here?"

Cole nodded to the man who entered with him and strode over to their group. "Peggy," he said and kissed her on the cheek. "I'm so sorry for your loss."

"Thank you," she murmured.

"Tony," he said and stuck out his hand.

"Cole," he acknowledged and shook it warmly. "What brings you here?"

Jeremy answered for him. "I sent him the information and asked him to get in touch with the local police."

"Why?"

"I wanted to make sure Peggy was safe."

"Why wouldn't she be?" Tony asked.

"We don't know why her brother left and we don't know why he was killed."

"I hadn't thought of that," Tony said, pulling Peggy close to him.

The other man walked over. They didn't recognize him as he introduced himself. "I'm Officer Horace Langford with the Chicago Police Department and I'll be meeting the body when it arrives by train."

"Cole? Is this an official investigation with the Pinkertons?" asked Emma.

"I've requested that we co-ordinate with the Chicago PD, since it's a family thing," he said. Tony had been a member of Emma's team since the beginning and had always been treated as family. When he married Peggy, she was included in the larger family circle.

"Thank you," Peggy said as she wiped a tear away.

"When will the body arrive?" asked Tony. He was thinking ahead about preparations for the funeral.

"It should be on the way here, but the first step will be the morgue," Horace stated.

"Why not the funeral home?" asked Peggy anxiously. She

wanted this whole business over with. Teddy was gone, and she felt that dragging it out just seemed more painful.

"Because it was murder," supplied Emma. "We'll need to confirm the cause of death. After that, they'll release the body."

Tony murmured in her ear, "It's the right thing."

Peggy nodded, slumping against him. "It's just… I'm just so tired."

Tony looked to the group. "I need to get Peggy home. Do you need anything else from us?"

Emma looked to Jeremy, and he responded, "I don't think so. Cole?"

"The next step will be the body identification."

"It is required," Horace stated.

Peggy moaned a bit at that comment and buried her face into Tony's shoulder. Tony picked her up. "She needs to rest. I'll be in touch later."

They watched as he carried her out. As the door shut behind them, Cole looked around and observed, "Nice place."

"I hear it was even nicer filled with his things," stated Emma.

"Expensive," Cole said and walked over to the marble mantle.

"Very," Jeremy said.

Cole turned to them. "When did they see him last?"

"Tony said he disappeared a few days ago," Jeremy replied.

"How did they realize he was gone?" Cole inquired and stroked his gray goatee absently.

"They had standing plans to meet here and go to dinner every Thursday."

"And this is what they found when they got here," added Emma as she turned her gaze back to the great expanse.

"Hmmm," Cole murmured, his gaze following hers around the room. "What do we think?"

"I think he was running," suggested Emma.

Jeremy nodded. "It makes the most sense."

"From what though?" Jeremy asked.

"That's the question," Cole said. He looked at the room and turned his gaze to Horace. "We'll be leaving for the rail station." The man nodded and started toward the door; Cole followed him out.

"Cole," called Emma. He stopped and turned back to her. "Could you let us know when Teddy's ready for viewing? We'd like to accompany Tony and Peggy." He nodded and exited the apartment.

Jeremy and Emma took one last look around and turned to leave. "Do you want to go to the office with me?" asked Jeremy.

She nodded and glanced around the room one last time.

He took her hand, and they headed through the lobby to the exit. Tom saw them and grabbed the sleeve of the man he was speaking with to stop him from turning toward them. While Tom distracted the man, Emma and Jeremy understood they shouldn't be seen and hurried out. "Must be the manager," murmured Emma.

Jeremy waved to a nearby carriage; when it pulled in front of them, they climbed in and rode toward the Pinkerton office. Once there, they paid the driver and went up the stoop and inside the office. The men in the outer office called out a welcoming. "Hey, Emma. You going to hang out here today?" Jones, one of the detectives, asked.

"For a short time," commented Emma.

"We're expecting a message from Pops, Jones," Jeremy told the detective.

"I'll let you know when it gets here," he promised.

They moved to Jeremy's office to wait. It was about an hour later when Jones knocked on the door. "The note arrived."

Jeremy went over and retrieved it. "Thanks, Jones." He opened it and read it quickly. Emma was watching him. "Teddy's at the morgue. They want Peggy to come and identify him within the hour."

Emma frowned but didn't comment as they got organized to head to Peggy and Tony's home.

When they arrived, Carmichael let them in, and they waited in the foyer while he let Tony know they were there. He came down the stairs quickly.

"Do you have news?"

"We do," said Emma. "Teddy's ready to view and Cole would like us to head over there."

Tony looked up the stairs with a frown.

Jeremy noticed and asked, "Is something wrong with Peggy?"

"Is it the baby?" asked Emma; worry colored her tone.

Tony shook his head. "No. It isn't that. She doesn't need the excitement right now."

Emma drummed her fingers against her lips, Jeremy turned to her "What were you thinking? Something bothered you at the office."

She wasn't surprised he saw that. "I was thinking of what Cole said about Peggy's safety. What if the murderer didn't get what they wanted and are still around?"

"Why do you think they didn't get what they wanted?" Tony asked.

"Simple. They killed him."

"Or It could've been they got what they wanted and still killed him," reasoned Jeremy.

She shrugged. "Maybe, maybe not, but I don't think we want to risk it."

Tony moved back to the stairs and sat heavily on the bottom step. He looked dazed. "You think the killer might still be here and could come after Peggy?"

"Right now, we don't know," said Emma as she sat next to him.

"You're right." Jeremy eyed Tony, who sat opposite him. He looked over at Emma. "How are we going to keep them safe?"

"I have some ideas," said Emma.

"Peggy shouldn't go," said Tony. The events had already been too stressful for her.

"I agree with you. Peggy shouldn't go," stated Jeremy.

"Oh, she'll go, or at least everyone will think she is there," murmured Emma.

Both men frowned at her.

She returned their looks and turned to Tony, "We might have an issue with you."

Jeremy caught on. "If we refer to Emma as Peggy Latimer, we can provide another layer between the case and your family."

"How will this work?" asked Tony.

CHAPTER 4

he morgue

"You can bring them in now," the coroner said to Cole. Cole moved to the door and opened it.

A woman dressed in a black dress and large hat, her face covered with black netting, entered the room.

The coroner stood by the body and said, "I will need you to come over here."

Cole moved over to escort her to the body; he held out his elbow. "Miss Latimer."

"Thank you," she murmured.

Horace stood nearby to witness the identification. Jeremy and Tony stood with them.

She approached the body and, as she got closer, Horace's eyes went wide. He looked at Jeremy, who subtly shook his head and kept his eyes on the body. Horace followed his example.

The coroner pulled back the sheet and she turned her head to bury it in Cole's chest.

"Miss Latimer?" the man prompted. He needed the identification confirmed.

Tony coughed, and Miss Latimer responded, "Yes, it is him."

The coroner moved to cover the body when the corpse's arm and hand were exposed to the room. The coroner quickly moved it back under the sheet. "Is that it?" Cole asked. "Is there anything else you need?"

The coroner said, "Just a moment more. Would you like to know how he died?"

Horace asked, "Wasn't it a fall from a train?"

Cole answered the question. "He was shot in the back, then pushed off."

The room was silent after that information was shared.

"Before you leave, you must sign for the personal effects." The coroner walked over to a table and picked up an envelope.

Cole walked her to the desk and assisted her with a pen; she signed quickly.

"Of course," the coroner said and took the signed form and handed over the envelope to Miss Latimer.

"Horace, please walk Miss Latimer out," Cole requested. He nodded and went over to her. They moved slowly out of the room as they left, and Cole said, "Jeremy, wait a second."

He held back while Tony nodded to them and left via the other exit.

Horace escorted her to the carriage located outside the building. He helped her climb in, where she waited for Jeremy to join her. It was a short period of time when the door opened, and Jeremy moved to his seat. "What did Cole have to say?" she asked after he got settled.

"Just that he'll meet us at the house," he responded and tapped the carriage roof to tell the driver he could go on his way.

The carriage jerked a bit as it headed toward their destination. They had set up several carriages to distract anyone that might be following them. The two stayed silent as they entered the house. Once inside, "Miss Latimer" removed her large hat and veil to reveal Emma. She held her hat in one hand as she fluffed out her hair with the other one.

She moved to Jeremy's side. "Did you notice the size of Teddy's hands?"

"Yeah, kind of odd." Their large size was noticed by both when it was accidentally shown by the coroner.

"Was it him?" Peggy asked, her voice trembling. She held onto the banister as she walked down the stairs toward them.

Tony walked in from the back hallway, moved quickly over to her, and assisted her down the last few stairs. "Was it him? Was it Teddy?" she asked again once they reached the foyer.

He took her hands in his and looked into her eyes. "My love, it was him."

She didn't cry, she sighed and looked at Emma. "Well, did the masquerade work?"

"It did. Thanks, Tony, for signaling to me." The cough had been prearranged.

He nodded and kept his eyes on Peggy.

"Except," said Jeremy, "did you notice Horace's reaction when he saw you?"

"No, my head was mostly turned away. Why? Did he see something?"

"He noticed you weren't Peggy right away," Tony agreed.

"Hey now, that's not fair," a voice called from the hallway behind the staircase. Horace was standing in the doorway with Cole. They must have come in the back way. "I wasn't aware that it'd be Emma instead of Peggy."

"How did you know it wasn't me?" asked Peggy.

"Well, you see," he stuttered, trying to explain without offending her.

"Stop teasing him, Peggy," said Tony. Everyone knew he meant that Emma was obviously not about to have a baby.

"Ah, we decided to keep it quiet," Cole explained to Horace. "We want to keep Peggy from becoming the focus of the potential murderer."

Tony gripped Peggy's hand. "Do we think the person might still be around?"

"It's better to be safe," stated Emma. The group nodded.

Peggy looked at the group. "Okay, what do we do now? What are the next steps?"

Emma spoke up. "We have Teddy's things, if you don't mind reviewing them with us."

Peggy took charge. "Let's move to the study." She pulled her hands from Tony's. "This way." She turned and walked to the room across the foyer. Emma smiled slightly as she watched her. Peggy could still carry herself regally even in her advanced state of pregnancy.

Hats and jackets were handed to the butler before they followed her. They all moved into the large room. Bookcases covered the walls and a large table sat in the middle of the room with chairs around it. At the far end of the room, there was a seating area with heavy furniture and a dark red rug.

They followed her to the couch. Tony sat beside Peggy and Jeremy, Emma, Cole, and Horace sat across from them.

Tony handed the envelope containing Teddy's personal effects to Emma. She knelt down by the table, located in the center of the sitting area, and emptied it onto the surface. Everyone was silent as they took in the contents. A watch, a white piece of cloth, toothbrush and tooth powder, a wallet, a train ticket, a steam ship ticket, and what appeared to be a receipt.

Peggy reached for the watch and opened it to look at the inscription. She closed it and held it tightly to her chest and explained, "This was our grandfather's watch. It isn't worth anything and hasn't worked in years."

Emma took out her notebook and documented the different

items. Tony picked up the wallet and looked through it. He counted out fifty dollars and found a small picture of Peggy in it. He handed the photo to her. Tears that she'd repressed trailed down her face. Tony handed her his handkerchief. She took it, grateful for his support.

Horace picked up the bent tickets and unfolded them. "It's two tickets. His train ticket and a steam ticket to Europe."

"Well, now we know his destination," commented Cole.

"Just the one ticket? He'd be going alone?" asked Peggy.

"Was he seeing anyone?" Jeremy asked.

"Not that we met. He never mentioned anyone," commented Peggy.

Emma picked up the white piece of cloth. "Is this what I think it is?"

Tony reached for it. "It's a clerical collar. Why would he have that?"

"Was he religious?" Emma asked.

"When we were children, church was somewhere we could get away from our father. As an adult, I didn't think so," Peggy answered.

Jeremy picked up the paper and unfolded it. "This appears to be the sale of all of his things." He handed the list to Cole.

Horace commented as he looked at the list with Cole. "He sold all of it, even his clothes."

"Traveling light," murmured Emma.

Cole turned to Peggy. "Was he afraid of something?"

"I don't know." She turned to Tony. "Tony?"

"He only talked about family and his childhood when he visited us."

"Nothing else?" Horace asked.

"No," murmured Peggy. "He seemed to want to stay in the past. I'd hoped that he and I would grow closer." She'd taken off her shoe and rubbed her foot on the embroidered rug under their feet.

"The apartment appears to be part of the sale," Cole observed.

"And there was the art," commented Tony. "So much of it was originals. I wasn't able to study them in detail but, even at a distance, the quality was evident." He looked over to Jeremey. "May I?"

Jeremy handed him the list. Tony looked at it. "The art I saw in the apartment appears to be all here. But there's one thing I don't see."

He handed the list to Peggy; she moved her finger down the list. "It isn't listed."

"What isn't listed?" asked Cole.

"Teddy had a picture of me commissioned. He told me he planned to move it to his home for display."

"Where is it currently?" Jeremy asked.

"Here," said Tony. "Upstairs."

"Can we see it?" asked Emma.

"Do you want me to bring it down or do you want to come up?"

"We can come up," she said, and Jeremy nodded.

"Will you be okay here?" asked Tony, stroking his wife's hair.

"I think I'll be okay for the few minutes it'll take you to go up and come back." She smiled at him.

"We'll be back," he said and guided Emma and Jeremy up to the third floor. The picture was part of a larger group of art. "That one," he said and motioned to the large painting that was a center point of the wall.

Tony had turned up the gas lights, but the picture was still quite dark.

"Is it valuable?" Emma asked.

"It is well done, but the artist is not well known," Tony replied.

Emma and Jeremy gave the painting a final look and then they went back downstairs.

When they were seated, Emma asked, "What caused him to run and did the person who threw him from the train get what they were looking for?"

They let that question hang. The group didn't know the answer.

Emma took a deep breath. "The key is the funeral. If the person didn't get what they were looking for, they may show up there."

"Is it the money they were after?" asked Jeremy. "This isn't a small amount. Was he carrying it with him?"

Cole rubbed his goatee and sat back. "We interviewed the train personnel and there was no luggage found in his room. The only items were the ones we have here."

"No answers, only questions," Peggy lamented.

"We take this a step at a time," said Cole. "Emma, I think we'll continue with you playing the part of Peggy at the funeral."

Peggy started. "I understand me not going to see the body, but I need to be at the funeral; he was my brother and my only family."

"Teddy wasn't your only family," said Tony. "You have me and this one." He touched her belly.

She smiled softly and put her hand on his. "Yes. Yes, I do."

Cole looked at her and then her stomach. "We don't want to take a chance with you and the baby."

"Can't I go as a friend?" Peggy asked desperately. She wanted —no, needed—to be there for Teddy.

When she saw Cole hesitate, Emma spoke up. "I don't see why she can't be there as my friend. I won't let anything happen to her."

"And I'll be there," said Tony.

"Only, you can't come with them; we need Peggy to stay single," said Cole reluctantly.

Peggy sat back, the lines on her face smoothed out. She reached over and took Emma's hand and said, "Thank you."

Emma squeezed her hand back.

Cole looked at Jeremy. "If the killer shows up, we may need you to be the unknown factor. So, don't come to the funeral."

Horace said, "We'll have people undercover watching the comings and goings."

"Jeremy, check with Jones and get some of our detectives to provide support."

Jeremy nodded.

Emma asked, "So, me and Peggy."

"Yes, Tony will come in once we close things down."

"What about you, Pops?" Jeremy asked.

"I'll be in the room with Peggy and Emma, as some type of police presence will be expected."

Horace directed his next comment to Peggy and Tony. "It would be easier if you do not mention the death to your friends. We don't need anyone extra at the event."

"That's fine, we didn't tell anyone he'd moved back," said Peggy.

"Whose idea was that?" asked Jeremy.

"Teddy's," Tony replied. "He said he wanted to settle in first."

"What about the newspapers? Will they carry the story?" Peggy asked.

Emma said, "I think I can help with that; I'll offer them the bigger story."

"Good thinking," commented Cole. "This thing is bound to resolve into something bigger."

"Yes," Emma agreed.

"We also need to keep this separate from Tony and Peggy's home," Jeremy said.

"I was thinking the same thing," Emma replied, drumming her fingers on her lips. "It'd be better to have a different location, someplace we can control. The smaller the better."

"We've thought about Peggy and Tony, but what about Tim,

Dora, and the rest? We don't want to bring them into this," Jeremy said.

"No, we don't want to involve them," Tony replied. He looked over at Peggy and whispered to her. She turned red and nodded. He said to the very interested group, "There's a small hotel, very French inspired, near the museum. I know the manager there and we can trust him."

"I know the place and the man. I'll arrange it," Cole said.

Jeremy frowned at him, and Emma quickly hid her smile as she thought, *Amy*. Emma saved Cole an uncomfortable question and asked quickly, "Would you be able to get us rooms?"

"Yes, I can do that," he murmured and avoided Jeremy's gaze.

Emma nudged Jeremy and said in a low voice, "Interconnecting rooms."

"I'll talk to him after," he said in the same low tone.

She nodded and said to the group, "Okay, we have a plan." *That reporter*, she thought. *I must get that taken care of.*

"We'll have all the arrangements completed, the funeral and the hotel," confirmed Cole.

Jeremy's thoughts were on Hen. *We'll need to see about her for the length of the case.*

CHAPTER 5

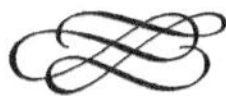

Tony's carriage was provided as transport for Emma and Jeremy. Cole had left separately to approach the hotel manager.

Jeremy and Emma's first stop would be the Pinkerton office to drop Jeremy off, where he would begin organizing the funeral. "What are your plans?" he asked Emma.

"Off to the Tribune first. I need to strike our bargain."

He nodded and went quiet until they pulled to a stop. He stepped down to the ground and leaned back in. "We need to make sure Hen is taken care of for the time we're gone."

"I agree. After the newspaper, I'm going home to talk to Dora and Tim about how we can manage this."

"You know they might say no. They said they wouldn't raise Hen for us," he reminded her.

She sighed and said, "I know they may turn us down. All I can do is try." She reached out to touch him. "We won't leave her on her own. I promise."

"Thank you," he said, and she leaned down to kiss him good-bye. He called out the Tribune's stop to the driver.

When Jeremy stepped back from the carriage, Emma waved

to him and sat back as it started to move. She sighed again as she thought of Hen. Jeremy's first thought had been of the girl. Hers had been the next step in the case. They'd always gone onto the next case without a thought. Even before she and Jeremy had taken responsibility for Hen, she'd been accused by her family of hiding things that could affect them and their safety. *And,* she admitted to herself, *sometimes it had.* Facts had been kept from Dora in their mother's death and again their trip to Paris. Could sharing what she knew earlier have helped either case? She couldn't be sure.

The carriage stopped and Emma jumped down before the driver could make his way to her. "I'll be a moment, can you wait?"

"Mr. Marella instructed me to take you wherever you need to go. I'll be here when you need me."

"Thank you." Emma turned and walked quickly up to the building. She had previous ties with the paper, some good and some bad. This time, she hoped it would be good. She took the side stairs off the dock and made her way up to the press room. Her eyes darted around for a reporter she'd previously worked with. *There he is,* she thought, seeing the man bent over his type-writer, *John Hoover.*

"Hoover!" she called over to him.

He looked up and saw who it was heading toward him. "Emma! It's been a while."

"It has," she said and looked around. "I need to talk to you."

"So, talk," he said and sat back in his chair.

"Privately," she muttered as she scanned the crowded room.

"Really? Hmm." His gaze followed hers. "How about the manager's office?"

Emma grimaced. That office generated bad memories: her mother's death and her own kidnapping. "What about over there?" She pointed to a conference room near the entrance.

"Yeah, that'll work. Follow me." She did as he asked and, once in the room, she waited for him to close the door.

"Is this private enough?" Hoover asked.

"It'll do." She sat down at the table. "I need to make a trade with you."

"What do ya have?" They had made similar deals in the past.

"We're working a case where a man was thrown from a train."

"Couldn't it have been suicide?"

"He was shot in the back first."

"I guess that fixes that. Why can't I write about that now?"

"We need time to find the murderer and to protect a local society hostess who was related to the victim."

"Will this be exclusive to just us?"

"Of course."

"I can get it assigned to me and I'll hold off on any articles."

Emma let out a long breath that she didn't realize she'd been holding. "You'll be helping a family."

Hoover laughed suddenly. "That sounds like something you said last time."

"It does, doesn't it? And I was able to trust you at that time."

"And you can trust me now."

"Thank you, John," she said, holding her hand out to him.

He took it. "Let me know when I can get the full story."

"You'll be my first stop," she promised. "Right now, I need to head home. Lots of things to arrange."

Hoover held the door open for her and she exited quickly, moving to the staircase. He watched her leave, took out a cigarette, and lit it. Hoover noticed Joseph Medill, the editor-in-chief, had returned and he walked toward the door. It was time to set this up officially.

***

The stairway was empty, and no one was there to impede Emma's progress. Hen was on her mind, and she moved quickly; she wanted to get home. The driver anticipated her, and this time was able to get the door open before Emma reached him. She started to pull herself up and the driver cleared his throat. The sound reminded her, *Ladies are supposed to be helped in and out of carriages,* she thought to herself. "Yes, of course." The driver gave her his hand and she climbed into the carriage.

"Where would you like to go?" he asked.

"Home, please." She gave him the address. He closed the door and climbed up to get the horse started to their destination.

Emma collapsed back in the seat, thinking. She didn't know how to approach the conversation with Tim and Dora, all of the scenarios seemed to end negatively. Before she knew it, the carriage door opened and pulled her out of her thoughts.

"Can I help you out, Miss Evans?" the driver asked as he opened the door.

"Yes, please." She moved to the door, and he put his hands on her waist and lifted her out to the sidewalk. "Thank you."

He tipped his hat at her and climbed back onto the top of the carriage.

She watched him drive away, delaying her entry into the house. When she could no longer see the carriage, she took a deep breath and walked up the stairs and into the house. The hurry she had been in to get home was gone now. She stood at the door for a few minutes, trying to calm her nerves. Finally, there was nothing to do but to take the next steps and enter the house. The foyer was quiet as she reached up to remove her hat pin and laid the hat on the small side table. She heard a glass rattling, a tell-tale sign that lunch was being set up in the dining room, but still she delayed.

"Aunt Emma, lunch," Patrick called from the doorway.

"On my way." She walked toward the dining room, forcing a smile on her face as she entered. Tim, Dora, baby Lottie, and Patrick were all sitting at the table. What she didn't expect was

Abbey and Papa to be there. Her smile no longer forced, she moved quickly to them, kissing Abbey and Papa on their cheeks.

Dora waited for Emma to sit and filled her plate. "How's Peggy?" she asked. Everyone waited for the answer; Dora and Tim had told their visitors where Emma was that morning.

"Better than expected given she's going to give birth soon," Emma replied.

"Poor girl, were she and her brother close?" asked Abbey.

"They were when they were kids, but not as adults. He had moved back into town, and I think they were trying to move toward a stronger relationship."

"Do you have any suspects?" asked Papa.

"Right now, we have no one. We did get new information at the coroner's office. The brother was shot, then thrown off the train."

"Shot? Were there any other surprises?" Tim asked.

"Yes, it looks like he was already running and whoever caught up with him killed him."

"Do you think the murderer is still around?" asked Dora as she cut up sandwich bites for Lottie.

"We think that, if they didn't get what they wanted, yes. We're preparing for that just in case."

"How so?" Tim asked.

"The funeral is going to be small and private. We want to keep Peggy safe, so I'll be undercover as Peggy and she will play the part of a friend."

"And if someone turns up?" asked Papa.

That part was harder to explain. Emma hesitated again and looked down, moving her food around the plate, not eating. She didn't raise her eyes when she said, "That's the concern. We're going to need to move into a hotel for at least a week to protect everyone involved. It would be me and Jeremy, with Cole's support, of course."

"But..." Dora looked at Tim. This was their worry come to

life, that Hen would be abandoned by the two. He reached over and patted her hand. "Emma, given this is our team, our family, Peggy is one of us. We'll take care of Hen while you're gone."

Relief washed over Emma, and she started, "Thank…"

Abbey interrupted, "Oh, we can have Henrietta stay with us. What do you think, Ellis?"

Papa looked surprised but happy. "You know," he suggested, "I think that we could also have a night with all of the children." He turned to Tim, Dora, and Emma. "What do you think?"

Tim smiled. "A night out with my special girl? Uh, yes, please!" Dora laughed.

"Grandpapa, does that mean we get to spend the night?" Patrick asked excitedly.

"Yes, sir. Would you like that?"

"Yippee! I can't wait."

Emma laid her head back on the chair, happy that her family understood. "Thank you all. I think Hen would love that, Abbey." Hen and Abbey had been enjoying time together and spent a number of weekends going to different bookstores and clothing shops.

"When will all of this start?" asked Dora.

"As soon as the funeral's scheduled."

"What hotel are you staying in?" Tim asked. "We'll need to know in case of an emergency."

"Yes, it's the Cambria Hotel, located near the museum."

"Oh, I know that one." Abbey smirked, with a side glance at Ellis.

Ellis grinned back. "That's one of the locations she's broken into."

Abbey was examining her nails and said, "There was a set of lovely jewels being housed there and I thought it would be nice to take them out for the evening."

"Which you did," he reminded her.

"I returned them, didn't I?" she teased.

"Yes indeed, after you went out to a party with them around your neck."

"Well, it was a dare. You said it couldn't be done."

"Well, you certainly proved me wrong," he said ruefully. The dare had been in jest, luckily she had not been caught.

Emma knew about Abbey's background as a jewel thief and her knowledge of the hotel might come in handy. "Abbey, can I speak with you after lunch? I'd like to learn how you got in and out of the hotel without being seen?"

"Of course. I have a few things that might help you."

"Now, everyone eat, before it gets cold," commanded Dora.

They followed her direction and forks could be heard hitting plates at the same time. With the first bite, Emma found she suddenly had an appetite and ate everything on her plate.

After lunch, Abbey asked Emma, "Would you like to go outside to talk?"

"Please."

Abbey kissed Ellis on the cheek. "I'll be back soon, dear."

"I'll be with Patrick in the study." Ellis put his arm around his grandson and accompanied him to the study to review the boy's schoolwork. He'd set up his curriculum the same as he did for his daughters, and he monitored it closely.

Everyone else pitched in to clear the table to the kitchen. Emma and Abbey handed over the plates to Amy and Ethyl and went to sit on the stoop outside that led to the backyard.

Abbey sat and patted the step next to her. "Sit, my dear."

After Emma sat, Abbey asked her, "You and Jeremy will be on a case where a murderer, or murderers, knows your location?"

"That's the plan. Tony, and especially Peggy, need protection since the baby will be coming soon. Our family will need protection, too, if our identities are found out. The best way to do that is to be in a remote location away from both families."

Abbey considered that and finally nodded; she knew Jeremy

and Emma could take care of themselves in almost any environment. And, having been previously married to Cole, she knew if anything did happen to the two of them, he would rain hell on anyone who caused the duo trouble.

"Now, what can you tell me about the hotel?" Emma asked.

Abbey leaned toward her and gave her all the details. Emma listened intently, just in case she needed the information later.

"Is that all of it?" she asked as she closed her notebook. The information was recorded in shorthand so that, even if it was found, it would be difficult to read. It was a skill she'd picked up in business school that had come in handy during several investigations.

"That's everything I know." Abbey reached out to take Emma's hand. "Thank you for letting us take Henrietta. I do so enjoy her company."

Emma got that. Abbey and Hen had similar backgrounds, having learned early to take care of themselves. Emma squeezed her hand. "No, thank you for volunteering to take her. She enjoys your company, too, and Jeremy and I are still adjusting to the parenting thing."

"I know the feeling. When I came back, it took time with Jeremy learning to be a mother again." When Abbey and Cole had been married, life choices and a stint in a French prison for Abbey had led to a separation. When she returned, Abbey and Jeremy had spent time rebuilding their relationship. "I just tried to be there when he wanted to talk."

"Yeah, we're trying to do the same thing with Hen." Emma slapped her notebook against her leg. "I think I need to go talk to Jeremy and find out if any of the plans have moved forward."

Abbey walked her stepdaughter into the foyer and watched as she put on her hat. Emma kissed her on the cheek and left quickly. Abbey could hear Ellis in the study and moved to join him.

CHAPTER 6

*E*mma smiled. So many doubts about Hen and where she'd stay for the week had been made clear. She pushed the pedals on her bicycle to move her faster through the busy streets and made her way to the Pinkerton office. She stepped off the bike to the stoop, hefted it on her shoulder and trudged up the stairs to the Pinkerton offices. Jones, who was exiting at the same time, shook his head, took the bike from her, and carried it to a storage closet.

"Emma, I've told you many times to let me, or someone, help you carry this monstrosity upstairs for you."

"Thanks," she said. Of course she ignored the instructions every time.

"Any time," Jones said sardonically. "You'll find Jeremy in his office," he called over his shoulder as he left.

She nodded and headed down the long wood-paneled hallway to Jeremy's office. She knocked quickly and was called in. Jeremy sat reading a file in his hand, feet propped on his desk. He grinned when he saw her, and she returned it with one of her own.

"Good news I hope?"

"Happily, yes. Abbey and Papa want to take Hen for the week."

"Thats great."

She moved to his side of the desk and leaned on it. "We still need to make sure Hen doesn't feel that we're leaving her without a choice."

"We will," he said, leaning his back on his chair to think.

"Has Cole returned yet?"

"Not yet," he said, still staring at the ceiling.

She moved to sit on the corner of his desk and swung her legs back and forth. She didn't say anything as she waited.

He finally looked at her. "We can talk to her tonight."

"And if she doesn't agree with the plan? You know she can be unpredictable."

"Just like a certain someone we all know and love."

"Ha ha."

He sighed. "Then we work on another way, a plan B."

"You know, even without the Hen situation, there's lots of unknowns with this case."

"Nothing we haven't seen before this," he reminded her.

"There is that. Although, if the murderer's gone, we may be doing all of this for nothing."

"So, we play it out, see where it goes, protect Peggy."

"And if nothing comes of it?" she asked as she worried her lip with her teeth.

"We take a few days in the hotel for ourselves," he teased and stood to take her in his arms.

"Mmmmm," she said, sinking into him. "Now that sounds like a plan. You know, maybe I hope the villain got what he was after."

"Me, too." Jeremy lowered his head to kiss her when a "humph" sounded from the door. He looked up, regretful. "Hey, Pops." He moved back to his chair.

Cole walked into the room and sat in the heavy chair in front of the desk and turned to Emma. "I've set up the funeral for the day after tomorrow."

"I'll have a small paragraph put in the paper to announce it," Emma said. She glanced at Jeremy. He was smiling at her and puckering his lips as if giving her kisses. She crossed her eyes at him and stuck out her tongue at him.

"Were you able to get it organized with the Tribune?" Cole asked, seemingly oblivious to his son's behavior.

"I did. I arranged it with John Hoover."

"Good man, we have used him before," commented Cole.
She nodded.

"You didn't mention Peggy?" asked Cole as she moved to the chair next to his.

"No, we just talked about Teddy."

"Good, right now we don't need the connection communicated to anyone."

"Especially if the murderer shows up at the funeral."

"Or not," Jeremy murmured. Emma blew a kiss to him. He winked at her and blew one back.

"When you two stop playing kissy face, can you stop by and go over the plans with Tony and Peggy?"

"Kissy face?" Jeremy asked in mock indignity.

"He means you," Emma said.

"Oh, in that case, mooshy mooshy, babe."

"Mooshy mooshy," Emma replied.

"A-hem!" Cole started.

"Sorry, Pops," Jeremy said. "We can run by their place. I think Tony's off until the baby's born."

"Is there anything else we need to do there?" asked Emma.

"No, the only thing left was the hotel. I confirmed that the rooms have been sorted," said Cole, looking down at his list. The details were wrapped up and, as they stood to leave, Cole said," Remember, Emma, the reservations are under Peggy Latimer."

"Got it," said Emma. "We need to drop some hints on where she will be."

Cole stroked his goatee. "That's a good point. I'll drop a comment to the mortuary that Peggy will be temporarily housed at the hotel while she settles her brother's estate."

"That works," Emma said. Jeremy led them out. Cole stopped at his office and waved as they exited the doors. "My bike!" she exclaimed, turning around.

"No worries," offered Cole from his office. "I'll drop it off on my way home."

"Thanks," she called back. They walked down the stoop and to the trolley. At their stop, they jumped off and walked the many blocks to get to Peggy and Tony's home. Once there, Emma stopped and stared at the grand structure.

"It is nice," commented Jeremy, his gaze following hers.

"Yes, but it's not something I want."

He smiled. "I'm glad to hear that. I don't think this is in my budget."

"Oh, you do all right," teased Emma, and she took his hand to accompany him to the door. Jeremy knocked and they waited.

The door opened and, instead of Carmichael, it was Tony who answered the door. His hair was uncombed, his shirt untucked and rumpled, and he looked like he hadn't slept in days. Emma stepped toward him. Jeremy snagged her arm.

"Tony are you okay?" she asked worriedly.

"Yeah, I'm fine. Peggy had a long night. Her back is bothering her."

"And when she doesn't sleep, you don't sleep," guessed Jeremy.

"Exactly. Come in. You have news?"

"We do," Emma said as they followed him further into the foyer.

A soft voice could be heard from the stairs. They looked up and saw Peggy dressed in a loose dress holding onto the rail.

Tony ran over to her, reaching her as she stepped on the final step. "Peggy, you shouldn't be up,"

"No, I want to see them."

He knew she could be stubborn. "Okay," he relented, "but I get to say where." He picked her up and called out, "Carmichael!"

The butler appeared out of the shadows, "Yes, sir."

"Can you get some pillows and a cover for Peggy?"

"Oh, Tony, don't make a big fuss over me," she muttered.

He didn't spare her a glance. "Carmichael, meet us in the study."

"Yes, sir." The butler left to get the requested items.

Tony carried Peggy to the room and to the couch. As he set her down, he said firmly, "Don't move from that position."

"Yes, sir." She mock saluted her husband. She looked over at Jeremy and Emma. "He worries."

"We can tell," said Emma. "Tim behaved this way when Dora was carrying Lottie."

Carmichael entered with the requested blankets and pillows. Once Peggy was settled, the others sat—Emma and Jeremy in chairs facing Tony with Peggy. Peggy asked the first question. "When are we having the funeral?"

"Two days from now," said Emma.

Jeremy took it from there. "We got it all organized and Emma will have her contact at the paper run a paragraph about the service."

"Will there be any mention of me?" asked Peggy, looking down at her hands.

"It's better that we don't call attention to you in case Teddy's killer is still in town," said Tony. He looked over at Emma and Jeremy for confirmation.

They nodded.

"Okay," Peggy said, "what's next?"

They all looked at her.

She smiled and asked, "What? You expected tears?"

"Kinda," admitted Emma.

"No, I'm done with all that, at least until the funeral."

"We move on to the plan," Emma said.

"Did I need to contact the hotel for you?" Tony asked them.

"Cole wanted to take that off your hands," said Emma.

"That's good. I was distracted," he admitted.

"Why a hotel?" Peggy asked.

"Just another layer of protection for you both," said Jeremy.

"What'll they say if only Peggy is there? And not me?" Tony asked.

"Cole told the mortuary that Peggy Latimer will be staying there until her brother's estate is settled."

"Oh, I am single now?" asked Peggy as she sent a sideways glance to Tony.

"For the duration of the case," confirmed Emma.

They stayed and talked through the afternoon, the topics switching to babies and families. They ended the day with a promise to confirm the time they'd arrive for the funeral.

Emma and Jeremy stood and Tony said, "I'll have the carriage ready for you." He walked to the foyer and spoke to Carmichael.

"Thank you," Jeremy said when Tony rejoined them.

A small time later, Carmichael stepped into the doorway. "The carriage is out front, sir."

"We'll see you both at the funeral," Tony said.

Emma and Jeremy nodded and watched as they left the room. Carmichael continued to hold the door as they exited.

"Good day, sir, madam," the butler said.

"See ya, Carmichael," Jeremy told him as he moved to the outer door. As they walked outside and toward the waiting carriage, Jeremy added, "Hen next?"

"Yes." Emma knew they had everything lined up, except for the one person they should've spoken to first. *Will Henrietta go along with our plans? What will we do if she doesn't?* Emma gripped Jeremy's hand tightly.

He squeezed hers back and released it to help her into the carriage. After he called their destination to the driver, he joined her. The ride didn't take long, and the building for the foundation where Hen worked in the afternoons became visible. Since the girl hadn't had much structure and purpose growing up, Emma and Jeremy had decided that, after school, she'd work at the foundation. The job was under the supervision of Clair Callahan, the manager, and Lily, Clair's secretary. So far, Hen had been thriving in the environment.

"Would you mind waiting?" called Jeremy up to the driver.

"Mr. Marella said I was to take you where you wanted to go. I'll wait."

"Thank you," Jeremy said and offered Emma his elbow. She took it as they walked into the building. They gave a wave to the guard and entered the elevator. The operator was silent as he pushed the button to take them to their floor. The foundation owned the building; Jeremy and Emma were well known by the staff.

As Emma watched the numbers ascend, Jeremy asked, "Is the new accountant in place?"

The operator answered before Emma could. "Yes, sir, they're all settled."

"I'll have to check in with him soon," commented Emma.

"Just don't accept any party invitation while you're there," Jeremy noted drolly. The previous accountant, Geoff, was no longer with them after he and his friend, Gregory, had thrown their infamous Christmas party. Geoff was fixated on trying to prove he was smarter than Emma and tried to use a murder of Ethan to prove it. It turned out Geoff wasn't smarter. He and Gregory were currently in prison for life. The duo had used their Christmas parties as cover to murder people across the country for years. Bodies had turned up at their farm; the digging was still going on in that location.

"I wouldn't mind the challenge," she admitted. She enjoyed the battle of intellect but not the impact on friends and family.

The elevator reached their floor, the doors opened, and they exited the elevator. The long hallway led them to a set of large double doors at the end. When they entered, who did they see leaning over Lily's shoulder? None other than Nathan Lombard, their new accountant. Lily laughed at something he said as Emma murmured, "Hmm."

Jeremy smothered a laugh and cleared his throat in a loud manner. Lily jumped at the noise and smiled when she saw who it was. Nathan walked quickly over to Jeremy and Emma. "Good to see you. Emma, how are you?"

"We're good, Nathan. How's the new job?" asked Emma.

"I'm enjoying it." Nathan had been hesitant to accept the job because of his prior history as a thief. The life he wanted had begun to come together after he started to work with the Pinkertons. Emma saw his skills in accounting when he uncovered a scam where Geoff was stealing money from the foundation. She recommended him to the board. They agreed and hired Nathan as their full time accountant. Albeit with oversight from Tim for the first year.

"I'm glad," said Emma. "We're looking forward to a long relationship."

"Me, too," whispered Lily into Nathan's ear when she joined him. He turned red at the comment but looked like a happy man.

"Hey, Nathan," Jeremy said idly, "are you planning on throwing any parties in the future?"

"Uh, no. Not planning any."

"Good. Good."

"Jeremy!" Emma said, swatting his arm. "I can't believe you asked that!"

Nathan commented, "I don't want to be confused with Geoff, so no parties, I assure you."

A door opened from behind Lily's desk and Henrietta stepped out.

"Jeremy and Emma!" She ran over and hugged each of them. "What a nice surprise! Are we all going home together?" Normally, it was just Emma or Jeremy depending on their work schedules.

"We are," he said and ruffled her hair. "And we have a nice carriage waiting to take us."

"Really?" she said and ran to look out the window. "Wow, is that for us?" It was far grander than the rented carriages they normally rode in.

"Tony, a friend of ours, loaned it to us," Emma supplied.

Clair came out. "Well, hello. Family outing today?" she asked.

"A nice ride home as a family." Over Hen's head, Emma mouthed, "I'll tell you later."

Claire nodded.

"We shouldn't keep the driver waiting too long," Jeremy reminded Emma.

"We'll see you tonight."

Hen took one each of Emma and Jeremy's hands in hers. She chatted about school and work on their way to the carriage. As they made their way home, Emma and Jeremy listened and waited to talk to her. At the house, the carriage pulled away from them and Hen started to run in. Jeremy called, "Hen, can we talk to you for a minute?"

She paused at the base of the stoop and turned to them with a frown on her face. "Have I done something wrong? You know the noodle incident wasn't my fault."

"What noodle incident?" started Jeremy.

"It doesn't matter," said Emma, her eyes narrowed at him. "What matters is that we have something to share with you."

"You're right. Hen, let's sit," Jeremy suggested. They sat and Hen waited, her foot tapping.

Emma started. "Jeremy and I are working a new case that will take about a week to complete."

"Oh, is that all?"

Jeremy smiled slightly and clarified. "We'll be gone the entire time, and we won't be able to pick you up or help you with homework."

"Okay," Hen said.

"I thought this was going to be traumatizing for you," Emma said sardonically.

"Me, too," commented Jeremy.

"I know you'll be back," Hen said confidently.

Emma laid her head on Hen's and held out her hand to Jeremy. He took it and they sat there together for a few minutes. Hen broke the silence with a question. "Will I stay here with Dora and Tim?"

Emma lifted her head and tilted her chin to look her in the eye. "How would you like to spend the week with Abbey and Grandpapa?"

"Really?" she asked excitedly. "I'd love that. Abbey is so much fun and Grandpapa shows me different experiments. I'd have them to myself for a whole week!"

"Well," Jeremy said, "as I understand it, they want to do a sleepover one of the nights with Lottie and Patrick."

Hen grinned widely. "How fun! Will we sleep on the floor?"

"You'll probably be in a bed," commented Emma.

"Oh, well." She shrugged. "It still sounds like so much fun. When can I go over to their house? Tonight?"

"No, but probably tomorrow, is that soon enough?" asked Jeremy.

"Yes," she said, standing up. "Don't worry, I know you have work to do that doesn't involve me."

"We're family. We wanted you to feel a part of the decision," said Emma. Jeremy nodded.

"I do," she assured them.

As she ran up the stairs Jeremy remembered something and called out to her. "Hey, Hen, what's this about a noodle incident?"

Hen stopped and turned around. "Um... Well... I..." Suddenly, she turned back toward the house. "What's that, Dora?" She glanced at Jeremy and Emma. "Sorry, Aunt needs me for something." With that, she rushed into the house.

"Wonder what that's about," Jeremy said with a frown.

"No telling," Emma replied.

Jeremy grinned. "Well, noodle incident aside, I think that went well." He stood and held out his hand to help her up.

"It did," she said with relief. She took the proffered hand and accompanied him in.

As they got to the door, they saw Hen speed past Dora in the foyer.

"Why is she in such a hurry?" Dora asked, bouncing Lottie on her hip, watching the girl bound up the stairs. She raised her eyebrows as she turned back to Emma.

"She's very excited about spending the week with Abbey and Papa," Emma said, taking off her hat and handing it to Jeremy to place with his in the closet.

Dora stayed where she was and stared at Emma. Jeremy saw that Dora wanted to talk and decided to make himself scarce. He kissed Emma quickly and said, "I'm going up to read some before dinner."

Emma nodded and turned back to Dora. She could tell by her sister's downturned mouth that Dora wanted to talk. "What's wrong?" she asked as she took the giggling Lottie from

Dora. She held the baby up to blow a raspberry on her tummy, which made Lottie laugh even more.

"Emma, I would've watched Henrietta for you this week."

"Really?" she said and lowered Lottie to look her sister in the eye. "Because I distinctly remember someone not being happy about Jeremy and I becoming Hen's guardians and saying they would need advanced notice to help out."

"I know," Dora said. "And I am sorry. Tim and I have seen that you and Jeremy have been responsible for Hen and taking care of her. You two have made great strides in being parents to that little girl. She's really come around."

"Thank you, but you were right," Emma admitted. "We had no idea how much responsibility we were taking on."

"I just didn't want you to think we wouldn't have stepped up for you this week."

"Rest assured, we'll be asking again at some point," Emma said dryly.

Dora smiled more easily now and reached for Lottie. "Let me take her; she needs a nap."

"Oh, by the way," Emma said, "what's this about a noodle incident?"

Dora's face turned red. "Oh… Um… Well… I…What's that, Tim dear?" She turned to Emma. "Sorry, sister, Tim needs me to do something." With that, she turned and rushed out of the room.

"That was weird," Emma said to herself. "I think I'll go see what Jeremy's reading and if he's interested in a nap." She walked upstairs to her bedroom door, opened it, and stepped in quickly. She closed it behind her and locked it swiftly.

Jeremy watched her quizzically from his reclined position on the bed. "Everything okay with Dora?"

"Yes, she was concerned that we thought she didn't want to help with Hen this week."

"Oh, okay." Emma sat down on the edge of the bed and

started to take off her boots. "And what're you doing?" he asked when he saw her drop the boots and move her finger to the buttons on her shirt.

"Who me? I thought I might take a nap," she said with a wide yawn, spreading her arms wide and showing her undergarments. "Want to join me?"

"Well, I'm almost at the end of my book," he said and held it up.

Emma sat on the bed and took the book from him and looked at the cover. "*Moby Dick*? Haven't you read this a dozen times already?"

"Only eleven."

"Then you know how it ends."

"Well, yeah, but I like reading the subtle nuances," he said, watching her further disrobe.

"Well, okay. I guess I'll nap by myself."

He started unbuttoning his shirt. "What're you doing?" she asked teasingly.

"Who me? I thought I might join you for a nap."

Once they were undressed and lying in bed, he asked, "Still tired?"

"Surprisingly not. Got any ideas of what we can do to occupy the time?"

"I have a few ideas," he said and pulled her on top of him.

A while later, there was a knock on the door. Jeremy and Emma went still in bed, talking in low voices. They'd yet to get dressed. Hen's voice called, "Emma, I want to show you my bags that I packed to take to Grandpapa's and Abbey's."

She started to answer but stopped when she heard Dora's voice. "Hen, baby, why don't you show me? Emma wanted to lie down a little while."

"Okay," the girl could be heard saying cheerfully.

"Whew," Emma said, lying back in the bed.

Jeremy pulled her close. "You know she's going to find out eventually."

"I know, but for now we keep it this way. Maybe when she's a little older we'll tell her."

He looked over at the clock and said reluctantly, "Ugh, time to get up."

"I know," she said regretfully. "I'll miss this next week."

"Yeah, me, too."

CHAPTER 7

*inner that night at the boarding house*

Abbey and Ellis had stopped by to spend some time with Hen and joined the family for dinner. Cole had accompanied them. "I didn't want to be left out."

Emma looked at Dora and winked. "Amy," she called, "we have guests for dinner."

Amy came out of the kitchen. "How many more?" She stopped abruptly when she saw Cole. She blushed and patted her hair.

Emma glanced at Cole and saw him smile just for Amy. She turned to Jeremy; he hadn't noticed his father and Amy's mutual interest.

Abbey had. She moved her gaze back and forth between Amy and Cole but didn't say anything. She looked at Dora and Emma. The three women met each other's eyes and nodded. They wouldn't bring it up to their men.

"I'll get back to dinner," Amy said. She smiled sweetly at Cole and went back into the kitchen to organize the extra food.

"Come on, everyone, sit," said Tim. "We have plenty."

Hen called to Abbey, "Sit next to me!"

Abbey laughed. "Of course, we must make plans for next week."

Emma grabbed Jeremy's hands and squeezed. *Family*, she thought He squeezed back, understanding.

"Can I go with Abbey and Grandpapa tonight?" Hen asked Jeremy. She'd packed and was ready to go.

"You're sure you want to go tonight?" he asked. "We can take you to school in the morning."

Hen bit her lip. She wanted to start her adventure, but she didn't want to hurt Jeremy's feelings.

Emma spoke up and said, "Hen, you can go tonight."

"Can I? Can I really?"

Emma looked at Jeremy and squeezed his hand once more. He responded with, "Sure, you can go." He tried not to show it, but he'd miss the girl. She'd become someone he liked to see every day, spending time with her and all the little things that went into being a parent.

Dinner continued with Hen taking up most of the conversation with her plans for the week. Abbey, Ellis, and Cole contributed to the list. When dinner was finished, they all helped move the dishes into the kitchen.

Jake took a seat at the round worktable and pulled out a book to read while he waited on Ethyl, Amy's assistant, to finish her evening work.

Everyone pitched in to clean up and, when the last dish was placed in the cabinet, Amy got her jacket out of the closet and started out the door. Cole called to her, "Amy, just a minute. I wanted to get some air; would you mind if I come with you?"

Amy nodded. "The company would be nice."

He followed her out. Dora bumped Emma on the hip. She bumped back.

The door closed with a loud bang, Abbey turned to the two sisters, and said in a low voice, "Girls, you owe me an explanation."

Before they could respond, Ellis came through the kitchen door. "I think Hen's ready. She's brought her suitcase downstairs."

Abbey turned to him with a smile. "Then we must go. I'll meet you in the foyer."

He nodded and left. She turned back to Dora and Emma. "And you both owe me a conversation." She left the room.

Emma and Dora watched the door swing shut behind her.

Ethyl put her hand on Jake's shoulder. "Ready to go?"

"Yes." He stood and held out his hand to her. She took it and started toward the door. She pulled on her jacket and prompted him with, "Jake, you're forgetting something."

"Oh, yes." He turned toward Emma and Dora. "I'll be back after I drop off Ethyl." Ethyl waved and they left through the kitchen door.

"She's been good for him," commented Emma.

"Are they serious?" Dora asked.

"I think they might be, but I think Ethyl is giving Jake plenty of space," she teased, knowing where Dora's mind had drifted.

"Oh you, you know I'm asking about Cole and Amy. What's going on there? Are they just enjoying each other's company?"

"I don't know why they're keeping it from us right now. I guess they'll let us know when they're ready." Emma sat at the table. "It's odd that Jeremy hasn't picked up on anything."

"How can he not?" asked Dora, joining her at the table.

"Probably because it's his father. We don't see our parents as people, especially in romantic situations."

"That's true," Dora said, remembering how she and Emma had felt when Ellis got serious with someone. That someone turned out to be Abbey and the perfect person for Papa. "Are you going to tell him?"

"Not right now. Let's give Cole and Amy this time to be together without family interference."

"You're right."

Jeremy stuck his head into the door. Dora and Emma jumped when they saw him. "They're ready to leave."

Emma answered for them, "On our way." Jeremy sent her a puzzled glance, but she just smiled. He nodded and went to join the family. Emma and Dora strolled out together and joined the group to say goodbye to Hen.

"You have your books and your homework?" Jeremy asked as he helped Hen on with her jacket.

"Yes, Jeremy."

"We'll make sure she keeps up with her homework," promised Abbey.

Emma walked over and whispered in her ear, "She's still having nightmares. Reading to her after helps."

Abbey nodded, and whispered back, "I'll keep my eyes out for it."

Emma and Jeremy stayed in the foyer at the door after everyone had said their goodbyes and the house had gotten quiet. Emma felt the immediate emptiness. "She'll have a nice week," she said reassuringly to Jeremy.

"I know." He stared a long time at the closed door. "I miss her already."

Emma took his hand. "Come on, let's go sit with the family."

They moved into the sitting room where Jeremy joined Tim and Patrick in a card game on the floor. Emma moved to the settee where Dora was playing dolls with Lottie. She laid her head on Dora's shoulder. Dora patted her back but didn't say anything.

CHAPTER 8

he next morning

Emma and Jeremy walked downstairs and into the dining room. Dora was already there, tearing up a biscuit for Lottie. "Emma, the paper came."

"Oh, good," she said and went to retrieve it from her. She flipped quickly to the obituaries.

"Is it there?" Jeremy asked. He paused as he reached for the tray of eggs.

"Here it is." She read it aloud. "Theodore Latimer died from a fall off an evening train from Chicago. The services will be held at the Kingsley funeral parlor."

Jeremy filled his plate with eggs and sausages and observed, "Hoover kept it simple."

"We didn't share anything in connection to Peggy." Emma folded the paper and took her seat next to Jeremy.

"Hmm," he said.

She looked up. "We start tomorrow."

"Packing and organizing tonight?"

She went silent, picking up a biscuit and adding butter to it. "I was wondering if we shouldn't move over tonight. That way, we don't have to rush moving into the hotel and to the funeral. That'll keep tomorrow easier." She took a large bite and waited.

"That makes sense. I'll stop by and see Cole this morning to confirm we can go to the hotel a day early."

"Let me know and we can go over after dinner tonight."

Savannah and Ethan walked in together. "Are we late this morning?"

"No, we started a little early. Sit and eat," Dora replied.

Tim walked in behind them and sat beside Lottie. "Top of the morning to everyone."

"Good morning," the group responded.

"Emma, will you be at work today?" asked Ethan, picking up his fork to dig into his eggs.

"I will," she confirmed. "I'll try to give you a schedule update."

With their day started, Emma retrieved her bike and walked Jeremy to the trolley. They kissed quickly and Emma said, "See you soon." He ran and jumped on the trolley as she climbed on the bike. She pedaled quickly to the Pennington law firm. Her job as an assistant and investigator allowed her flexibility to work other cases.

As she pedaled, she saw how much had changed in the last five years; hers was not the only bike on the streets now. The winter months had made cycling dangerous, but the warmer weather allowed cyclists to move about the city. They were calling the bicycles "noiseless steeds." What used to be a morning of her dodging horses and wagons now included dexterous movements around other less experienced cyclists. In the early mornings, bikes were utilized by many members of the community: the Tribune newsboys distributing papers; craftsmen carrying carpentry tools, carpets, chickens, cameras, and even shotguns as they pedaled around the area. Other riders, called scorchers because of their highly aggressive riding, risked crashes with other riders and pedestrians. They were creating most of the concerns, cycling too fast in areas where caution should've been utilized.

Later in the day, women and girls would be seen riding bikes around the parks. *Not just me anymore,* she thought. She didn't know if she liked the bloomers everyone wore; she still preferred her split skirt.

The day would begin with an investigation involving George Streeter, aka Skipper. In her opinion, the case wasn't winnable, but she knew her opinion wouldn't matter. Skipper had seen an opportunity when the local government started to purchase land for the upcoming World's Fair, being held in Chicago three years hence. His case involved his schooner; it had been stranded three years ago near the shore, at the foot of Superior Street and Lake Michigan. The city had allowed the boat to remain and Skipper still lived on the defunct boat. Now, he wanted the court to say it was his land to sell. His land was perfectly positioned in a location with very aristocratic neighbors. From his back stoop, he could watch the haughty carriages and even hear the chimes of the St. James.

Skipper was willing to move if paid eight million dollars for the forty acres around his defunct schooner. The problem was the case was based on squatters' rights. Mr. Pennington knew that the man had no case, but Skipper was adamant that they go to court and push the facts that the city had allowed him to stay where it was, making it his land.

Things had gotten out of hand when a writ of forcible detainer was sworn out, requiring Skipper to relocate. He'd violently responded when they tried to force him and his family from their home.

Her investigation would be used during jury selection and

opening arguments. The case would keep Mr. Pennington out of the office for a few weeks and allow her some time off.

She arrived at the office, stopped her bike, and placed it on her shoulder to enter the law office and saw that Mr. Pennington wasn't in yet. She was surprised to see Ethan had beaten her there. He already had his face buried in his files. "You were fast," she remarked.

"I didn't have to walk anyone to work," he countered. Ethan engaged in very little small talk at work and said in a sour voice, "The Skipper case starts today." He normally supported Mr. Pennington in all things and the fact that he had an opinion on this case was startling.

She hadn't discussed it with him yet and looked over at him, surprised. "Is there a reason you don't want us to do this case?" She knew her reasons but was curious about his.

"It's unwinnable," he said. His thoughts mirrored hers.

Emma agreed. "Skipper's passionate, but the law isn't on his side."

"I told Mr. Pennington the same thing," Ethan commented as Emma took her bike to the closet.

"You did?" Emma paused and asked, surprise coloring her voice. "What was his response?"

"He said that Skipper's been told he gets one chance and then he'll move on. They're friends."

"Skipper isn't going to stop if the first one doesn't win. From my conversations with him, he wants to fight and keep fighting as long as it takes."

"I hope the first trial is over quickly and we can move on to something else."

"That'd be nice. Oh, by the way, I'll definitely be out the rest of the week on our current case."

"We should be okay, but will you be at the boarding house in the evenings?" Ethan thought he could bring her work if needed.

"No, but I'll be in town, so if something comes up you can contact me through Cole."

He frowned. "Do you think Tim could provide temporary help if I need it?"

"Of course. Let him know to have someone available, if something comes up."

"I will. Will you be here the rest of today?"

"Ye, I'll be cleaning up my open investigations."

Mr. Pennington walked into the office; the door slammed shut behind him. "Good morning," he said and retrieved the current case files from Ethan. Emma took the opportunity to give an update on her schedule. "That should be fine," he said. "Check back in with me once your case is concluded."

"I will," she promised.

Emma worked through the day. She had her lunch laid out on her desk when Savannah stuck her head in her door. Emma put down her sandwich and said, "Hey, are you headed out for lunch?"

"We are," her friend confirmed. "Could you watch the office for Ethan?" Mr. Pennington had already gone to the courthouse.

"Of course. Leave my door open."

Savannah opened the door wide, and Ethan called out, "Thanks!"

"Sure! Have fun."

She concentrated on the files in front of her, absently eating her sandwich. The outer door opened, and Emma hurried to the main office. A young man carrying a courier bag had entered and Emma went out to greet him. "Can I help you?"

"Yeah, I have a note for Emma." He opened the bag he'd slung over his shoulder.

"That's me," she confirmed.

He nodded and took out the envelope. "Here you go. Do you want me to wait for a response?"

"Let me review it." She opened it quickly and saw it was

from Jeremy. Cole had confirmed they could move to the hotel tonight. He had one question for her. "Can you meet me at the house at 4pm to get packed and have dinner before moving to the hotel?"

"I have something for you to take back." She retrieved her notebook and quickly jotted her response and placed it back into the same envelope. She added Jeremy's name to it. She pulled out her pocketbook and gave him the money for the delivery and a tip.

"Hey, thanks!" he said as he took the money.

"Thanks for waiting. "

He tipped his hat at her and grinned. "I'm saving up for a bike."

"I hope that helps!"

"It will," he said and walked out of the door as Ethan and Savannah were returning. "Good day," he said as he passed them.

"You, too," the duo responded.

"What was that?" Ethan asked abruptly. "Was it something for Mr. Pennington?"

"No, it was from Jeremy. He was confirmed that we'll be starting the case tonight."

Ethan released Savannah's hand and walked to his desk. Savannah followed him and sat on the corner of it. She asked Emma, "Do you need anything from me?" Savannah worked at the local theatre and contributed make up and wigs when disguises were needed.

Emma thought about Abbey's comments about the hotel and said, "Not just yet. I might contact you later."

"Let me know. I need to head over to the theatre now," she said, hopping up. The new show was starting that evening and she wanted to be there to manage the final rehearsals. She leaned down to Ethan. "Meet me after the show?" she asked.

"Of course," he said and took the opportunity to kiss her. "I'll bring you dinner."

"Love you," she murmured. "Bye."

"Bye," he mumbled and watched her leave. He stared for a long moment after the door was closed. When he turned back to his desk, he realized Emma was still there. "Is there something I can do for you?"

"No, no, I wondered how the hours are affecting you. You leave here and go to the theatre until late into the night. How do you do it?"

"I sleep in the green room."

"Green room?"

"Where the actors rest in between scenes."

"Do they disturb you?" she asked curiously.

"I can sleep through anything."

She nodded. He and Savannah were working together to figure out how to make their marriage work for them. She started to go back to her office, but turned back. "I'll have to leave before four. Jeremy and I need to pack and get dinner before we head out to the hotel."

"No problem," he said absently, no longer looking at her.

She smiled, noting her dismissal. The afternoon wrapped up and she took her files to his desk. "Here they are."

He took them. "I'll keep them with me until you return."

"I appreciate that."

Emma retrieved her bike and pinned her hat into place on her head. She placed the bike on her shoulder so she could navigate the steps. She walked out the door and down the stoop. Once at the bottom, she lowered the bike and climbed on to start homeward. The day was so nice that she slowed a bit to enjoy the weather. At that moment, another biker flew by her at a fast pace, just missing her.

"Scorcher," she muttered. "Guess I need to get moving," She

pedaled faster and started to overtake the biker. It was a woman; she wore the standard bloomers and a cloth hat. Emma couldn't see who it was because the woman's head was lowered as she tried to race past her. They were in a head-to-head race when a horse pulled out in front of them. They skidded to a halt.

"Close call," the other woman said.

"Yes," Emma agreed. She had been mistaken. The other person was a girl, not a woman. She couldn't have been more than sixteen or seventeen years old.

"What's your name?"

Emma didn't know what caused her to say it, but her response was, "I'm Peggy."

"Peggy," the girl said, her eyes narrowing for a moment. "Well, *Peggy*, I hope our paths cross again sometime."

"I bet you do," Emma said and watched her ride away. "Hey!" She yelled, she hadn't got the girl's name. She shook her head started toward home. She slowed the bike, not wanting to guide the girl to the boarding house. *Did I overreact?* Emma thought. *Maybe, maybe not. We don't know who's who in this case and this strange girl just shows up out of nowhere. It's suspicious.* She turned the bike and took the back roads and alleys toward home. At the boarding house, she stopped the bike and climbed off. She looked around, no-one was in the area so she quickly took it to the back of the house.

The noise of dinner being prepared greeted her as she entered through the kitchen door. Amy was stirring a big pot on the stove; Ethyl was snapping green beans. "You're a little early, aren't you?" Amy inquired.

"Jeremy asked me to come home early; we need to get moving to the hotel tonight."

The kitchen door swung open, and Jeremy walked. "Ready?" he asked.

"Ready."

As they walked upstairs, she said, "I think we need to get organized and get out of here quickly."

"Why?" he asked. "Has something happened?"

"Maybe."

He stopped her and demanded an answer. "Tell me."

She detailed the bike ride and the race for him.

"You think she's involved?"

"I don't know. It seems likely. I've never seen her before."

"And you said your name's Peggy?"

"I went on instinct. If she is a threat, I want her directed at me."

"Now that's something I trust. Let's go get packed."

They held hands as they walked to their rooms. They split up at their doors and Jeremy said, "See you on the other side."

Emma laughed as she opened her door and moved toward her closet. Her bag was inside under her dresses. She pulled it out and started to add items from her drawers. She took out several dark dresses from the closet, folded them and placed them with her undergarments in the bag. She moved to her desk to retrieve her brush and other personal items.

Jeremy opened the door between the rooms and pushed back the bookshelf. "I got my stuff packed. Yours?"

She held up her bag in confirmation. "Dinner isn't for another two hours. We need to go now. If someone is watching, we need to move."

"We can make some sandwiches and take some fruit."

"Sounds like a plan."

They walked to the kitchen and told Amy what they needed.

"I can help get things together," she said. "One of you, come here and stir the soup for me."

"Thanks!" Emma said, moving to the pot to take the spoon from her. She stirred while Amy put together their sandwiches. Jeremy loaded them into the lunch cans.

"Don't forget some fruit," reminded Emma. He nodded and grabbed a couple of apples. "Where's Dora and Tim?" she asked.

"They're in the study with the kids," commented Ethyl.

Amy relieved Emma at the soup. "Thank you," Emma said and kissed her on the cheek.

"Anything to help."

Jeremy moved the cans of food to the foyer and Emma walked toward the study. Patrick was reading to Dora and Lottie while Tim worked on his books. "Emma, you're home early," Dora said.

"We decided to leave early for the hotel."

"But dinner…"

"Amy took care of us. Everything is packed."

Dora went over to her. "So, you'll be gone a week?"

"About that. I'll let you know if it runs longer. "

"Be careful," Dora said, putting a hand to her sister's cheek.

"I will. It's Jeremy you should worry about. He's always getting up to something."

"Oh, you." Dora grinned. "Do you have your knives?"

"Of course." Emma kissed her on the cheek. "Tim, see you in a week," she said over Dora's shoulder.

"Bye, Aunt Emma," called Patrick.

Jeremy had come up behind her. "We need to get going."

They moved to the front door and, as he put out his hand to grasp the doorknob, she grabbed his hand to stop him. "You know, if that girl is involved, they'll be watching for me."

"You're right. We probably shouldn't arrive together."

"You go first. I'll follow on my bike."

"Your reservations under Peggy Latimer," he reminded her. "And now we don't know each other. See you on the other side." He used the familiar phrase, kissed her, went out the door, down the steps to the street, and started walking toward the trolley stop to take it to the hotel.

"See you." She reached for her black hat with the netting and pinned it on. She grabbed her bags and walked to the kitchen door. "See you in about a week," she said to Amy and Ethyl. They waved goodbye.

She grabbed her bike and put her bag and bucket in the basket. Jeremy had given her the hotel's address. It was near the museum, so she had time to get over there before it got too late.

Since Jeremy had taken the trolley, he should be there before her. The roads were teaming with people all still doing business. It took time to maneuver through the crowds and she was happy when she saw the small hotel in the distance. She stopped her bike in front of it. It looked like it had been plucked out of France and put into Chicago. The architecture was intricate, and it had had many lives before finally settling down as a hotel. She studied the building, thinking of Abbey's information.

Now or never, she thought. Her bag and can in one hand, she lifted her bike onto her shoulder and made her way into the building.

There was a long hall that led to a small desk at the far end of the room. She made her way to it and set her bag and bike down. "I need to check in," she told the clerk.

"Your name?" he asked, looking through his glasses at her.

"Peggy Latimer," she supplied.

He flipped through his stack of cards and pulled one out. "Yes, I have your reservation. You're on the third floor, please sign here."

She took the pen and signed the large book.

He handed her a key. "Room 302, here's your key."

"Is there somewhere I can put this?" she asked and motioned to the bike.

He frowned and muttered, "Women are everywhere on those things."

"More and more every day," she said cheekily. She had a thought suddenly and asked, "Is there another girl staying here who also has a bike?"

He didn't look up from his desk. "No guest staying at the hotel has a bike. Until now." He motioned to a closet near his desk. "You may move it over there." She placed the bike on her shoulder and took it to the closet. Once it was opened, she saw it wasn't big enough to wheel it in so she stood it up and laid it against the inside wall.

"Thank you," she said, returning to get her bags from the desk area.

"Third floor," he said again and turned his attention away from her.

She looked at the bag and back at the clerk. When no offer of help came, she took the bag and the can and walked to the elevator. The elevator operator, a young man with shaggy black hair and big brown eyes, was there. He opened the outer door for her and slid the inside iron gate opened. He used white gloved hands to help move her bag inside.

"Thank you," she said.

"Sure. Floor?" he asked and moved to his lever.

"Third please."

"Hmm, I took a gentleman up there earlier."

Jeremy, I hope, she thought.

Once they reached her floor, he opened the inner gate and the door to the floor. He looked at the number on her key and pointed. "That room is across the hall."

She followed his pointed finger. "Thank you."

"Need help with the bag?" he asked.

"No. I have it. Thanks, though." Emma started toward the door, paused, and turned back to him. "Hey, would you mind telling me if anyone is asking about me?"

"Who would they be asking for?"

"Peggy Latimer," she supplied.

"Nice to meet you. I'm Pete Townsend."

"Nice to meet you also."

"Why would anyone be looking for you?" he asked curiously.

"I don't know."

"I'll let you know," he promised.

Emma took her bag and lunch bucket with her and walked to her door. She inserted the key, unlocked the door, and pushed it open with her boot. She walked into the room and set her things down. It was a rather simple room with an iron bed, armoire, and a small desk. *No bathroom. Must be down the hall,* she thought.

She took the bucket and bag to the desk. She pulled out her dresses, shook them out, and started to hang them in the armoire.

There was a sudden sound behind her and, as she turned toward the wall, she saw the doorknob from the interconnecting room turning. She watched it turn again and she reached for her knife as she approached the door. She released the lock and, when the knob turned again, the door eased open. As a form entered, she placed her knife against their neck.

The form stopped cold and said, "Hey, babe, wanting to relive our first meeting?" On that first meeting, Emma had threatened Jeremy with a knife to his neck in an alley. She lowered the knife slowly. "Hi, Jeremy. You managed to get our rooms together?"

"Of course I did. You hungry? Wanna eat?" he asked and held up his bucket.

"Sure, come on in." She looked through the door curiously at his room. "Same layout."

He looked around her room. "Seems like."

"Bathroom must be down the hall," she mused.

"Yeah. Not a great set up. Not looking forward to stumbling down the hall in my drawers during the night." They moved to the bed and opened the cans.

"So, big day tomorrow," Emma said as they dug into the buckets.

"Yeah, Peggy will be there as support."

"And Tony?"

"He said he'll be there; Cole will make sure."

She laid back on the pillow. "Going to stay with me tonight?"

"Mmmmm. I don't know," he said and looked around. "Seems well built but can we be heard from other rooms?"

"Let's test," she suggested. He walked into his room and closed the door.

She spoke loudly. "Hey, Jeremy!" And waited for and response. He walked back in. "Could you hear me?"

"Not a thing."

"Me either."

"So yeah, I guess I will stay with you tonight."

"Great." She grinned. She didn't like them to be apart.

The evening passed slowly; they stayed in the room and read until bedtime.

CHAPTER 9

The next morning

The funeral would be at ten AM. They got up and left separately
to get breakfast, as they felt they shouldn't be seen together.
Emma started across the street to a small café that served breakfast. As she made her way there, she thought she saw the same
bike rider as the day before speed by on a cross street. She
turned toward them. *Was that the Mystery girl?* she thought. *It
could've been anyone.* She shook her head and entered the
restaurant. The small place was bright and a little crowded.
Time wasn't an issue, so as she waited, she watched the other
diners.

Couples and families took up many of the tables and her
eyes settled on one table taken up by four men. She looked
closer and saw one of them was Jeremy! *What is he doing here?
Who are those men?*

A server approached her. "Table?" he asked.

"Yes, please." She was relieved when he guided her further

away from Jeremy and the other men she'd been observing. She deliberately sat with her back to them and ordered breakfast. The service was good, and she finished in a short period of time. A quick look at her timepiece told her she had some time to go back to the hotel to rest until it was time to attend the funeral.

Emma had the interconnecting door open for Jeremy when he returned. When she heard his door open and close, she headed to his room.

"Good breakfast?" he asked as he removed his hat.

"It was fine. Who were those men and how did you end up at breakfast with them?" she asked bluntly.

"That happened as soon as I left the hotel. They nabbed me by the collar and encouraged me to join them."

"To breakfast?" she asked incredulously.

"They were hungry. Turns out so was I. I think one of those men killed Teddy. Or maybe all three did, I am not sure."

"What makes you think that?"

"They seemed to know who I was."

"They know you are Jeremy from the Pinkertons?" asked Emma as she dropped on the bed. Were they already found out?

"Nope. They assumed I was someone else."

"And who did they think you were?"

"Arthur Smith's brother."

Emma shook her head. "I feel like I'm missing a large part of the story. Who's Arthur Smith?"

"I don't know, but apparently I'm his brother," he commented. "What I gleaned from the three men is that Teddy and Arthur were part of something. And they're here for their cut of whatever money Teddy had."

"So, where is Arthur Smith and why assume you are his brother?"

"Not sure," he admitted, "but I get the idea they don't expect him."

She thought about the new information and asked, "Will they be at the funeral?"

"They will be, but I won't. I'll keep my distance on the outside. Like we planned."

"So, now you're Arthur and I'm Peggy," Emma pondered.

"No, I'm Arthur's brother."

"Oh, shut up," she said and Jeremy laughed. "And there's not just one suspect, but probably three."

"We'll be busy," he confirmed.

Emma moved to sit up on the bed. "I think I saw the girl on her bike."

"Near here?"

"Just outside. What's her part in this?" she wondered aloud.

He noticed the clock. "Time for you to get organized." He plopped down on the bed and grabbed his book.

She nodded and moved to her room. "What about you?"

"I'm okay here. Got my book," he said, holding up the volume.

"Oh, you," she said and threw her boot at him. "Still at the end?"

He dodged the boot and stayed where he was. "Yeah. Maybe now I can finish it since I was so rudely interrupted the other day."

"Oh, you enjoyed it."

"Did I, though?" He blew a kiss at her.

She shook her head at his antics and walked to the closet to take out a dark mourning dress. It was the right dress for the occasion but a little boring. She sat in her chemise and drawers and pulled on her stockings; they were attached to her corset. That particular piece of underwear had shown itself to be invaluable in a knife fight in Paris. Next, she pulled on her dress. It buttoned up the front, making getting in and out of it easier, as Jeremy could attest to.

Once she was done dressing, she added her small knife to

her right leg. "You never know," she said to Jeremy's cocked eyebrow.

"Sure. 'Cause funerals are so dangerous."

She reached into her pocket to make sure she could access the knife. Her other one, the bigger one, would have to be left behind. Her large hat would go on next; she inserted the hat pin carefully. It had been sharpened and could be used in an emergency if needed.

The knife probably wouldn't be needed. Cole would be in the room with her, and Jeremy would be watching from outside. Other Pinkertons and Chicago policemen would be stationed around, too. If there were mourners, each would be investigated. *Will the three men pay their respects? Jeremy seemed to think so.*

She moved to the connecting door and motioned to him that she was closing it. He waved. She locked it and listened for his side; he did the same. Jeremy would go on foot to the funeral parlor and her transport that day would be her bike. They'd initially thought about using a carriage, but Emma knew a bike would give her more freedom.

She exited her room and locked the door before heading to the elevator. Pete was already there waiting. "Hey, Pete."

"Hi, Miss Latimer. Where are you headed? Somewhere special today?"

"My brother passed. I'm on the way to his funeral," she explained.

"Oh, I'm sorry," he said quietly, his head down.

"Yes, it'll be a sad day," she murmured.

The atmosphere was solemn as the elevator descended to the lobby. It came to a stop, and he turned to her with a downturned mouth. "I hope you have a better day."

"I hope so also, thank you," she returned in a similar tone.

He lifted the inner gate and pushed the outer door open for

her. She exited and went to get her bike from the closet. The lobby was empty, and the clerk wasn't at the desk.

After she retrieved it, she stepped out on the sidewalk. Jeremy had given her directions, and the funeral parlor was about five blocks away. Once on the bike, she pedaled into the road. It didn't take long to reach her destination and, when she arrived, she got off her bike and looked at the building. It was tucked in between two much larger buildings and was small and painted in ivory tones. She pushed her bike into the hall of the building, and inside the door.

"Can I help you?" A small man ran over to her. "I'm Jeremiah Kingsley, owner of this establishment."

Emma had to tilt her face down to look the man in the eyes. "Yes, I'm Peggy Latimer."

Kingsley's eyes widened. "Oh. Dear, I'm so sorry for your loss."

"Thank you. Can I put this somewhere?" she asked and tapped the bike handle with her hand.

"Yes," he said and looked a little panicked. "I-I know, my office. We can move it there."

"Thank you," she said gratefully. "Has anyone arrived for my brother?"

He looked around and said in a low voice, "Just Mr. Tilden."

"Oh, good."

"Follow me to my office and we'll get that stored."

She followed Kingsley and, once at the door, she pushed the bike into the room. Once the it was stored, Kingsley asked, "Would you like to view the area where we have your brother?"

She pulled her netting down across her face. "Let's go in."

"Wait for me," a voice sounded from behind her.

She was ready to play the part of grieving sister when she turned and saw it was Peggy. "Oh, thank you for coming!"

Peggy ran over to hug her. Emma pulled back and said,

"Please walk in with me." They gripped each other's hands and Emma murmured to her friend, "Hold on tight and pull your netting down. It'll help."

Peggy listened and moved to lower hers.

As they walked into the room, they saw it was cozy with four rows of chairs and an open casket at the front with flowers at the end of the casket.

Cole sat in the back, holding his hat in his hands. He inclined his head toward them in greeting.

They returned the greeting and walked slowly to the front to take their seats. Emma gave Peggy a moment to settle before she asked, "Ready?" Peggy nodded and they stood to move toward the casket. Once there, they looked down at the man. Peggy started to tremble, and Emma gripped her hand tightly to steady her. Emma made a show of taking her handkerchief out and lifting her face cover to wipe her eyes.

They spoke in low voices so that no one could hear them. "Oh, he doesn't look like he's dead," Peggy murmured. "He looks like he's sleeping."

"He does," Emma agreed. They stayed up there for some time before moving to their seats in the first row of chairs. They sat with Emma playing the role of chief mourner. Peggy was there as her friend to help her through the funeral. Cole waited in the back, watching the very empty room.

Emma asked in a low voice, "Did you know your brothers' friends?"

"By the looks of the room, he didn't have any," Peggy replied as she looked around the room. "At least, not here anyway."

"You didn't socialize with him?"

"Other than our weekly dinners, no. Even as a child, he had few friends. He left home as soon as he turned sixteen. The work in the factories was hard and he wanted out."

Emma looked surprised.

"I'm not the helpless flower you think I am. Before my marriage, I worked in the clothes factories."

"I never…" Peggy looked at Emma with a raised eyebrow. "Okay, so I did. But I'm changing that opinion now."

Peggy grimaced and held her stomach.

"Are you okay? Is it the baby?" Emma asked.

"We're fine. He's just active."

"They say that's a good sign."

They both turned to stare at the open coffin, wondering if the day would provide any information. At that moment, the sound of heavy feet dragging on the floor made them turn toward the aisle. The man charging forward was almost as tall as he was wide, his shoes making a loud scuffing sound as he walked. It was one of the three men Emma had seen with Jeremy that morning.

Peggy and Emma looked on, fascinated. What would he do?

He passed them without comment and moved to the coffin. He leaned in so far that Emma and Peggy stood to see what he was doing. He reached into his pocket and took something out. The object Emma saw was a small mirror; it caught the light as he moved it back and forth under Teddy's nose. The outcome must have pleased him, because he smirked as he placed the mirror back into his pocket. He turned to head back up the aisle. Emma and Peggy continued to stand and watch him. He stopped next to Emma and glared at her before stomping out of the room.

They sat again.

"What was that?" asked Peggy, perplexed.

"I think he wanted to make sure Teddy was dead."

"Is he a friend?" Peggy asked hesitantly.

"No, I don't think so," Emma said, staring straight ahead.

The room grew quiet again.

Next, the sound of quick steps coming up the aisle caused

Emma and Peggy to look over their shoulders. A second man passed them by as quickly as the first.

"Now what?" Peggy muttered.

"We watch."

This man, short and thin with a bowler hat that sat too low on his head, pushed it back as he also leaned into the coffin. They stood again to watch.

He was another of the men from that morning. What he did next caused Emma to hold Peggy's arm to stop her from going over to him. Emma pulled her back with a shake of her head.

"But, but... he pinched him," Peggy whispered fiercely.

"Yes, it was another test."

That pinch seemed to satisfy the man that the brother was indeed dead. He glanced at Emma and moved back down the aisle quickly to make his way out.

They sat again.

"Why did he have to do that?" Peggy asked, her hands clinched tightly.

"Teddy didn't feel it."

"Yes, but it wasn't right," she said stubbornly.

"No, it wasn't." Emma looked back at Cole. He shook his head. He appeared as puzzled as they did about the happenings.

"Do you think that's all?" Peggy asked.

Emma looked around. "I believe there are three."

At that moment, another man walked in. He was tall and thin. Emma and Peggy watched as the man strolled up the aisle. "What're those on his feet?" asked Peggy.

Emma looked at the man's strange footwear. "I think cowboys wear those."

"Cowboys?"

"People out west who work with cattle. They're boots."

Just as the other two had done, the new arrival didn't spare them a glance as he approached the coffin. He did exactly as the other men had and leaned in. He didn't pinch or pull out a mirror. What he did do caused both Emma and Peggy to jump. He yelled "HEY!" into Teddy's ear and, when he received no response, he turned and started out. He stopped by Emma and glared at her for a long moment, then took his time leaving the room.

"Will there be anyone else?" asked Peggy.

"That's all the ones I expect," Emma replied.

"That was certainly enough for me," Peggy said, rubbing her belly.

They waited another hour and, when it looked like no one else was coming, Cole closed and locked the doors. There was a light knock from the side door and, when Cole opened it, Tony rushed to Peggy's side. Kingsley stood and lowered the shades. Prayers were offered for Teddy's soul and Peggy's welfare, and the small group said a final goodbye to Teddy.

Peggy wiped her eyes with a handkerchief and held onto Tony's hand. "What now?"

Emma answered. "Jeremy and I are in the hotel. I expect, given that performance today, those three didn't get what they wanted."

"Did one of those men kill my brother?"

Emma looked at Cole. "We don't know. But they're our first suspects."

"Did they believe you were Peggy?" Tony asked Emma, continuing to hold Peggy to him.

"I think so. The three men we saw today already made contact with Jeremy."

Cole nodded. "Jeremy's going to work both sides for us." He'd met with his son before the funeral began.

Peggy nodded. She was so grateful that Emma was in their lives. She reached over to grip Emma's hands.

"We'll find out why your brother died and who killed him," promised Emma.

"Thank you."

They separated and Cole opened the doors. Emma put her handkerchief up under her netting and held it to her face on the way out. Tony headed out the back with a promise to meet Peggy back at home. Cole would get Peggy to him, and Emma would take her bike back to the hotel. Jeremy would stay to watch if anyone else came and where the three visitors went.

CHAPTER 10

The road was clear as Emma biked back. She took a moment to think about the three men. Whatever Teddy did in life gave him enemies. The three tested to see if he was alive, but did that remove them from the suspect list? After all, if they shot and threw him off a train, wouldn't that have confirmed he was dead? And if they didn't do it, who did?

Someone stepped out in front of her, and she skidded to a halt. "What're you doing? I could've hurt you!" Her nerves were a little on edge.

The individual was an older man, solidly built in a heavy coat, hands in his pockets. He was also a stranger to her. "Miss Latimer, I need to speak with you."

"Right here and right now? Out on the street?" she demanded.

"Where else?"

She looked around and saw a café. "How about there?" she asked and inclined her head to the café.

"Good a place as any."

Emma didn't see Jeremy anywhere. She'd have to keep this meeting public. She couldn't trust anyone going forward. *We need information,* she thought, *and this man didn't show up at the funeral. What part did he play in Teddy's murder?*

He motioned with his cane for her to go in front of him. She followed his direction and headed into the restaurant. A server ran up and took her bike for her; after it was stored, Emma kept a safe distance from the man as they found their seats and sat down. He had an odd gait, he had cane and was dragging a his left leg behind him. *An injury of some sort?* she wondered.

"Now, who are you and why must we talk immediately?" asked Emma.

"Your brother passed, and I wanted to offer my condolences."

"Did you know him?" she asked curiously.

"No, no. I'm Max Winsten," he said as he handed her his card, the long sleeve of his jacket covering his hand.

She looked at him and reached out to take the proffered card and read it. "You're a private investigator? What's this about? How would this be related to my brother?"

"It's the money, Miss Latimer. It isn't his. It doesn't belong to him or to you."

"There's no money, nothing. He left nothing behind."

"What do you mean? Didn't he live well while he was here?"

"He did," she mentioned, thinking of that nice apartment and the list of goods that had been sold.

"Have you asked yourself where the money came from?" Winsten continued.

"He was a businessman," she said in a low voice, trying to play the hurt and grieving sister.

"Business? Hah, his business was theft. And the people he stole from want that money back."

"I don't understand what you want from me. I don't have your money."

"But, Miss Latimer, you have to have it. Where else would it be?"

Emma thought about the three men from the funeral but didn't say anything further to Winsten. She needed to find out who they were and what their connection was to Peggy's brother.

"I need you to let me know if you have anyone else contact you about the money."

"Who else would there be?"

He sat back and gave her a long look. "We shall see, Miss Latimer. We shall see."

Danger signs were going off about this situation, so she kept her mouth shut.

She thought of the money from the auction. *Where had it gone?* "Whoever it is you're looking for," she told him, "why do you think they will show up here?"

"Because your brother and three other men were part of a larger group that stole from various jewelers around the country. And that money Theodore used to set up his life here, the men think that it belongs to them."

Winsten stood with his hands in his pockets and demanded, "You need to tell me if you find anything out about the money."

"And if I do not do as you ask?"

"You will do as I ask," he said, his body seeming to vibrate with anger.

"Are you threatening me?" she asked idly, running her finger along the rim of her glass.

"Let's not call it a threat, shall we? How about I'm just stating the truth?" With that, Winsten moved in an agitated manner toward the door; his cane tapped the floor as he dragged his leg behind him. Emma stared after him.

She heard a polite cough beside her, and she turned to see the waiter looking at her expectantly. "Madam, would you like to order?" he asked. He'd avoided the table during their intense conversation.

"Oh, yes. I'd like to take a dinner special to go." She thought again. "Could you double that?" He looked doubtful, so she added, "I'm very hungry. And could you add some cookies, please?"

She waited for the meals, paid for her bags and headed back to the hotel on her bike. When she entered the lobby, she found the three men arguing in the lobby. They quieted immediately when they saw her. The larger man punched the small one in the back, trying to push him toward her.

"Hi. We wanted to talk to you," the small man stuttered.

She frowned and kept her netting pulled down low. "I've had a long day. I'm sure you understand."

The larger man pushed forward. "No, no, we don't understand," he said loudly. "We want to talk, and we want to talk now!"

As Emma tried to decide on a course of action, fight or flight, she heard Pete the elevator operator call from the elevator. "Miss Latimer! I'm holding it for you."

Flight! she thought as she ignored the three men and quickly dashed toward the elevator. They yelled at her to stop and fell over each other trying to get to her. The doors of the elevator closed, stopping them. She leaned on the wall. "Pete, you're a lifesaver."

"Anytime," he said over his shoulder.

The elevator arrived at her floor. "Could you delay in letting the men upstairs to their room?" she asked, wanting a few moments to gather her thoughts.

"I'll do my best," he said and opened the gate for her.

She moved into the hall and opened the door to her room. She knocked quickly on Jeremy's door. *Is he there?*

She didn't hear anything and moved to the bed and sat. The food smelled amazing and, just when she started to get into it, a knock sounded on the connecting door. *Finally!*

She unlatched it, and he walked through and kissed her. His

hair looked like he'd been running his hands through it. "Well, they took the bait."

"Bait?" she asked and followed him to the bed.

"Cole told the funeral director where you were staying. That is why the men were here this morning."

"I wondered how they all ended up here. Did Cole see Peggy home?"

"Through a circuitous route," he confirmed. He sighed and rubbed his neck.

"Come on. Sit down and eat," she said and tapped the bed next to her.

"I'm so glad you picked up some food. Those guys were moving faster than I expected to get here."

"Did they look like they were on friendly terms?"

He sat back on the bed with his plate. "I would say friends is the wrong term. In fact, several fights broke out even before they entered the hotel."

"Hmm."

"What about you? Any observations?"

She picked up her plate and unwrapped it. "Yeah, I think we have a motive in the killing."

He sat up quickly at the news. "When did you formulate that?"

"On the way back to the hotel. A man stepped right in front of me when I was riding here. I almost ran him down."

"Who was it? Not one of the three men we were following?"

"No, it was someone else."

"Why did you stop?" he asked, sending her a heavy frown.

"Like I said, I almost ran him down."

"What happened?"

"He said he needed to talk to me."

"It could've been dangerous," he commented, unwrapping his plate.

"I can take care of myself, and we went to a café to talk, hence the food."

He took a bite. "Well, I approve of the outcome if not how it came about. Okay, what did he tell you? Who is he? And what's his part in this?"

"He gave me this." She handed him Winsten's card.

"Max Winsten. A detective?" He turned the card over. "What's he investigating?"

"He said he represents the businesses that are owed money from theft."

He frowned. "Did he mention theft of what?"

"Something to do with jewelry stores; he didn't say more than that."

"Hmm, what else?"

"He says the money didn't belong to Teddy. No, I take that back, he called him Theodore. And then he said, 'Your brother took what wasn't his!'"

"We don't have any money."

"I told him that. He didn't believe me."

"Did he know anything about the three men who are also here?"

"He said there would be three men who would be after me for money owed to them."

"So, we don't really know if he is lying about representing anyone. He could be another suspect?"

"Agreed," she said and thought about the man's agitation.

"Did he say how we could contact him?"

"No, just that he'll be in touch. Those three men today, why did they approach you this morning? Why did they think you were Arthur's brother?"

"I let it slip that I was looking for Teddy."

"To whom?"

"Everyone I could talk to, the maids, the clerk at the desk, the manager, the elevator operator. The butcher, the baker, the candlestick maker."

"Very funny. You think one of them told the men?"

"I do. Someone who works here might have a connection to Teddy or to who killed him."

She laid her head back and groaned. "So, a bigger suspect pool."

"Yeah. What about the girl you mentioned? You saw her earlier?"

"I think so. It was a flash of hair on a fast bike."

"Probably her."

"Probably."

"Any other contact?"

"Not yet. You know, Jeremy, just staying here won't make this case move forward. We need to get to know the suspects."

"How 'bout dinner out this evening?" he suggested.

"Perfect, but I thought we'd planned to pretend to not know each other."

"Oh, I fixed that."

"Oh, you did, did you? How did you manage that?"

"Well, I mentioned in passing to the desk manager that I'd planned to approach you for a night out to get your mind off your brother's tragic passing. I also told the three men, and they think I'm going to pump you for information about the money."

"Then we meet downstairs for dinner?"

"Yeah. You know, it's gonna be a long night. We should probably nap," he suggested.

"You always want to nap," she teased.

"You don't?" he asked, sounding disappointed.

Emma stood and stretched her arms. "Well, I guess I am feeling a little tired."

He grinned and grabbed her by the arm. He lowered his head for a long kiss.

After their nap, they read and readied to go out for the evening.

CHAPTER 11

*E*mma dressed carefully, still wearing primarily black colors, but adding a lighter blouse insert in the top. Under her dress was her corset; it felt like the right night for it. She patted her hair, ready for an evening out.

A knock sounded on her door, the main one that led to the hallway.

She frowned at it. Jeremy had suggested they meet downstairs, *not* at her room. She walked to the door and called out, "Who is it?"

"Open the door Miss Latimer," a booming voice called.

"Why should I?" she called back. *Which one of the men is at the door? Or is it all three?*

"You don't want to know what I might do. Open the door!" the man demanded.

She looked around the room and quickly pocketed her clutch knife. She walked back to the door and slowly turned the knob. Once it released, the man on the other side slammed the door open and it crashed into the wall, barely missing her. It was the first man to enter the mortuary today, the wide, tall man who had put the mirror under Teddy's nose. He was so big the room seemed to shrink with him in it.

She backed up further into the room to get away from him. She sent a short glance toward the connecting door and saw a shadow moving under it. Jeremy would be there if needed. It was time to be Peggy, not Emma. "I saw you at the funeral for my brother," she told the man.

"We had to know," he muttered, still glaring at her.

"Know what?"

"If he was really dead or if he had found a way to keep the money for himself. Teddy's pulled tricks before this."

"Of course, he was dead! Someone shot him and threw him off a train! You can't get much deader than that."

"We had to be sure. Where's the money?" the man asked, advancing on her again.

"I don't have it," she said as the back of her legs hit the bed. She held out her hands. "Stop! Or I'll scream."

"I need that money. Teddy shouldn't have done what he did."

"What did he do?"

He ignored her question. "Where's the things he had with him?"

"They're there," she said, pointing to the brown leather bag, "but you won't find anything of value."

He turned away from her and Emma took a deep breath. The man seemed to take up all of the air in the room. He grabbed the bag and she thought he meant to take it, but instead he poured the contents out on the desk. He opened the wallet, and he pocketed the cash that was there. She didn't stop him; it was only a few dollars. He glanced at the list of items that were sold and asked, "Where's the money from these sales?"

"I don't know. I really don't." She rubbed her hands together and looked down.

He wadded up the receipt and kept it in his fist. "Miss Latimer, you need to find the money."

She lifted her eyes to him, her expression stony. "And if I don't?"

"You will. If you know what's good for you." He threw the wadded-up paper on the desk, turned and stomped out, slamming the door behind him. She collapsed on the bed. That was man number one. How many more confrontations would there be?

The connecting door opened. "All clear," she called.

"Good."

"You heard him?"

"I did. But I knew you could handle yourself."

"Everyone seems to think that either I have the money or it's here somewhere." She walked over to the pile of things and sifted through them. "Jeremy, is the answer here in front of us?"

He walked over. "If it is, it's hidden well. Enough of this. For now, meet me downstairs for dinner."

"All right. Let me get things reorganized."

"I'll meet you in the lobby," he said and went back into his room. "Lock your side," he called.

She walked over to the door and engaged the locks. She took her hairbrush and smoothed her hair. When she finished getting ready, she turned to the desk. The items were still strewn about, and the leather bag sat in the open. *Where to put it?* She glanced around the room and stopped at the armoire. *That's it.* Next, she moved to the desk and added all the items back into the leather bag. She took the chair and moved it to the front of the armoire. The top was still too high for her, so she shrugged and tossed it up. It landed softly. She stepped down and put the chair back in its proper location.

It was time to go meet Jeremy. Emma walked to the door and opened it slowly. She stuck her head out and glanced up and down the hallway before she cautiously left the room. No one was around, so she walked to the elevator and pushed the call button, waiting impatiently as it slowly ascended from the lobby to her floor. As the numbers changed, she counted the floors. When it finally came to a stop, the doors were opened, revealing Pete. "Going down?" he asked. He had the same bright smile she'd come to expect.

First, she checked the car and, when she saw it was empty, she let out a sigh and boarded. "Lobby, please."

Pete pulled the lever, and got the elevator moving. This case was slow moving and her impatience was coming through. She'd like nothing more than to take her knives and corner each man as they came to her. Her fists were clenched as she fought her growing frustration. For now, she'd play her part as Peggy. She was Peggy Latimer, sister of the deceased Teddy Latimer. She watched the floors go by and wondered what the night would hold for them. Pete stopped the elevator and opened the doors for her.

"Thanks, Pete," she said and started to step off.

He touched her arm. "Those men, they were asking about you."

"Which ones?" she asked. Their pool of suspects had gotten bigger than just the three men.

"The three who are staying here."

"Pete where are their rooms located?" she asked.

"All are on your floor," he replied.

"All three of them?" she asked in surprise.

"Yes."

"How did that happen?"

"The manager may have allowed the request. We aren't very full right now."

"Is that unusual?"

"Not really, no," he admitted.

"What did you tell them?"

"Nothing. Just like you said."

"Thanks, Pete," she said and reached up to kiss him on the cheek.

He turned red and stepped back into the elevator.

She entered the small lobby and looked around for Jeremy. "Over here," he called.

She turned toward him. One of the three men, the short one, sat opposite Jeremy, hiding behind a paper.

"It was nice of you to ask me to dinner," Emma murmured as Jeremy approached.

"It's my pleasure, Miss Latimer. Are you ready?" he asked and offered her his elbow. She took it and they walked out of the hotel. "Do you mind walking?"

She took in the pleasant evening and said, "That would be nice." After they walked for a few minutes, Emma asked "Is he following?"

"Probably. I wonder what his approach will be."

She thought about that as they made their way to the restaurant. Jeremy had gotten their reservation and, when they reached the establishment, they were immediately led to their table. There was a small band playing in the corner and the room was lit with candles.

"This is a perfect location."

Jeremy looked around. "We should do this more often."

"Is he here?" she asked, her back to the door.

He watched the man enter and argue with the host. "For now. I don't expect he has a reservation; we'll probably see them after. Their patience seems to be waning."

"They want the money."

"The money that you don't have," he reminded her.

"The money. I'm wondering about that. Teddy sold everything and disappeared. He had to have the money with him or some way to get to it."

Jeremy thought about that. "The only other thing not included on that list was that painting."

"Yes, but it was painted by a local artist and hardly worth the amount that the apartment, furnishings, and clothes would've sold for."

"I agree."

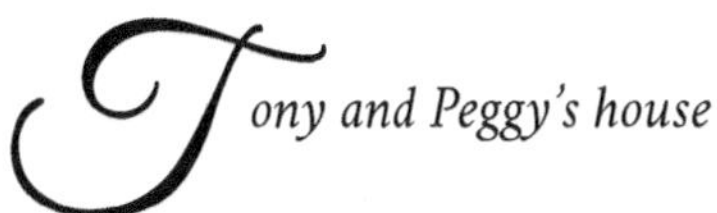

ony and Peggy's house

Peggy stood and walked to the bookcase and, after a few minutes, returned without any reading material. She sat down and suddenly stood again, returning to the bookcase.

"Can't find what you're looking for?" Tony asked. He put his pencil down in the account book he was reviewing.

"I'm just on edge. Emma's out there pretending to be me. I don't want her to get hurt."

He smiled. "I think you should worry more about anyone following her."

"I know. Have you made any progress on the artist who did my portrait?"

"He's no longer at the studio."

"Did he leave a forwarding address?"

"No, Cole checked. His place was as empty as your brother's place."

"Does Phillip know of him?" Phillip was Tony's boss and manager of the local museum.

"He's always interested in local talent, but until I mentioned his name, he hadn't heard of him."

"So, both he and Teddy disappeared without a trace. Were they in this together?"

"For what reason? Why would Teddy come back into your life at this time just to disappear?"

"Oh, Tony, I miss him so much," she said and moved to sit on his lap. He pulled her close to him.

"The man that came back or the boy you remember?"

"I'm not sure," she admitted. "When we talked, I could see a hint of that boy, the one who wanted so much more than what we had. It gave me hope."

"It turns out we didn't know him at all."

She laid her head on his shoulder. "What next?"

"The artist might be the key. We have to keep looking for him."

CHAPTER 13

Emma and Jeremy at the restaurant

Their dinner was wonderful and relaxing. As Jeremy paid for their meal, she looked at him with a raised eyebrow. "You up for an adventure?"

"Sure, let's give them what they want. You go first, I'll follow."

She smiled slightly and picked up her hat. "See you on the other side."

He grinned and waved to the waiter to pay the bill.

She stepped into the small hallway that led to the ladies' room. Emma knew the small man was there almost as soon as she entered the long, narrow hallway. "You know it isn't your money," the man said in a clipped voice.

They really need a new line. "I don't know what you're talking about," she said, still playing her role.

He was smaller than her but approached her aggressively in the small hallway. She retreated and, as he got closer, she stopped suddenly. The man hadn't expected that and jerked to a halt. "What?" he said, startled.

Emma tested his mettle and took a step toward him. This time, it was him who took a step back. "Hey! Stop that!" he said when he realized *he* was being intimidated. When she didn't stop approaching him, he held up his fist and shook it at her. "We'll be watching, and we'll get that money. Your brother had no right to take all of it. No right at all." He slammed his hat on his head. She put her hand in her pocket and pulled out just enough of her knife so the man could see the handle. She raised an eyebrow, and started toward him. He turned and ran away from her.

"Did you scare him?" asked Jeremy from across the hall.

"Yeah, I think I did," she mused.

"Not quite a Peggy thing to do," he commented.

"Well, I think Peggy would be getting fed up with the intimidation."

He smirked. "Ready to go back?"

"How about a walk around first?"

"I'd enjoy that. How about a carriage ride by the river?"

Her eyes lit up. "Yes, please."

He hailed a carriage, and they climbed in to enjoy the night. "So much is changing around here," she said, looking at the area. "Roads are being expanded; the land is being repurposed for the upcoming fair."

"The World's Fair," he commented. "All eyes will be on Chicago."

"Yes, like we saw in Paris at their fair." They sat quietly and Emma commented, "Mr. Pennington started the case with Skipper this week."

"Is he going to win?"

"He doesn't have a chance." She looked at the river and thought about the fair. "It will be magical. The plans show so many changes and improvements."

"You've been reading too much," he commented dryly.

"It'll improve the areas," she argued.

"And bring in more people. You see Chicago has gotten so much bigger."

Their trip complete, they were dropped off by the restaurant. They stood under the gas light for a long moment. "Time to get back."

"Yes, I've been approached by the big guy and the small one. Will the cowboy be next?"

"Probably. I wonder when he's going to approach you?"

"What're these guys' names?"

"Let's see," Jeremy said. "Eddie is the large man, Louis is the small man, and Harvey is the cowboy."

They mulled that over and walked to their hotel. They passed a stoop just before the hotel's entrance and heard a low voice drawl, "Gettin' kind of cozy, ain't you?"

She turned toward the voice and saw it was Harvey, sprawled on the stoop. *Well, that answers that question,* she thought. "And just what business is that of yours?" she asked.

He stayed where he was and didn't move to stand. Smoke trailed from his cigar. They watched as it floated up and dissipated into the air. "It's only my business if he's also after the money." He looked at Jeremy and said, "You ain't part of this and I think you should get lost."

"I don't think so," said Jeremy. "I think we're all concerned about where the money's located."

Harvey came slowly to his feet and flicked his cigar at Jeremy. Without thinking, Emma kicked him in the stomach.

Harvey stayed bent over and finally pulled himself up slowly. He looked closer at Emma. "Well, little lady, you're stronger than I thought."

"You deserved it," she said as Jeremy grabbed her arm and pulled her back from him.

He rubbed his stomach and said casually, "You may not make it through the night with that attitude."

"Are you threatening me?" she demanded, ready to go after him again. Jeremy held her back.

"No, it wasn't a threat. It was promise. You better not get in our way. Whatever happens, we'll get our money back."

Jeremy said to Emma, "We should go." He pulled her with him, but she continued to watch him over her shoulder.

As they left, Harvey called after them, "Think about who he might be, Miss Latimer. Is he who he says he is?"

She stopped suddenly and turned. "Why not mind your own business?"

"You are my business. That is, until the money's found."

"The money you keep mentioning, is it really yours or was it stolen?" she demanded.

He stood motionless and pulled out a new cigar and lit it. He finally said, "I don't know what you're talking about. We earned that money."

"Did you, though? Or are businesses owed the money you stole from them?"

He looked nonplussed at her. "Who've you been talking to?"

"All right, that's enough. Peggy, let's go," Jeremy said and led her away.

Harvey watched them move away. He exhaled the smoke in rings and started to follow them. When they entered the hotel, he was close behind.

The lobby was empty except for the clerk who was at the desk talking to Pete.

"Sit for a moment?" Jeremy asked.

She nodded and they moved to the small couches and sat.

"You lost your temper back there."

"Worried I am blowing my cover?"

"Yeah, can't see Peggy kicking someone in the stomach."

"Oh, I think it would've been exactly how she behaved if a lit cigar was thrown at Tony," Emma replied.

"Maybe, maybe not."

"Her upbringing was rougher than we thought. She's got some fight in her."

He thought about that. "Well, that's all three now, and they're all asking the same question."

"Four including Winsten. And we still have no idea where the money is located. We need more information on what they did to get that money."

"Is there a way to get more information from Winsten?" he mused.

"I don't have a way to contact him. His card didn't have an address."

"I bet we don't need one," he said, looking around the small lobby.

"You think he's watching also?"

"I don't think he wants those three clowns to know he's here." He looked over her shoulder. "Pete's trying to get your attention."

She glanced over with a quick nod. "Just a second," she said to Jeremy and went over to Pete. She listened to his low voice and took the proffered paper. "Thanks."

Pete nodded and watched as she returned to sit with Jeremy.

"What is it?" he asked.

"Let's find out." She read it and looked up. "Winsten, he's here and wants to talk."

"That's a coincidence. Where does he want to talk?"

"Out back in the alley."

He stood to accompany her. She stopped him with her hand. "I don't think he'll talk with you there."

He looked torn. Eddie, Louis, and Harvey had stepped into the lobby and were huddled together, gesturing toward them. "You go, I'll stay here and deal with them."

She nodded and headed to the desk. Pete met her there and commented in a low voice, "The door's that way."

"Thanks," she said. She exited into the dark alley and waited.

"You owe me an update," Winsten said as he stepped out of the shadows.

She ignored the statement. "You need to tell us what exactly these men did to get that money," she said, tapping her foot and putting her hand in her pocket. She was ready to pull out her knife to get the man to talk.

Winsten pulled at his coat and jerked his shoulders back. "What'll that give you?"

"Maybe the reason these men believe it's their money and not anyone else's."

His patience at an end, he shouted, "Those three men are killers!"

She hadn't expected that response. "I thought they were thieves."

He looked over his shoulder. "They are both. We can't talk here. It might not be safe."

"Then where?" she asked. Emma turned back to the hotel. "How about the hotel office?"

"I don't want to be seen by them," he muttered.

The detective needed to stay in the shadows to be effective. "Wait here." She stuck her head in and looked around. She spotted Jeremy, who seemed to be in an argument with all three suspects, so he was out. She looked around and saw Pete leaning on the desk, a twisted smile on his face as he watched the interaction.

She tapped on the wall next to her to get his attention. He turned toward her; she mouthed, "Office?"

He motioned with his hand toward the office. She held up a hand and went back out the door. "Come on," she said in a low voice. She turned to the door, and he followed close behind her.

Once inside, she held him up and waited for Pete. His eyes

widened but he immediately moved to block the view of the suspects. They went in low and into the office. She shut the door behind him.

He stood by the door, not moving further into the room. She didn't have the same apprehension and walked directly to the desk. "Over here," she directed. "We need to talk. I need the background on those men who are here in this hotel."

He grunted. "Miss Latimer, I think you're the wrong person to be sharing this information with. I don't want to put you into further danger."

She leaned back in the chair. "You know what? I think that time's passed, and it's time for you to fill in the facts I don't know." Winsten made a move to leave the room. "If you leave, I won't tell you if I find any of the money," she said. Her voice was low and had an edge to it.

He looked at the door and back at her. He moved reluctantly to the chair in front of the desk; his cane tapped as he got close and sat heavily, the chair screeching under his weight. She watched him with narrowed eyes, his hands were always in his pockets.

Finally, he started to talk. "It started years ago. They were involved in a con. That's where the money came from."

"You mentioned jewelry theft. We're all of them involved?"

"Not initially," Winsten admitted. "It started with two. Theodore was one the original members."

Now that's interesting, thought Emma. *Again he is using Theodore, not Teddy. Everyone else from Peggy to those three men called him Teddy.* She asked, "And the other one?"

"Harvey."

When she started to ask a question, Winsten continued. "Harvey was the key."

"How so?"

"Harvey was in a jewelry store when Teddy first saw him."

"Shopping?" she asked sarcastically.

"Yeah, well, scoping out the store for a quick score. That's when Harvey came in."

"What was he there for?"

"At that time, Harvey was a full-fledged priest."

She sat up suddenly. The chair creaked in response, and she asked in disbelief, "That cowboy, who smokes and threatened me, was a priest?" *Though,* she thought, *the clerical collar in the bag makes more sense now. Was it something Teddy kept as a reminder of that time?*

"He was, and when Theodore watched him walk up to the counter and ask for jewels for the cardinal to review, he couldn't believe it; they just handed them over. Why wouldn't they? Everyone knows priests are above reproach. And when Harvey left, Theodore followed him out."

"Did Harvey immediately drop his faith and join Teddy?" Emma was having a hard time wrapping her head around this scenario.

"Let's just say that Theodore was very persuasive and showed Harvey that the money was there for the taking."

"Just like that?"

"You'll have to ask Harvey for the rest of the story. Anyway. Harvey provided the resources they needed to start."

"Resources?"

"He knew where to get the robes and how to walk and talk like a priest. Theodore wouldn't be questioned."

"I guess no one asks a man of the cloth if he's honest. They just assume he is," she said, tapping her pencil. "The other two, why were they needed?"

"Initially, it was small jobs, and they were constantly on the move. Theodore knew that the larger churches had access to larger amounts of money, jewels , antiquities, and the like. They have it all."

"So, how did Eddie and Louis get involved?"

"You're mistaken there about the number of men."

Emma frowned and asked, "How so? Three of them showed up at the funeral and have been demanding money."

"There was a fourth man, Miss Latimer."

"A fourth? Now there is another person involved in this. This is getting out of hand," she said. *Is he talking about Arthur?* she wondered and played ignorant of this fact.

Winsten stood and leaned on the desk toward her, his voice raised. "The missing man is Arthur. They left him to die!" He pulled himself up and explained. "It was their last score, the big one. The con was becoming too well *known*. They were getting famous."

She watched him stalk up and down the room with that cane. Each time it struck the floor, she jumped. *His hands remained in his pockets, even to manage the cane,* she observed. He was wrapped up in the story and seemed to be talking to himself more than her. It was time to listen.

"That last score was in the diamond market in New York City. They'd decided it was time to end their association. They'd set it up so that they'd hit four diamond merchants at the same time, each taking a different location and meeting up after."

She had to ask. "What happened?"

He looked dazed when he turned to her. "The location picked for the final meeting wasn't far enough away and the store's security found them. They were surrounded and, once the shooting started, the four ran."

"And the fifth man, Arthur?"

"Left there to bleed to death."

She sighed and asked, "What happened next?"

"The jewels were pulled together and hidden until the heat died down. An agreement was made between the final four to meet up and divide the jewels. From what I understand, your brother took them to hide."

"Where did you get the information?" Emma asked suspiciously as she pulled out her notebook. *Why does he know this? This sounds like a firsthand account.*

"I've been investigating them for all these years. My first lead in a while was Theodore's obituary."

"What about the others? What do you know about them?"

"Harvey's from Texas, Harvey Simms. Louis' full name is Louis Charles, and the last is Eddie Swindel."

Jeremy, she thought, *I'll have to bring him in.* "What about the other man?"

"The one here at the hotel? Slim, dark curly hair?"

She nodded. "He wasn't at the funeral."

"Him, I don't know. He isn't part of this."

"I wonder why he's here. I saw him talking to the others."

"You seem to be spending time with him," he commented.

So, he is watching me. She shrugged. "I have no reason not to."

"Has he asked about the money?"

"No more than anyone else," she stated noncommittally.

Winsten asked the question that everyone had been asking her. "Have you found the money?"

"No. I don't know where to look. Any ideas?"

He shook his head. "Though the men themselves might know more. You might ask Eddie why he arrived here before everyone else."

"How do you know that?" she said.

He moved his gaze around the room and said casually, "I asked about the men here and the manager told me a messenger delivered Eddie's things from another hotel in the area. The other two arrived by train the morning of the funeral." He checked his watch without taking his hands out of his pocket. "I gotta be going." He put on his tall hat and left the room. As the detective strode off, his peculiar gate caused his long coat tails to flap against his legs.

Emma stayed where she was, tapping her pencil on the now closed notebook. *What a strange man,* she thought. *He seems more emotionally involved than a detective should be.* Moving to the door, she opened it more cautiously than Winsten had. "They're gone," Pete said. "You can come out."

She moved the door wide enough to ease her way out and saw that Pete was behind the desk.

"Where's the manager?" she asked, looking around.

"He went to get some food. I told him I'd cover."

She went over to the counter, leaned on it, and asked, "Are you always here?" So far, she'd seen him both early in the morning and now late at night.

"I need the money." Pete turned to her and looked her directly in the eyes.

Emma watched him closely and finally said, "Thanks for the help."

"Find out anything?" he asked, looking back down at the cards in front of him.

"Maybe," she said, looking around for Jeremy.

"I took him up to his room."

"Who?"

"The gentleman in the room next to yours."

Pete was anticipating her. She gave him a long look, but with his back toward her, he didn't notice her attention. "Can you take me up to my room? It's been a long evening."

Pete was all smiles when he turned and looked like the nice kid who'd been so helpful before. Was she seeing something that wasn't there?

"Are you ready?" he asked.

"I am." She followed him to the elevator and waited while he opened it for her to board. Once underway, they were silent. The doors were opened on her floor, and she started out.

"I'm sure there'll be more answers for you tomorrow," he told her.

She turned to ask him what he meant, but he was already pulling the doors shut on the elevator. She leaned over the iron guard and watched as it descended down the shaft. A low whistle distracted her. She turned toward it and saw Jeremy at her door. She nodded and headed toward it. They met inside and she quickly kissed him hello.

"That was an active evening," Jeremy said, moving into the room. "Who should go first?"

"I will," she said, dropping on the bed. He nodded and moved the desk chair close to the bed. She continued. "I got the background on why Eddie, Louis, and Harvey think the money is theirs." She went into the details she'd learned.

"Winsten's been trailing them for ten years? What kind of investigator does that?" he asked in wonder.

"I don't know. Maybe he trails them in his spare time?"

"Seems like he's fixated on those three."

"He does and he was overly emotional during different parts of the story. It was almost like he'd been there."

"He might have been, maybe a security guard on the scene. And does that make him dangerous?"

"That makes him someone we shouldn't discount. Though I wonder if he wants the money for himself. He didn't share any specifics on who hired him."

"Hmm," he said, thinking.

"What about you? Did you learn anything from the three men?"

"They're getting impatient. All they can talk about is the money they're owed."

"That's kind of a gray area," she commented.

"Not according to them."

She jumped to another subject. "How do you think Hen is?" Emma asked. "I don't want her to have bad dreams and we're not there to help."

"You told Mom to watch out for it, right? You don't think she can handle her?"

"You're right. I know you're right," she said, lying down and looking up at the ceiling.

"I think Hen's fine," he said reassuringly. "We haven't even been here a full day. She has only been gone one night; not enough time has passed to miss us."

She continued to study the ceiling. "I know, I miss her so much. I miss the routine we've settled into."

"So, this whole parenting thing isn't so bad?" he teased.

"You know what? Surprisingly, it's been rather wonderful," she admitted. "It feels like she's always been with us."

That was a big step for her to admit, thought Jeremy. *She's been against having a family and a traditional marriage, that's why we're still unmarried. Are things changing with her?* "It does," He mumbled, distracted by his thoughts. "You know what? I'm tired. It's getting late."

"It is," she said, pulling herself up and beginning to get organized for bed.

Jeremy had started toward his room and had a thought. "Where's the bag?"

"Up there." She indicated the armoire with her hand. He started toward it. "No," she said, "not inside but on top." He nodded and grabbed the chair he'd been sitting in.

"Did you think of something?" she asked, watching him.

"Maybe." He felt around the top with his hand and pulled the bag down to him. He poured the contents out on the bed, and they looked at the items again. They hadn't changed: a list, a train ticket, a clerical collar, and a wallet.

"Nothing's changed," she said, moving things around. "Though now we know why a clerical collar's here."

"That does seem to confirm Winsten's story, or at least it helps support it."

"Yeah. It's coming down to our three suspects. Harvey, Louis, and Eddie."

"Don't discount Winsten. He's also up to his neck in this."

"Yes," she said and drummed her fingers on her lips.

"What're you thinking?" he asked, reading her tell.

"I think what bothers me is the money and that they're all pressuring me for it."

"If they had the money, they wouldn't still be here," he said logically.

"You're right. I think we need something to move this case forward." She reached for the receipt. "I think we need to check out the auction house tomorrow."

"That sounds like a plan," he said with a wide yawn.

"Time for bed?"

"I never thought you would ask," he said and lowered his head to hers and held her tight.

CHAPTER 14

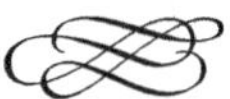

he next day

The sun streamed into the room and Emma snuggled deeper under the covers. Jeremy nudged her. "We have to get up soon. We're trying their patience by staying in."

"It's still too early," she muttered, burrowing down. "Why would they be up at this hour?"

BANG BANG BANG!

"Does that answer your question?" Jeremy asked in a low voice.

She sighed but didn't move.

BANG BANG BANG! This time, voices followed. "Get up! We want to talk!"

BANG BANG BANG!

Jeremy got up and quickly went to his room to dress. He'd meet them in the hallway.

Emma got up, pulled on a blue dressing gown, went to the

door, and flung it open. Louis' hand was raised and he was just about to bang on the door again.

"The next person who bangs on this door again," she growled, "I will break his fingers off, cut them up into little, tiny bits, and feed those little tiny bits to him one by one."

The man lowered his arm slowly and stepped away from her. "You, you got no right to be rude like that," Louis stammered. "'Sides, we want to talk."

"You'll have to wait. I'm not dressed."

"We ain't moving," Eddie said.

I guess the bathroom is out of the question. "Give me a few minutes," she said, and slammed the door in his face. Emma looked at the pitcher and water basin. *I'll have to make do.* She pulled off her dressing gown and quickly washed up. Once dressed, she pulled her hair into a high bun and the banging started again. *Now or never,* she thought and reached out a hand to open the door.

She pulled the door open as Louis started to bang on it again. Louis' fist was in midair and without the door, the momentum forced him to fall at her feet. He saw the look on Emma's face and scrambled upright, straightening his jacket.

The other men pushed their way past him and into the room.

She backed up, warily watching the three.

"Hey, guys, what have we hear?" Jeremy asked from the doorway. "Forcing ourselves into women's hotel rooms now? Tsk. Tsk."

Harvey turned toward Jeremy, his face the opposite of the priest he'd been purported to be. "You again. You're like a bad penny, always turning up."

Emma couldn't resist and taunted, "Don't you mean the prodigal son?"

The man turned the glare on her. "What do you know?"

"I know plenty," she said, lifting her chin. "I know that whatever money you guys' think is yours was stolen."

"It doesn't matter where the money came from. It's ours!" Harvey thundered. Louis and Eddie nodded.

She let that go. "Well, what is it? What do you want?"

"The money!"

"Yes, yes, the money. This is getting monotonous. I don't have the money."

All three started to protest.

"SHUT UP!" She pointed her finger at them and the three men fell silent. "Today, I am going to talk to the person who set up the auction for Teddy's belongings."

"Good, then we'll go with you," Eddie said forcefully.

"No, you won't," said Emma, "but I will take August with me."

"Why him?" demanded Louis.

"That's my decision. You'll just have to accept it."

Jeremy straightened from the doorway. "I'm Arthur's brother. Remember, the man you left to die in an alley? The man you abandoned to save your own skin?"

The men froze and looked at each other. They were silent; they had nothing to refute the claims. What he said was true.

Harvey shook his finger first at Emma and then at Jeremy. "You better contact us as soon as you get back."

"Fine," she said, and for the first time, she saw that they were being reasonable. "I think you should leave now. I need to finish getting dressed and go to breakfast."

They looked mutinous but finally filed out one at a time. Jeremy called from the doorway, "Knock on my door when you're ready to leave."

"I will, thank you."

Emma closed the door behind the men and leaned on it. Jeremy didn't come through the connecting door immediately and she could hear more arguing in the hallway. She left them to it and gathered up her items to go to the bathroom. She passed the still arguing men and made her way there, and once refreshed, she exited. The hallway was clear, and she was happy to see Harvey, Eddie, and Louis were no longer by her door.

She shrugged and entered her room. She was surprised to see Jeremy there. "Hey, babe, just about ready?" he asked.

"Just about. I heard more arguments?" she inquired.

"Aw, they weren't thrilled with me accompanying you and the possibility of my getting to the money before them." He shook his head. "Boy, I hope we find something out today. I'm afraid they may be ready to do something drastic to us for being in their way."

"No, I don't think so. We're too valuable right now. We're their only hope of finding the money."

"The auction house is a good lead. And one of the only ones that's connected to Teddy's bag."

"We'll need to get with Cole and let him know the lead we're pursuing," said Emma.

"I sent a message with Pete."

"Pete, huh. He's on duty again?"

He heard the tone and asked, "Do you suspect Pete of something?"

"He's just been right where I need him to be."

"So, another person to watch. You think he's another suspect?"

"I suspect everyone," she commented, and he responded with a low laugh.

"That you do."

"Those three know where we're going."

"You know they'll follow."

"Maybe we can sneak out without them seeing us."

"Maybe."

A knock sounded from next door. Jeremy held up his fingers to his mouth and moved quietly back to his room. She closed the connecting door behind him. It was a few moments later when the door opened again. "A messenger," he said and held up an envelope.

"From Cole?" she asked.

He opened it and read quickly. "Yes, he confirmed it's Smith Auction House on 4th."

"Then we go."

"How about a quick nap?"

Emma's stomach growled. "How 'bout food first, nap later?"

"Oh, all right," he said, kissing her cheek. "I'll meet you on the other side."

"You always say that," she muttered.

Emma pinned her hat on her head; she'd removed the netting but stayed dressed in black. She tucked the list into her pocket and tossed the bag back on top of the armoire. One less thing to worry about.

She heard another knock, this time at her door. She went to it and found Jeremy waiting and took his elbow to the elevator. The ever-present Pete stood waiting for them in the elevator.

"Good morning, Miss Latimer, Mister Smith."

"Good morning, Pete. Back on shift today?" Emma asked. Jeremy bumped her to stop her questioning. She bumped back and waited for the elevator operator's reply.

"Working to get money for my family," Pete said. "You'll probably see me a lot while you're guests of the hotel." *Did Pete's voice have an edge to it?* she wondered. She looked closer but just saw the same open boyish face. She dropped the line of questioning. They had too many other suspects to worry about.

The elevator slowly made its way down, the operator and passengers silent. When the elevator reached the bottom floor, Pete eased the door open and said, "I'm here to help. Nothing more."

What an odd way to say that, thought Emma. "Thank you," she said and followed Jeremy out. She could feel Pete watching them as they exited the hotel onto the street. "That was unexpected," she said.

"Was it?" asked Jeremy. "The boy's been helpful and protective of you."

"I know, and if he is part of this, he might be with us and not against us?"

"That's something to consider."

They walked across to the café. The restaurant was quiet as they entered. The initial breakfast rush had ended. Once they were sat at a table, they ordered quickly.

Emma asked when they were alone, "Is Cole going to meet us there?"

"No, he's on the train this morning. He wants to reinterview the people who were working when Teddy was pushed off."

"Does he think he missed something?"

"We have so little to go on; we need to go back over everything."

"The items in the bag were so sparse. If he was running, who or what was funding the trip? Again, where's the money?"

"He must have had a plan."

They stopped talking as the food arrived. She eagerly ate and was pleasantly full once the meal was over.

"Do you see them?" she asked, not looking around.

"No, but I'm sure they're around."

"Me, too. We need to move on to the auction house."

"I hope they keep their distance so that we can investigate."

"Patience doesn't seem to be their strong suit," she murmured.

Jeremy didn't answer, instead he stood and placed the money on the table for the check. He offered her a hand up, she took it, and they strolled outside, where Jeremy hailed a carriage and guided her to it. They gave the destination to the driver and sat back to enjoy the ride. The sun shone down on the open carriage. Emma closed her eyes and let the heat give her some calm.

The carriage pulled to a stop. Jeremy paid the driver and helped her down to the sidewalk. They stood in front of the building; it was mostly warehouses. "Why so big?" she asked.

"They need space for the wares," he explained. "They have them set out in the open space and then move them to the stage for bidders."

They walked to the door and entered. The space was wide open in front of them. The place was full of furniture, art, rugs, and other assorted oddities. It was the kind of place Dora would've loved. Emma would've liked to look at the assortment of goods, too, but focused on what they were there for. "Do you have a name?" Emma asked Jeremy.

He looked at the note from Cole. "Fredrick Kirtz." He spotted a man in a dark suit and white shirt; he was tall and looking at a woman from his imposing height about a desk. "This way, I think."

They made their way over and waited until the woman's questions were exhausted. "You may find another one over in that section," he said and waved over a young man to assist her. The woman moved on, and he turned to Emma and Jeremy

"Are you Fredrick Kirtz?" Emma asked.

"I am. Do you have a question about the auction?"

"Not this one," stated Jeremy.

Emma asked, "Is there somewhere we can talk?"

Kirtz looked torn. "I'm sorry, we're working to get the auction started. I won't be available until after."

Emma opened her mouth to argue the point and Jeremy leaned down to whisper. "We might observe the auction process."

Emma nodded, understanding the merits of his argument. She turned to Kirtz. "We'd appreciate your time after the auction. We have some things to discuss with you."

He gave them a long look and said, "See me after." He turned and strode off determinedly toward the stage. It was time to get the auction started. As he moved, people took it as their direction to take their seats.

"Let's take a seat," Jeremy suggested.

Emma looked around the room and saw Harvey at the back by the door. "Damn it," she said.

Jeremy looked and saw Eddie on the west side and Louis on the east. "Surrounded."

"Yeah," she said and continued to study them. "They're keeping their distance."

"They need us here," he said and turned away from them. The auction started with the first pieces of furniture moved to the stage. "Got the list?"

"Right here." Emma pulled it out and ran her finger down it. "What should we be looking for?" she murmured. "Furniture?"

"No. The art?" he suggested.

"We'll have to wait and see. Though I have my doubts. If the collection was as good as Tony said, it probably had private buyers."

He looked at Kirtz. "He may have set it up. It's something to follow up on."

"There's some jewelry listed here. We can keep an eye out for that."

"I'm not sure it would be of any value. Certainly not a clue to the money."

"True."

Objects were taken to and from the stage and a record keeper stayed on the side to document the final sales. Smaller pieces came up, but nothing matched the descriptions on the paper.

Kirtz announced to the crowd, "We'll be taking a two-hour break and then we'll resume." He stepped down from the stage and motioned to Emma and Jeremy to follow him.

As they stood, Jeremy asked, "Have they moved?"

"No. They seem to be staying put for now." Emma nodded and continued to the office.

When they entered the office space, they found Kirtz at a large ornate desk. Every corner of the room was stuffed with antiquities and art. It was hanging on all of the walls and ones that couldn't be hung were leaning against the walls. Emma thought, *Legally received?*

"Please, sit," Kirtz said. Emma and Jeremy moved to the heavy chairs in front of the desk. "What did you want to discuss that couldn't wait?"

Jeremy nodded toward Emma. She pulled out the list and offered it to him. "I have a list here of items you sold for Teddy Latimer."

Kirtz seemed startled at the topic. He sat back without taking the list and went silent.

Emma pulled her hand back and waited.

When he remained silent, Jeremy asked, "Are you aware that Teddy was murdered?"

He sat forward at that and asked, "Who are you?"

Jeremy looked at Emma with a raised eyebrow. She turned to the auctioneer. "We're investigators looking into his murder."

"Investigators! With the police?" The man's eyes darted around the room.

That confirmed Emma's suspicions: some of the items had come from non-legal channels.

"No," answered Jeremy. The man looked relieved and started to sit back. "We're with the Pinkertons."

Kirtz paled at that comment and stood in an agitated manner.

"Look, Mr. Kirtz," said Emma, "we aren't interested in anything not connected to our case." She deliberately looked around the room.

"You're not?" he asked and took out his handkerchief to blot his forehead.

"No."

Jeremy took the list from Emm and said, "What can you tell us about this?"

"I don't need it. I have a copy here with me." He opened his desk drawer and pulled out a black notebook. "What would you like to know?"

Emma started. "When did Teddy come to you?" They needed a timeline and, except for the night he disappeared and the week between dinners with Peggy, Tony, and Teddy, they needed to fill in the gaps in his activities in the city.

"He approached me about two months ago."

"Two months! His leaving was planned!" Jeremy asked. "What did he tell you?"

"Not much," Kirtz admitted. "He wanted to see if he could sell everything he had."

"Including the art?" asked Emma.

"Well, the art was what delayed everything."

"Delayed? How?"

"Teddy had planned to leave much faster, but the art had to be handled carefully. Special sales had to be set up. He was quite upset at the delay."

"Did he mention anyone threatening him? What was the reason for him leaving?"

Kirtz sat down in his chair and leaned back. "He was on edge, worried about something or someone. He only wanted to meet in his apartment and never here."

"Was there anyone with him when you met?"

"Never."

"We have information that the art was still on the walls as of last week."

"That was part of it," he admitted. "Once the sales went through, the art had to stay. On the day he left, I and a team of workers went there and emptied the apartment. They were then transported to their new owners."

"Do you have a list of the paintings?" Jeremy asked. He wanted Tony to review it and see if any weren't listed.

"I do." He looked down at the book and said, "The people who bought these won't want their names to be part of the investigation."

"If they have nothing to do with the inquiries we're making, we'll respect their privacy."

Kirtz looked relieved at that. He handed over the list to Jeremy.

Jermey took it, folded it up, and placed it in his pocket.

Emma asked, "How much money did he receive from this sale?" Kirtz jotted a number on a piece of paper and handed it to her. Her eyes widened and she handed it to Jeremy. He had the same reaction and asked, "Why so much?"

"Teddy had invested in very valuable art. He also had refined taste in furniture, clothes, and other items. The finer things."

Emma leaned toward Jeremy and said in a low voice, "I'm not sure those guys are aware of how much money might be involved in this."

"No, and we don't need to tell them. This is already messy enough," Jeremy replied in the same tone. He turned to Kirtz. "Did you know Teddy before he came back to Chicago?"

"I did," he admitted.

Emma pounced on that. "Did you sell diamonds for him?"

"You-you said you wouldn't look at other things," Kirtz stuttered.

"I just need you to answer the question," she said, standing to make her point.

He looked to Jeremy for help and Jeremy stared back at him. He sighed. "I did."

"When?" she demanded.

"It was years ago."

"Years?"

"We were friends back in the old days; we worked in the factories together. My way out and his were different. He left to find his way and I stayed."

"So, you know Peggy?" asked Jeremy.

"I did. I see her at the occasional auction and we're friendly."

"Did you ever talk about Teddy?"

"Occasionally. She wanted to know if I'd heard from him."

"Had you?"

"Yes," he admitted. "It was years ago, and he had several things to dispose of."

"Did he see Peggy when he came home?"

"Not at that time, no. He was very nervous and wanted the process to go fast."

"Like now."

Kirtz acknowledged that with a nod. "Yes, his manner during our current transactions was similar to that time."

"Where did he go after that?"

"I'm not sure. I didn't hear from him until he arrived in Chicago this last time." He looked at the clock "I need to get back. Is there anything else?"

Jeremy looked at Emma, and she shrugged. "We can come back if there are any other questions." Jeremy stood and offered Emma his elbow.

She reached over to take it and hesitated. "Mr. Kirtz, there are three men…"

"Maybe four," interrupted Jeremy.

"Four men…"

"Maybe five," Jeremy interrupted again. "Pete."

"*Five* men…" Emma started again.

"Maybe more. At this point, we're not exactly sure."

"ANYWAY," Emma said, shooting an irritated look at Jeremy. She turned back to Kirtz. "There are *possibly a number* of individuals who're getting desperate to find that money."

Kirtz swallowed nervously. "Will they, will they try to hurt me?"

"Is there someplace you can go for a short time?" Jeremy asked. "Until we resolve this case?"

"These are the men Teddy was scared of?"

"We think so. At the very least, they helped steal the diamonds, and they feel that any money from the sale is theirs."

"I'll make sure that I close down for a few days," Kirtz promised.

Jeremy handed him one of his business cards. "If you run into trouble, contact the Pinkerton office and we'll be there for you."

Emma stressed, "Don't find yourself alone with any of them. We can't trust anyone." They started to head out again.

"Wait," Kirtz said. "One more thing." He pulled open his desk drawer and pulled out a small ring box. "I need to get to Peggy, and I don't want to draw any unnecessary attention to her."

"What is it?" Emma asked. The small box drew her back to the desk.

Kirtz opened the box and showed her a lovely large opal stone set in gold.

"Jeremy!" she said, startled. "This is in the painting!"

Jeremy recognized it as well and commented, "We've seen that ring before. How did you get it?"

"Teddy gave it to me when he started preparations to leave."

"But Peggy wore it in a painting that he commissioned for her," Emma said.

"I don't know about that. All I was told was that I was to deliver it to her if anything happened to him. Can you do this for me?"

Emma said, "We can." He handed her the box. She took the ring out of the box and slid it inside her corset top.

Jeremy leaned over her shoulder and murmured, "Sure it's safe there?"

She looked serious and said, "We don't need those guys finding it." She turned back to Kirtz. "I'd like to examine the painting and ask Peggy some questions." There might be more clues in it than they originally thought. She wanted a good look at it.

As they walked towards the exit, Jeremy repeated the warning. "Make sure you aren't alone at any time."

"I'll finish the auction and make myself scarce," Kirtz promised.

They exited the room; people had returned and were strolling around the items being prepared for auction. "Do you see them?" murmured Emma.

He looked around the room quickly. "No, they may have gotten tired of waiting for us."

"Hmm."

"You concerned?"

"Some. I like to know where they are," she said simply.

"Where to next?"

"Back to the hotel, I think. We need to think about next steps."

"Let's go."

As they walked together, Emma slowed him and asked, "Do you think they're aware of how much money Teddy had?" The amount they'd seen had been life changing for whomever got it.

"I think they just want the money. I don't know if they have an amount in mind." They started to walk again, and Jeremy asked, "Any ideas on the ring?"

"Odd, isn't it? Why didn't Peggy already have the ring if she wore it in the picture?"

"And why deliver the ring to her now, only if something happened to Teddy?"

"It might be the link to the painting. I think it might be more valuable than we thought."

"So, not just a sentimental gift," he mused.

"No, I don't think so."

"Would you like to get a carriage?" he asked. They'd moved into a busier area and carriages were available.

"Not yet. I'm enjoying the walk," she said. "Though we should probably stop for lunch."

"Okay, there's a café down this street."

They continued down the street and into the café. A glance around the room assured her that there wasn't anyone she recognized in the room. She was able to relax and enjoy the meal. These moments alone would be treasured.

Once done, they walked outside, and Jeremy hailed a carriage; it was time to return to the case. They sat quietly and held hands as the carriage took them back to the hotel. Once they were there, they found the lobby full of people. "Must be something happening in town," Jeremy observed.

Emma looked around at the men, most of whom were in business suits and hats. Several had assistants taking notes and following them around. "As long as they aren't mixed up in our case. We have enough suspects now."

"Not quite the same league as our three."

They went to the elevator and waited with a group of businessmen. "This thing has been stuck forever," one of the men bitterly complained.

"Stuck?" Emma said. She looked up and saw the number indicated was on the floor where she and Jeremy were located.

She tugged at his coat and muttered, "Stairs?"

He looked up at the floor number and confirmed, "Stairs."

They both moved quickly to the door and up the stairs. They were out of breath as they entered the hallway and walked toward the elevator. Pete stood outside his elevator; he had a heavy frown on his face and was staring hard at Emma's door.

"What's going on, Pete?" asked Jeremy.

Pete jumped and turned to them. "You didn't wait for the elevator!"

"No," she murmured, "we came up to check and see why the elevator appears to be stuck here. You have a lot of people waiting for you."

Pete turned his gaze back to her door. "They can wait," he muttered.

"Uh, Pete, who's in that room?" Jeremy asked. Pete didn't answer and his gaze didn't waver.

Emma moved quickly toward her door. "Don't!" shouted Pete. "Wait!" He ran up behind her and grabbed her arm.

Emma whirled toward him and demanded, "Who's in my room?"

"No one now," Harvey said as he strolled down the hallway toward them.

Pete's eyes opened wide, and he continued to hold her arm tightly. Jeremy stopped the boy and pushed him back. "I think you should let the lady open her own door."

Pete's lips tightened and he started to push past him. Jeremy punched him in the gut, sending the air out quickly and doubling him over. He released Emma abruptly.

She took the moment to go to the door. The knob turned easily. She entered first warily, followed closely by Jeremy, Harvey, and finally a bent over Pete, who was still struggling to get his breath back. She had to step on the mattress to continue to check the room. It'd been torn apart. The bed had been moved to the center of the floor. She went to the armoire and checked her bags. "I don't think anything's been taken." She didn't move a chair to check for the bag on top.

Jeremy grabbed Harvey. "Did you do this?" he demanded.

"It wasn't him," Eddie said from the doorway. He stepped from behind Harvey.

"And Louis?" asked Jeremy.

"I'm here also," the man said and moved into view behind Eddie.

"Did you *all* do this?" Jeremy asked. He turned his glare onto Pete. Is *Pete covering for them?*

"No, we didn't," Harvey answered for the three of them.

"Really," said Emma mockingly. "Right now, you're turning honest?"

Harvey drawled, "Honest? No. We'd planned to do this, but we spotted the girl leaving the room by the fire escape. We waited around to see what would happen."

"Girl? What did this girl look like?" Emma asked. She turned her eyes on Pete. He squirmed under her glare.

"She was a pretty little thing," Harvey said and held up his hand about mid cheek. "She's about this tall."

"Long dark hair piled high on her head," Eddie added.

Louis contributed the last part. "And young."

"I think I know her," said Emma. She turned away from Pete and looked at the three men. "Have you seen her around here before?"

"Not since we checked in," Eddie replied. The other two men nodded in agreement.

"Why would she search your room?" asked Jeremy. He looked at the three men. They shrugged.

"Yeesh! Is she after our money?" Louis complained. "We don't need additional people involved in this."

"What money?" asked Emma sardonically, sitting on the bed.

"What did you find out at the auction?" pounced Harvey.

"Well, I ..." she started. She stopped as Pete started to slink out the door. "Whoa, hold on there!"

"I-I need to get the people moving on the elevator, or I'll lose my job," he stammered.

Jeremy said, "We know where to find him." He turned to Pete and stated, "You can go."

Pete ran out and they heard the elevator door slam shut.

The three men looked at her. "Well?"

"We only found out that the list was accurate, and that Teddy did receive cash in exchange for the merchandise."

"Yes! At least we know the money is real!" Eddie exclaimed excitedly.

"But we don't know where it is yet," Emma reminded him.

They all started to ask more questions and Emma finally put up her hands. "Fellas, I'm tired, and I need to straighten this up. Unless you want to help?" The three men all shook their heads no. "That figures. Can we start the active stalking of me later today?"

Jeremy's mouth twisted into a semblance of a smile. "I think Miss Latimers's right. We have nothing here to work on."

"How can we trust you don't already know where it is? Maybe you got more information than you're sharing?" Eddie challenged.

"Why would we come back here?" asked Jeremy reasonably.

That logic seemed to work on the three. They huddled together and finally nodded. They turned back to Emma and Jeremy.

"We'll resume this evening." They turned and started to leave. Harvey put his arm up across the door and turned back to them. "I assume you're also going to leave the lady as well?" he asked Jeremy.

"Ah, right, right. I'm right behind you," said Jeremy. He turned to Emma with a smile. "See you for dinner this evening."

"I'll see you then," Emma said. They finally filed out with Jeremy surreptitiously blowing her a kiss. Emma looked around at the mess and started picking things up.

Jeremy stood in the hallway and watched Eddie and Louis enter their rooms and shut the doors. Harvey stopped and looked back at Jeremy and cocked an eyebrow at him. Jeremy saluted and walked to his door, unlocked it, and went inside, closing the door behind him.

Emma's side door eased open, revealing Jeremy. "Help me

with this, will you?" she directed. The bed was organized first. They moved it back into position and lifted the mattress. Once it was in place, they moved about the room, picking up. Emma gathered the clothes and hung them in the closet. Jermey retrieved other things strewn about and placed them back where they'd been. They moved to the bed and put the sheets and covers back on it. Once everything was in place, he commented, "The girl."

"Yeah, what's her connection to Pete?"

"We need to talk to that boy."

"You did let him go," she said, wagging her finger at him.

He grabbed it and pulled her to him, kissing her quickly. "I didn't want him to become another target for the guys."

"Pete and the girl aren't old enough to be part of the original scams. What's their connection to this?"

"Are they the killers?"

"Unlikely. You saw how big Teddy was. I doubt she could've pushed him off a train."

"Even if she shot him first?"

"It would've made it harder."

"Then who are they?"

Emma looked out the window and drummed her fingers on her lips. Jeremy followed her gaze and walked to the window. "We need some questions answered, but how do we leave and not have the guys see us?"

"Fire escape?" he asked. "Down to the street."

"Not down, but up," she stated. Abbey had said that, if they needed to get out without being seen, they could go up. "The building next door is close enough to get to and we could use their exit to get out."

"Did Mom tell you that?" he asked.

"Definitely."

"Okay, let's do it. How do we get out of here if they can see the fire escape?"

"They're probably also watching the hallway."

"Harvey said they saw her going down, not up. Their view might be blocked the higher up we go."

"Let me change." Emma put on the split skirt she used for riding her bike and turned back to him. "Ready."

They walked to his room, and he eased open the window. "Be quick." She went out and started up the ladder that led to the floor above them. Jeremy eased out behind her and shut the window. They quickly make their way up to the roof. Once there, Emma asked, "Did we make it without being seen?"

Jeremy looked around. "I think so. We need to get moving." They walked to look at the building next door to them, Jeremy in the lead. "Whoops," he said.

"What's wrong?"

"Well, I think things have changed since Mom was here last." The neighboring building appeared to be of newer construction and there was a gap of about five feet between the two.

"You think so?" Emma asked sarcastically.

"We'll need to jump," observed Jeremy. "You up for it?"

"If we can get a good running start," she said, glancing around the rooftop. "I can do it."

"Okay, we go," Jeremy said. "I'll go first. See you on the other side." He backed away some distance and started to run. The ledge was low and allowed him to push off on it. He landed on the other roof safely. He was out of breath but called out, "Come on, your turn!"

Emma smiled. "On my way." She backed up the same distance and ran. As she reached the edge, she heard something behind her. She didn't stop and she jumped and landed in a roll next to Jeremy. "Hey!" called a voice from the rooftop they had just left. Jeremy helped her up and they turned to the voice. It was Pete!

"Where are you going?" he called rather frantically.

"We'll be back," she said. "We need to check on something."

"Promise you'll be back!" the young man's voice went higher.

"We will be, I promise. Watch our rooms. We don't want anyone else, and I mean anyone, in there."

He looked down briefly and back at the duo. "I'll make sure."

"You owe us an explanation!"

"Yeah, I guess I might," he said and turned toward the door.

Emma moved to follow Jeremy and they heard Pete yell out, "I know you're not Peggy!" They turned in surprise, but he hadn't waited for their reaction and had already left the roof.

"He knows," she said, studying the closed door that Pete exited through.

"We need to go," said Jeremy. She nodded and headed to the edge of the building. "Um, Emma," he called.

"Yes," she said, distracted by Pete's disclosure.

"I think the doorway might be easier to use."

She looked over at him. He stood by the door that led downstairs. "You might be right."

They hurried through the door and down the stairs. The building housed offices and they were careful to stay on the stairs and, once they reached the bottom floor, Jeremy opened the door to the lobby. He peered out and found the area vacant. "Let's go."

They walked out and started toward the door. Emma stopped him. "Alley."

"Right." They moved toward the back of the building and out to the alley. "We'll need a carriage to get to Peggy and Tony's."

They walked out of the alley, where Jeremy hailed a carriage. They climbed in and gave the address for Tony and Peggy's home. "Think we were followed?" she asked, looking out the small opening in the back of the carriage.

He turned and looked behind them. "I don't think so." He turned back and settled into the seat. "Still have the ring?"

"Yes, did you want to make sure?" she teased.

"I do," he said and smiled. It dropped off his face when he said, "So, Pete."

"Yeah, I thought he knew more than he let on. He was around too much."

"Not only that, but he is also mixed up with our Mystery girl. You know, we really need to get her name."

"Well, our priority now is to get this ring to Peggy and see that painting again."

Jeremy nodded.

The carriage pulled to a stop. Jeremy assisted Emma down and paid the driver. She took his elbow and they walked to the front door. It opened as they approached. Tony stood there. He immediately stepped back to let them into the house.

"You're back here so soon! Why?" he asked.

"Can we talk?" Jeremy asked as he shut the door behind them.

"I haven't had a chance to look into the art." Tony rubbed his neck and said, "I wanted to stay close to Peggy."

"We understand. We have some information to share and something to show Peggy."

"What is it?"

"Why don't we move into the study?" Emma suggested. Tony looked like he needed to sit down. His shirt was undone at the collar, his jacket was nowhere in sight, and it appeared that he hadn't combed his hair in a while.

They moved to the room and pulled the doors shut. "Well," demanded Tony, "what is it?"

Emma patted her chest and Jeremy motioned to Tony. "You'll need to turn around."

"Why?" Tony asked exasperated.

"Because I said. C'mon, Tony, help us out," said Jeremy. Tony turned suddenly and faced the bookshelf behind them.

Emma unbuttoned her top and reached into her corset for

the ring. Once she had it out, she handed it to Jeremy and secured her top. "You can turn around now," said Jeremy.

Tony turned and saw what Jeremy held in his hand.

"The ring! But I didn't think it was real!" He reached out and took it from him.

The doors slipped open and the three looked toward it. It was Peggy; she looked rested. "What have you got there?" she inquired as she walked over to Tony.

"You won't believe it," he said and showed her what he held. Her face lost color and Emma grabbed one arm and Tony the other. They walked her to a chair at the desk.

"The ring! I thought the artist painted it in. Can I see it?" she asked. Tony handed it to her. "It's the same." She looked at Emma and Jeremy. "Where did you get it?"

"We got it from the auction house that was referenced on the receipt."

"Fredrick Kirtz," Peggy said.

"That's right. He said the three of you knew each other as children," said Emma.

"Yes," she murmured, turning the ring over in her hand. "I've run into him over the years. Why did he have it and why did he give it to you?"

"Teddy asked him to hold it for you and, if something happened to him, Kirtz was to give it to you."

Peggy sighed and continued to study the ring.

"Peggy," Emma asked, "can we see the painting again?" She needed a chance to study it and see if the ring provided any clues.

Tony groaned softly and laid his head back on the couch.

Peggy reached over and touched Tony's hand. "You need to tell them."

He didn't lift his head when he said, "It was taken."

"When?" Jeremy asked.

"Last night. When we woke up this morning, I noticed it was missing."

"Was anything else taken?" asked Jeremy.

"No."

"Did you report it to the police?" Emma asked.

Tony sat up. "No, we waited. We did send a note to the Pinkerton office, but they said Cole was unavailable."

"Yeah, he's probably still on a train," Jeremy said ruefully.

"We didn't want to call more attention to us."

"No," said Emma. "You're right. How did they get in?"

"It was through a small window in the attic. I looked around and found it broken this morning."

Emma looked at Jeremy. "I don't think any of the three guys would have the smarts to pull this off."

"Or the size to get through a small window," Jeremy replied.

Emma's mouth twisted. "The Mystery girl, it must've been her."

"Girl?" asked Peggy. "I thought it was only the three men."

"We thought so, too, but the list of suspects has grown since the funeral."

"Grown?" Tony asked.

"Yeah," Jeremy said. "We got suspects coming out of the woodworks." He leaned down to whisper in Emma's ear. "We need to review the case with them."

She nodded. "We'd like to review our suspects with you and give you some of the background we found about Teddy."

Peggy started to shake her head; she didn't want any more bad news about Teddy. Tony saw the shake and tried to reason with her. "We need to hear everything. I know it'll be hard, but it's better we know."

"Better for who?" she demanded. Peggy sighed and took a deep breath. "I apologize. Tony, dear, can we get some tea and cakes?"

"I think we can manage that," he said. He stood and went to

call Carmichael. When the butler appeared, Tony mentioned Peggy's request. He nodded and left the room.

"While we wait," Tony said, "would you like to see where we think the burglar came into the house?"

Emma nodded. "I would."

"Would you mind?" Tony asked Peggy.

"No, go ahead. We need some answers."

Tony kissed her on the head and murmured something in her ear. She turned red and said, "I'll wait here, and I'll rest."

Emma grinned. From what she'd seen with Tim, husbands get very protective of their pregnant wives and Tony was no exception.

He walked out the door to the staircase, Emma and Jeremy following close behind. They ascended to the attic on the fourth floor. Tony pulled out a key and said, "I figured I should secure it after the break-in in case they try to come back."

"Good idea," Jeremy agreed.

Tony nodded. "I'll make sure it stays locked." He pushed the door open and gestured. "The window's on the far wall." He turned up the gas lamps as they moved through the large room; it seemed to take up the entire floor. There was furniture, rugs, paintings, and all sorts of knickknacks that blocked their path to the window. Tony guided them through the menagerie to the window and Emma and Jeremy saw it was blocked in by wood. "It's a similar size to that one over there," said Tony, pointing to the window next to it.

"Too small for our guys," commented Jeremy.

"I agree, but not our girl. She could easily make it through there," said Emma.

"That's the girl you mentioned earlier?" Tony asked.

"Yes."

Jeremy looked around the room. "Tony, is there anything of value that you might lose if she comes in again?"

"Most of this was Peggy's first husband's family items. We

haven't inventoried it, but I don't think there's anything of much worth up here."

"Sir," came a voice from the door.

"Yes, Carmichael?" Tony asked.

"Miss Peggy asked that you return to the study."

"Okay, we're on our way now." When Carmichael turned away, Tony stopped. "Please make sure this door is kept locked." The butler frowned in response. "We don't want anyone getting into the house," explained Tony.

"Yes, sir. I'll see to it."

The trio walked back downstairs and to the study. Peggy had the tea service set on the table in front of the couch. Tony moved quickly to her when he saw Peggy reach for the teapot. "Let me do that for you."

She smiled and let him have his way. While they loaded their plates and filled cups, Peggy turned to Emma and Jeremy. "Tell me what's happening."

Emma took her tea and plate and sat across from Tony and Peggy. Before she answered, she took a long drink, and said, "You know the three men that were at the funeral. Since we arrived at the hotel, we've also met a man who works there named Pete."

"You haven't mentioned him before. Is he Teddy's age?"

"No, he's a young man," said Jeremy. "Maybe 16 or 17."

"Why do you think he's involved in this?"

"I didn't initially," said Jeremy as he gave a side look to Emma.

"I did have my suspicions," Emma said.

"You suspect everybody," Tony told her.

"I know. But he just seemed to be around all of the time, trying so hard to be helpful."

"That doesn't sound like a bad thing," said Tony.

"Then there was the break-in at the hotel," Jeremy brought up.

"Your room was broken into?" Peggy asked in shock.

"Not his. Mine," Emma clarified.

"When was this?"

"Earlier today. The room was turned upside down. The difference between the two break-ins was that we know who was in my room."

"Who?" Peggy asked. She was on the edge of her seat with excitement.

"Mystery girl."

"Did you see her?"

"Well, we didn't see her," Jeremy reminded Emma.

"Then how do you know that she was the one?" Tony asked curiously.

"The guys saw her exiting my room by the fire escape." Emma didn't mention that the reason the guys were watching the room was so that they could enter themselves.

"The fire escape," said Peggy faintly. "But isn't that dangerous?"

"It is," Emma murmured, not mentioning their climb up onto the roof or how they got to the other building. Jeremy covered a smile with his hand.

"Did she take anything from your room?" asked Tony.

"Not that we're aware of," Jeremy replied.

"We only have a bag of Teddy's items that the coroner gave us."

"Did you find out anything about those?" Peggy asked.

Emma took a moment to fill her teacup and sat back. "Peggy, we need to be honest with you about your brother."

"What do you mean?" she asked, crossing her arms over her chest.

Tony saw the movement and said, "Peggy, give her a chance."

She slowly loosened her arms and sighed. "It's so hard to hear bad things about Teddy. I so wanted to have him back with me, us," she said, holding out her hand to Tony.

He took it and held it tightly. He looked over at Emma. "Okay, start."

"Teddy was involved in a scam, starting a few years after he left Chicago," Emma began.

"Scam? He stole something?" asked Peggy.

"Oh, he stole something all right," Jeremy said.

"He did?"

"Yes. Diamonds and other types of jewels," Emma said bluntly.

"You're sure?" asked Tony.

"He and the three guys at the funeral would dress as priests and take the diamonds and jewels."

"A priest," Peggy said faintly, holding her hand to her chest.

"That made it easy for them to get the items and get away before they were found," Jeremy explained.

"But how?" Tony asked.

"Think about it. Who's going to question a priest, a man of God?"

"How long did this go on?" Peggy asked.

"On and off for years."

"When Teddy came back, had he quit the business?" Peggy asked, with hope in her voice.

"He had. There was a final job and all the guys agreed to meet up at a later date. They were to split the money among themselves and parted ways."

"And did that meeting occur?"

"It didn't. Teddy took all the money and didn't try to contact them."

"That's why they're after money, even if Teddy's dead."

"We think he died because of that money."

"They want it," Jermey said. "And they don't care who's in the way."

"So, it's a treasure hunt now?" asked Tony.

"Yes," said Emma. "And that missing painting is the first clue in that hunt."

"We need the painting," Jeremy said.

"We also need Mystery girl. What's her role in this?" Emma asked.

"There's only one person who can supply that information," said Jeremy.

"Pete," supplied Emma.

"Yeah, they're in this together," confirmed Jeremy.

Tony said, "But, you think they're too young to be involved in the thefts."

"I know. But they're definitely involved; we just don't know how."

Jeremy tapped his watch. "Babe, we need to head back. The guys'll be looking for us."

"And we need to find Pete. Though, knowing Pete, he's probably still at the elevator."

They stood and Tony said, "I'll show you out. Will you need a carriage?"

"No," Jeremy told him. "I think it's best that we go back through the back alleys."

Emma leaned over and kissed Peggy on the cheek. "Get some rest and we'll try to figure this out."

"I'll try. Thank you."

Tony walked them to the door. Jeremy stopped and said, "You mentioned that an artist was brought in to do the painting."

"Yeah. It was someone Teddy knew."

Emma had a sudden thought. "What did he look like?"

"Rather young to be so talented."

"What was his hair color?" Jeremy asked.

"Dark black, straight. You know the type, hair in his face."

"How tall?"

"A little taller than Emma."

"I'll be damned," Jeremy exclaimed. "Sounds like Pete."

Emma raised her eyebrows. "Now there's all the more reason to find him."

They left with the intention of finding Pete and getting some answers.

Tony stood, shaking his head at the direction the case had taken. "Tony," called Peggy from the study. He closed the door and quickly went to check on her. She was his whole world and he'd protect her from anything that might threaten her.

Emma and Jeremy walked together through the back alleys. The trip took much longer because of the detours.

"Pete and Mystery girl. What's their connection here?" asked Jeremy.

"I'm not sure, but I do know we don't move forward without them."

They got closer to the hotel and came to a stop before exiting the final alley. "How do you want to enter the hotel?" He looked up at the side of the building they'd come out of.

"Yeah, but this time we take the stairs inside and up."

They went to the building and entered through the back alley. The lobby was empty, and they made their way to the staircase and went quickly to the roof. Once there, Jeremy jumped first and then Emma. They each landed with a tumble. They quickly got to their feet and walked to the stairway.

They took the stairs two at a time and, once at their floor, she opened the door and looked around. "Clear."

"You go first. I'll be behind you." She started out and he said, "Wait, is the elevator on the floor?"

She looked again. "No. Not that I can see."

"Okay, go."

Emma reached her room without incident. Once her door

was open, she was happy to see that it didn't appear to have been searched again. She moved to the bed and sat. It'd been a long walk.

She heard Jeremy's door open and close next door. He came into the room and joined her on the side of the bed.

"Now, we're where we're supposed to be. What now?" she asked.

"Why not take an elevator ride? See what our old pal Pete's up to."

"Sounds like a plan."

They separated and would meet in the hall. Appearance is everything, especially in this case.

She waited for the knock and headed to her door. When she opened it, Jeremy was standing there, alone. "Where is everyone?"

He looked around. "No idea, and I don't plan to investigate."

"Elevator?"

He nodded and they approached it. She pushed the call button and they waited. The car rose slowly from the lobby. "Do you know what you're going to ask him?" inquired Jeremy.

"I'll figure that out as we go."

"Oh, good. Normal protocol," he teased.

"Exactly." The elevator arrived at that moment. "Here we go." The doors were pushed open, and Emma was ready with her first question. Only, it wasn't Pete. The young man who stepped out had light blond hair.

"Boarding, miss?" he asked.

She frowned at him, and at Jeremy. "I'm not sure."

"I can wait," he said and folded his hands in front of him.

Distracted, she frowned and thought, *Something is different between him and Pete. What is it?* She shook the thought away and demanded, "Where's Pete?"

"It's his day off. He's allowed time off, miss."

"He's right," Jeremy agreed.

"But… but…" she started.

"Do you still need to go to the lobby?" the operator asked.

"No, no, I don't think so."

"Thank you, though," Jeremy said.

"Looney birds," the operator muttered and closed the doors. They watched the elevator descend to the lobby.

"Two days into the case and what do we have?" Emma asked.

"More questions than answers. And more suspects that we can shake a stick at."

"That Pete! The one time, the ONE time, we need him, and he chooses to be gone," she said, frustrated, and kicked the iron cage that housed the elevator.

"Look, it's close to dinner. We have an excuse to leave the room and find him," he reasoned.

"All right. Give me a few minutes and meet you in the hallway?"

He leaned over and kissed her. She settled into his embrace, enjoying the moment.

He laid his head on hers briefly. "See you on the other side," he said before entering his room. She sighed, moved to her door, and closed it softly.

Emma picked up her brush to straighten up the bun on her head. She grimaced at the black dress hanging in the armoire. It wasn't her favorite, but she had nothing else at the moment. She heard the door to Jeremy's room open to the hallway and the sound encouraged her to change quickly. Lastly, she did a quick check for her clutch knife. It was always with her and was already strapped to her leg.

She grabbed her hat and carried it with her to the door. As expected, Jeremy was waiting, but what she didn't expect was a still empty hallway. She pulled her door shut and said to him in a low voice, "No sign of anyone?"

"Not yet. It does make things easier."

"It's suspicious," she said. The guys had been their constant companions since the funeral.

"It is, but let's take advantage," he suggested.

They headed to the elevator. After he pushed the button, she murmured, "Here we are again." The elevator slowly rose and, when it stopped, they waited patiently for the internal gate to slide open and the outer doors to be pushed toward them.

"Going down this time?" asked the same young man they'd talked to earlier.

They ignored his attitude and stepped onto the elevator. Jeremy stated, "Lobby, please." He turned to the operator. "Have you seen Pete today?"

The young man didn't turn to them but stared straight ahead. "I'm not aware of his schedule."

Jeremy raised his eyebrows at that answer and Emma shrugged. At the lobby, they departed the elevator and walked to the desk. The manager stood there reading through his check-in book. He didn't look up as they approached.

Emma cleared her throat, and he glanced up. "May I help you?"

"Will Pete be on duty today?"

He frowned. "I'm sorry, madam, but what's your interest in my employee's work schedule?"

"We wanted to talk with him about something he said earlier today. Can you tell us how to get in touch with him?"

"Madam, I do not give out personal details about my staff."

Jeremy tried next. "Can you tell us how long he's been with you?"

The manager slammed his book closed. "You're here because of my friendship with a certain person; don't push me. I believe this conversation is finished." He stormed off to his office and slammed the door behind him.

Emma leaned on the counter. "Wow. What was that about?" she asked.

"Could be he just doesn't want his employees bothered."

"Could be. Dinner and a stroll?" She looked around the lobby. It was empty. "The men aren't here either?"

"I don't care where they are as long as they aren't following us."

"It bothers me that both they and Pete are missing."

"Do you think they took him?"

"No, I don't think they know about the connection."

"So, we don't worry for now." Jeremy held out his elbow to Emma and she took it. The evening greeted them with a breeze. They walked for a long while before stopping at a restaurant. "Want to go in?" he asked.

"Yes." They entered the restaurant and were taken quickly to their table; it was early, and the first seating had started. Flowers and candles adorned the tables, with tablecloths and dim lights. "Romantic," Emma commented.

"It'll be nice to have a little of that," said Jeremy.

"It will," she said as they sat. The waiter took their hats and jackets.

They were left alone, and Jeremy put out his hand to her. She took it. "It's nice to have a quiet moment like this with just the two of us."

"We need these to get us through."

"We do."

They chose not to discuss the case; instead, they ordered their food and enjoyed the time together. On the way back to the hotel, their mood shifted; it was back to business. What would be waiting for them tonight?

They entered the hotel and saw there were more people than before, new people checking in or current customers checking out. "No sign of the guys," said Jeremy as he looked around.

"Or Pete."

They walked to the elevator and saw the same young man who was there earlier. He was as quiet as before and took them up without comment. They split off at their rooms and Jeremy came through the door with a book. She did the same and sat on the bed, relaxing for the evening.

As the evening wound down, Jeremy glanced at the clock. "Want to get ready for bed?"

Emma yawned. "I do." She put down her book, gathered her things, and made her way to the door.

"Knock when you get back," he said from the connecting door to his room.

"I will," she said and waited until he closed his door.

She put on the only colored item she had, a blue dressing gown, the only article of color she had with her, and opened her door to make her way down to the shared bathroom. She knocked and, when she received no answer, she eased the door open a few inches. No one seemed to be using the facilities. Relieved she wouldn't have to wait, she pushed it the rest of the way open. The door caught on something and stopped. She pushed harder and whatever had stopped it loosened, and Emma stumbled into the room. She fell forward onto a dark object on the floor.

"What!" she yelped and sat there in wonder. It was a man; his neck was bruised purple. She leaned back in surprise and horror and put a shaky hand in her hair. She pulled herself back up and ran to bang on Jeremy's door.

He opened it and frowned when he saw her frightened face. "What happened?"

"He's dead," Emma said, she stuttered in a low voice.

"What? Who's dead?" he asked He kept his voice the same tone as hers. She raised her trembling hand and pointed down the hallway. They started down the hall and two other doors opened on their right. Harvey and Louis looked out at them.

"What's going on?" Harvey drawled. Emma pointed again to the bathroom. They all went in and looked at the dead man on the floor. It was Eddie!

Emma looked at the two men closely. *Did they do this?*

Harvey, his mouth twisted, shook his head. "Another one. I don't get it. There was only the three of us left." He turned to Louis. "Did you do this?"

Louis looked nonplussed at the question. "No! Did you?"

"Naw, I didn't." They turned to Emma and Jeremy. "What about you two?"

"I just wanted to get ready for bed," Emma said. The men turned their gaze on Jeremy.

"Wasn't me. What would I gain?" he asked and held up his hands.

"That's true," Harvey said begrudgingly.

"We need to stay on our guard," said Jeremy. "Someone's after us."

"You think so?" Harvey asked sarcastically.

Emma's shock had worn off and she assumed a detached review of the corpse. "Look, someone dressed him like a priest." Eddie had on a black suit and a clerical collar. They even put a cross around his neck.

"Yeah, someone's providing reminders of how we all got here," said Harvey. "Someone's holding a grudge."

"What do we do?" Louis asked.

Jeremy looked at him. "Unless we want to be locked out of the bathroom tonight, we move him to his room."

Emma hid a grin. Jeremy played his part and couldn't report the murder. That would give up the game.

"That sounds like a plan," Harvey agreed. "Louis, check the hallway."

Louis turned and stepped out into the hallway. The others waited. He came back. "All clear." The three men got together, picked Eddie up, and moved to his room. They laid him on the bed and stood around him.

"He wasn't a bad guy," said Harvey. Louis nodded. They left

him in his suit and covered him up. "We should not be seen." They nodded and moved quickly to their rooms.

"Block your doors after you're in the room," Emma called to the duo.

"Don't worry. That won't happen to us," Louis replied.

Emma went back to the bathroom while Jeremy sat outside and waited for her. He wasn't taking any chances. There was no way to notify Cole. The hotel maid would find the body in the morning. He expected they'd be questioned tomorrow. When she finished, he went inside, and she waited by the door, her clutch knife at the ready. No one approached and, when they went back to their rooms, each put heavy furniture in front of their doors.

Jeremy came in and helped to push the dresser in front of her door. He collapsed against it and said, "Wow. The second day here and another person murdered."

"You think Harvey or Louis did it?" she asked.

"No, they seemed honestly surprised about Eddie's murder."

"I agree. Do you think it was the Mystery girl?"

"No. Eddie was small and thin, but I don't think she could strangle a man of that size and dress him."

"I don't expect dressing a dead man would be easy."

"No, no. I do believe, though, that she ransacked your room and is involved in this up to her eyeballs."

"Definitely." She yawned broadly. "Bed time."

"Want some company?"

"That would be wonderful."

Going to bed was a relief. The bed was so small that Jeremy stayed wrapped around her all night. Surprisingly, they slept and were only awakened the next morning by a scream.

"Sounds like someone found Eddie," she commented, sitting up.

"Sounds like. I guess Pops will be here soon."

"If he's back. Will he question us?"

"Probably. At the very least, we'll get to see Pops in action," murmured Jeremy. "Should be entertaining." He stood up, stretching. She admired his shoulders as he moved back to his room.

She ran quickly to the bathroom for her morning ablutions, then back. The hallway would be crowded soon.

Jeremy did the same. They were both dressed and waiting in their separate rooms when a knock sounded on each of their doors.

She took a deep break, opened it, and saw Jones standing at her door. He'd been told by Cole that Emma and Jeremy were undercover. "Miss if you would step out, we have questions about what happened here last night."

"Happened?" she asked, feigning confusion. "What's happened?"

Jones didn't answer her; he just moved to Jeremy's door. He knocked and waited for him to answer and told him the same instructions. She and Jeremy stood in the hallway with Harvey and Louis. She asked again, "Excuse me, why are we here?"

"We have some questions for you," he responded.

Cole appeared at the entrance to the stairs down the hallway. "You two," he waved at two of his detectives, "follow me." He turned and walked toward Eddie's room, Jones and another detective following closely behind. He didn't glance toward the people in the hall. Once inside the room, Cole gestured for Jones to uncover the body.

The detective uncovered Eddie and the room went quiet. The man next to him exclaimed, "He's a priest!" He quickly crossed himself.

Cole stroked his goatee and said in a low tone, "No, I don't think he's a priest. I think maybe that's a costume."

"Costume?" Jones asked. "Someone dressed him up like that?"

"Probably. Strangulation," Cole observed, his gaze drawn to the purple neck. "Definitely murder."

The other detective walked around the bed and said, "It's too neat and orderly and he was covered up."

"I agree. I don't think this happened here," he said and looked around the room.

"Why move him?"

Cole didn't answer. "Gather the people up," he directed. "We need everyone at the station for questioning. One or more of these people moved this man."

"Did one of them kill him?" Jones asked.

"It's possible."

"Everyone?"

Cole got Jones' meaning. "Everyone on this floor, for now." He gestured to his officer. "Meet with the manager to get a list of the other occupants."

Jones went and told Harvey and Louis that they'd need to go downtown for questioning. Louis and Harvey grumbled but went along. "You, too," he told Jeremy and Emma. They nodded and followed him to the stairs.

As they neared the elevator, Emma nudged Jeremy. "What is it?" he asked.

"Pete's here." The man stood in his elevator, watching everyone being escorted out. Emma raised her hand and shook her finger at him. She mouthed, "We need to talk."

Pete didn't answer. He looked around the hallway and back at her. He slowly nodded.

They were escorted to the lobby and had to wait for paddy wagons to arrive. Cole kept his distance from them.

A bike buzzed by. It was the Mystery girl. Emma saw her and squeezed Jeremy's arm, nodding toward her. "It's her!"

He looked over and saw her, his eyes wide. "She must be all of sixteen. Is she on her own?"

"It looks like." They watched as she pedaled down the street.

The paddy wagons pulled up and blocked them from seeing where she went.

"Let's go, everyone in," Jones called out. The wagons were loaded, and they were transported downtown to the precinct. They pulled to a stop and were helped out and told to move inside. The group was escorted to the hallways by the interrogation rooms.

"You and you first," Cole barked, indicating for Emma and Jeremy to move into the first interrogation room. They nodded and followed his direction without question.

"Hey, what about us?" asked Louis. "We don't want to be here all day."

Cole gave them a long glance and replied in a low, menacing voice, "Don't worry. I'll get to you."

That shut him up, and he and Harvey sat on the benches across from the doors. They watched silently as Emma and Jeremy went into the room and shut the door behind them.

Louis asked in a raspy whisper, "Hey, can you hear anything?"

Harvey stood slowly, looking around, and moved to the interrogation room door. He placed his head against it. *Wham!* He grabbed his head. It was ringing from the impact of something on the door.

"What was that?" Louis asked, running over to him.

Wham! The loud bang forced them back to the benches.

"Getting violent in there," commented Harvey.

"Yeah." Louis nodded, watching the door. He was suddenly not so eager for their interview.

Inside the room

Emma walked to upright the chair that had been tossed at

the door by Cole. "Well, that was fun, and it was a good idea," she said.

"It'll keep them from listening in to our conversation," he replied.

"And it gives you the upper hand when their interview starts," commented Jeremy.

"It does."

They picked up the table and put it back into its correct position. Jeremy moved the chairs back and they sat.

"Good to see you, Pops," said Jeremy with a grin.

"Hi, Cole," said Emma, her tone more guarded as she waited for Cole's reaction to their questions.

He shook his head at them. "I left you with one dead man and now there's two."

"Yeah," said Jeremy. "Eddie."

"When did this happen?" Cole demanded.

"Near as we can figure, it was some time last night," admitted Emma.

Cole looked thunderous and Jeremy inserted, "We needed to show that we were willing to bend the law."

"And we needed access to the bathroom," Emma said practically.

Cole shook his head, but he understood they were undercover. "The priest outfit? How did that happen?"

"He was already in it," Jeremy explained. "We found him that way."

"Funny. That links back to something found on the train."

"What was it you found out, Pops?"

"The men I interviewed said the only thing out of the ordinary was that a priest was on the train and asked about Teddy."

"A priest? The killer dressed like a priest? That does link back to Harvey and Louis."

"How?"

"They were a group con that involved priest outfits," Emma added. She explained the scam that the five men had been running and the detective who delivered the news. "There's a detective, Max Winsten, looking to recover the money that Teddy had taken."

"Hmm, this detective. When did he approach you?" Cole asked, stroking his gray goatee.

"On the way from the funeral to the hotel."

"The guys were all part of the con. They were supposed to meet up at a later date and divide up the money," Jeremy supplied.

"And they left that one man behind to die," said Emma.

"What happened at that final meeting?" asked Cole.

"Everyone showed up at the meeting place, except Teddy. It was only Louis, Eddie, and Harvey."

"So, instead of going with the plan, Teddy disappears," Cole filled in. "Any more guesses on who killed him?"

Emma looked at Jeremy and back to Cole. "Our main suspect was just found dead in the bathroom."

Cole rubbed a hand on his face and sat back. "What made you suspect him out of the three?"

"We have information that he was the one who was in town before the other two arrived."

"Who told you this?"

"Winsten," she admitted.

"I'd like more than his word. I'll check train schedules. Okay, where do we go from here?"

"Back to the hotel and let this play out," Jeremy said.

"And if another body appears?" Cole asked wryly.

"Well then, we'll see you at that time."

They started to stand when Emma stopped them and said, "We have two more people to discuss. Pete the elevator operator and the Mystery girl."

"Start with Pete," instructed Cole.

"Initially, he seemed like what he appeared to be, a helpful hotel worker."

"Then," prompted Cole.

"He was around too much. Never took off; always available if we needed anything," she explained.

Jeremy added, "We also found out that he has a connection with the Mystery girl."

"He let her into my room so that she could search it," Emma explained.

"Have you had a chance to talk to him since that time?"

"No…" she started.

"Don't forget about the roof," reminded Jeremy.

"What about the roof?" Cole asked.

"Ah, we needed a way to leave the hotel for a bit without being seen," Jeremy began. "So, we took the fire escape to the roof and jumped across to the next building."

"That's right, and that's when Pete admitted to knowing I wasn't Peggy."

"Any more follow-up from that?" Cole asked her.

"No, too much has happened, what with the murder and all."

"We'll get with him as soon as we return," Jeremy promised his dad.

"What about this Mystery girl you mentioned?" asked Cole.

"She's about 16 and has been showing up at different times since this case started. The first time I saw her, a few days before the funeral, was when she tried to race me on my bike. Next, she ransacked my room."

"You're sure it was her?"

"The description Harvey gave us when he saw her exit our room, confirmed my suspicions."

"And don't forget she's our lead suspect in the theft of the painting at Tony's house," reminded Jeremy.

"How does that tie into this case?" Cole asked him.

"We followed up on the auction that had been held from Teddy's belongings and there's a connection between Fredrick Kirtz the auctioneer, Teddy, and Peggy," Emma replied.

"They grew up together," Jeremy put in.

"And he gave us a ring from Teddy to give to Peggy," said Emma.

"What's significant about that?" Cole asked.

"The painting was one that Teddy had commissioned, featuring Peggy wearing that ring. It was stolen. But she'd never seen or owned that ring. Tony and Peggy thought the ring was just an artist's addition to the painting," Jeremy supplied.

"But it was real. What does that signify?"

"We don't know yet," Emma admitted. "But that painting needs further evaluation."

"So, the Mystery girl and this Pete probably have it," mulled Cole. "Both are too young for the priest con. They may be working together."

"Yeah," Jeremy agreed. "What about a relative? A daughter perhaps?"

Emma drummed her fingers on her lips. "But whose?"

"You said that the three guys saw her in your room?" asked Cole.

"Yes," said Emma, dropping her fingers.

"Could she be Teddy's daughter?" Jeremy asked.

"The age fits. He left and was gone about 16 years. I'll check with Peggy and see if she knows anything."

"What about the guys? Shouldn't they recognize Teddy's daughter?" asked Cole.

Emma grimaced. "We haven't thought to ask."

"Follow up on that," he instructed.

"We will," promised Jeremy.

As they started to exit the room, Cole commented, "You might look a bit beaten down. After all, I am intimidating."

"Yeah, Pops, you're a real bulldog." Jeremy shot him a grin as they left. They lowered their heads and their mouths turned downward as they were escorted out. Harvey and Louis watched them file out.

"You two, now!" Cole thundered at them. They hastily stood and followed Cole into the room, the door slamming behind them.

Jeremy laughed lightly. "Man, Pops is intimidating."

"They were quaking in their boots," Emma said as she looked at the closed door.

"Ready to go?" Jeremy asked.

She pulled her eyes from the door. "Yeah, we should head out."

They made their way to the front of the precinct. Jones spotted them and asked, "Would you like a ride back to the hotel?"

Jeremy looked at Emma and raised an eyebrow. "No, I don't think so. I could use a long walk," she said.

"And we haven't eaten yet this morning," reminded Jeremy.

"That's true." She looked over and said, "Thanks for the offer."

"Gonna be here a while longer, Jones?" Jeremy asked.

"Yeah. The boss wants me here to be all intimidating and all."

"Good luck with that."

Jones waved them off and they headed out in the direction of the hotel. "Food first," Emma said.

"Over there," he said and pointed to a restaurant.

"Perfect."

They entered the café and were seated. Once they were alone, Emma said, "It's been an active case. Who do you think killed Eddie?"

"Could be any of the three."

"Three?" she asked.

"I think we have to include Winsten in the equation. Especially if money's the motive."

"Fair point. He's as intimidating as they are," she said, thinking of the detective.

"And he turns up at the oddest times."

Emma looked over and said, "You know, Harvey and Louis seemed genuinely surprised at Eddie's death."

"Could be a cover," he reasoned.

"True, they could be killing people and increasing their share."

"Guess we'll wait and see." They ordered breakfast and took their time finishing.

"I guess we should go back," she said reluctantly.

"Do you want me to get a carriage?"

"No, not yet. Let's walk."

"We should order lunch and take it with us."

"Good suggestion." They waved down their waiter and put their order in. After it arrived, they started back toward the hotel. The hotel lobby was empty as they made their way in.

Pete stood at the hotel desk. Emma nudged Jeremy and nodded toward him.

They walked to him. The manager at the desk said something and Pete turned. "Back so soon? Did they find out who killed that man?"

"Not yet. The police wanted to talk to everyone," Jeremy answered.

Emma was tapping her fingers against her leg. "We need to talk."

"Do we?" Pete murmured and looked toward the elevator. "Can I take you up to your room?"

"To start," murmured Jeremy.

They walked to the elevator and boarded. Pete started the elevator moving up. When they didn't stop at their floor, Emma asked, "Where are we going?"

"The roof seems like the best place to get some privacy."

Emma and Jeremy nodded. Jeremy sat down the food bags and when they came to a stop. The three walked into the top floor hallway to the stairs to the roof. Pete was first through the door and onto the roof followed by Emma. Jeremy exited last; he closed the door behind him and leaned back on it. They needed some answers before anyone else got killed. He nodded to Emma to begin.

Emma started boldly. "So, I'm not Peggy?" Pete's eyes widened and his mouth opened and closed. "Well?"

"Okay, okay. I've seen Peggy and know you aren't her," he said, offering little explanation.

Jeremy asked, "Pete, what's your role in this mess? Are you the killer?"

"NO!" he said loudly. "I'd never do that!"

"What about the Mystery girl?" asked Emma. "Did she do it?"

"NO!" he said again in the same tone. "She would never," he muttered and looked down at his feet.

"Pete, when did you arrive in Chicago?" Emma asked, trying to assemble a timeline.

At that question, he looked up. "About six months ago."

Emma looked to Jeremy; it was the same time that Teddy had returned. "Did you know Teddy Latimer?"

He looked down again and shuffled his feet.

"Answer the question," Jeremy demanded.

"I did know him," Pete admitted.

"What was the nature of your relationship?"

"I don't want to answer that."

Emma sighed and let it go. "Why are you at the hotel?"

"You were all here. I know the manager from a previous job, and he was willing to work with me."

"When did you start here?"

"Right before you arrived," he admitted.

"How did you know that we'd be here?" asked Emma.

He looked mutinous.

Jeremy supplied his answer. "Jeremiah Kingsley, the owner of the funeral parlor. He was the only one we told where you'd be staying after the funeral." Pete nodded, looking down.

"What confuses me," said Emma, as she continued to study him, "is how integral a part of this hotel you seem to be."

"The protectiveness of other employees and the manager. That made us think you had a longer relationship than just a few days," Jeremy supplied.

"Yes, can you explain that?" Emma asked.

Pete finally looked up. "They are good people; they understood that I needed help."

Jeremy looked at Emma.

"Are you here for the money?" asked Jeremy.

He looked more secure in this answer and looked at Jeremy. "Aren't we all?"

Emma continued. "What about the girl you let into my room?"

The openness Pete had earlier displayed vanished, and he turned away from them. "I don't want to talk about her."

"Okay," said Emma, "tell us where she's stashed the painting."

"Painting?" he asked faintly. The comment was so faint, she barely heard him.

"Yes. We were at Peggy's house today and there was a break-in. The only thing missing was the painting that Teddy commissioned for Peggy," Jeremy said.

Pete's lips were moving, but Emma couldn't hear the words. "What're you saying?" she asked a bit impatiently.

"Why do you think it was her?" he said loudly.

"The window size; it would've taken a small person to get in and out of that window."

Pete put a hand up to rub his neck. He dropped it back to his side and said, "I didn't know she did that."

"Where were you last night?" Jeremy asked.

"I needed some time off to sleep. Having all you people running around is tiresome."

"You haven't had much of that lately, though, have you?" observed Emma.

"No, I thought I could take a few hours to myself." He looked at her and said, "I had nothing to do with that man dying."

Emma watched him closely and finally nodded. "I believe you. I also believe that you're more involved in this than you're saying."

Jeremy pushed himself away from the door and walked over to them. "Pete, were you the artist who painted the picture of Peggy?"

Pete's face was tense when he responded. "Yes. Yes, I did that."

"That explains how you knew I wasn't Peggy," said Emma.

"Yes. I sat and sketched with her daily until the painting was completed."

"Was there anything out of the ordinary about the painting?" asked Jeremy.

He frowned at that question. "Teddy instructed me to add certain things to the picture."

"Did he tell you why he wanted that?" Emma asked.

"No."

"What were those things?" Jeremy prodded.

Pete walked to the edge of the roof and said, "I can show you. I have the sketches."

Emma stepped toward him. "Can you bring them so we can review them?"

He sighed. "I can." He turned back to them. "I don't know the meaning behind some of the items."

"When can we view them?" Emma asked excitedly. She felt that the key to the case was within their grasp.

"I have some things to finish up here, so it'll have to be later tonight."

Emma started to push him for a definite time when Jeremy stepped in. "We understand. Tonight is fine."

"Can we go back down? I need to return to my elevator post."

"Sure." Jeremy moved out of the way and let Pete walk to the door. They followed him back down the stairs and into the hallway to where the elevator waited for them.

"Pete, did the other elevator operator who works nights take anyone to our floor?" asked Emma.

"He didn't mention anyone."

"Hmm."

Pete took them down in the elevator. Once out, they separated, going to their separate rooms. Jeremy entered her room through the connecting door and dropped down on the bed. "Do you think…" he started when a loud BANG was heard on the door.

Emma stood and looked at him. "Are you going to go to your room?"

"Not this time," he said. He had a feeling that it was Harvey and Louis at her door. Cole must've finished with them. "They can deal with both of us at the same time."

The pounding started on the door again.

"Here we go." She walked to the door and opened it. Harvey and Louis were standing there, as they'd expected, and another person they didn't. Peggy! "Why do you have my friend?" Emma asked, not saying her name aloud.

Jeremy moved quickly to the door. "Are you okay?" he asked her.

Peggy's face was pulled tight, and her hand rubbed her belly as she leaned heavily on Louis. Emma took one of Peggy's arms, Jeremy the other, and they led her to the bed. Once she sat down, they scooted her back so that she was reclining.

"Well, well, what're you doing in here?" Louis asked Jeremy. Jeremy didn't respond.

Harvey glanced at the open connecting door and drawled, "That's convenient."

Once Peggy was settled, Emma turned and put her hand into her pocket; she was ready to cut someone. "What the hell is this?" she demanded, "Why did you bring her here?"

"Hey now, hold up," Harvey protested. "It wasn't us. We found her outside."

"They're telling the truth," Peggy said faintly from the bed. "I was worried about you and came over to see if everything was okay."

Jeremy looked at the two guys with narrowed eyes. "And you two were just being perfect gentlemen when you brought her up here."

"Why sure, we're good guys," Louis stated.

"Though I didn't plan on coming in," Peggy said, pulling herself higher up on the bed.

"We thought she should come up," explained Harvey.

Louis contradicted him and said, "We want the money and we figured she could be leverage."

"Hey, Louis," Harvey scolded. "Shut up!"

"What'd I say?" Louis complained.

"You gave away our plan, dingus."

Emma shook her head at the duo.

Jeremy leaned over to Emma to whisper in her ear, "We need to send a note to Tony and let him know where she is."

"I agree," she said and gave Peggy's hand a squeeze before she stood and started toward the door.

"And where do you think you're going?" Louis asked as he moved to block her path.

"I need to get a note to her husband. As you see, she's in a delicate condition."

"No! You need to stay here. We need to work this out now. We want the money!" Louis yelled.

"Peggy doesn't have it, and her friend doesn't either," Jeremy said, reaching the end of this tether.

"Well, if she doesn't, why don't we look at you, smart guy? The stranger in this whole event. Why are you here? And why were you in *her* room? Are you working together, planning something? Maybe planning to kill another one of us?" Louis demanded.

"Yeah," drawled Harvey, "we didn't kill Eddie or Teddy and we don't trust either of you."

"Oh, sure," said Jeremy, his voice turning sardonic. "First, I murder a man I don't know by shooting him and throwing him off a train. Then I murder a man I barely know and put him in a priest suit. All for what? Money that I have no idea the location of? From a series of cons that took place years ago and hundreds of miles away?"

Harvey whispered to Louis. Louis nodded and said, "Yeah, how would he have known about the con? And where would he have found a priest outfit?"

"I don't know, but something's up with him," Harvey muttered. "I don't trust him. And I don't think he is Arthur's brother."

"That was your idea, not mine," Jeremy retorted. "I don't trust either of you."

"Just who are you anyway?" asked Louis.

Emma spoke up. She wanted to antagonize the duo to see if they would give up some clues. "That doesn't matter now. I think one of you did both murders."

"Why us?" asked Louis.

"You had the most to gain," she reasoned.

"If it was us, why would we stick around?"

"So that we wouldn't suspect you," she countered.

"Stop confusing me." He jammed his finger at her and said desperately, "You have our money. I know you do!"

Harvey looked around. "We need to search their rooms."

"That's fine," said Emma, "and we'll search yours."

"Fine," the two men said. They separated into two teams, Louis and Harvey on one and Emma and Jeremy on the other. Before she left to start the search, Emma leaned down to Peggy. "Will you be okay here?"

"Yes. I just want to close my eyes. I'm sorry I caused you any trouble. Can you get word to Tony?"

"I'll get word to him," Emma promised. She glared at Harvey and Louis. "You disturb her during your search and you're going to wish you had never even heard of Chicago! You got me?" Both men nodded. Something about her tone scared them to the bones.

Emma grabbed her notebook and pencil and moved to the hallway. She left her door open and, before entering one of the men's rooms, she called for the elevator. The elevator slowly rose and, when the doors were pushed open, she saw Pete. "Good, can you get a note to Tony for me?"

He saw her door was open and could see who was in her room. "Um, is everything okay? Why is *she* here?"

"You brought her up," she countered.

"I did."

"Did she recognize you?"

"I kept my head down," he admitted.

She glanced back over her shoulder and said, "Right now, she's resting. The note is the important thing."

He took the note and assured her, "I'll get this to him now."

"Check the museum. If he's not there, go to his home. I couldn't imagine she'd be here if he'd been at home."

He took the note and she started to hand him a tip. "No, it's okay. I'll take it anyway."

"Thank you, Pete," she said sincerely, putting the money back into her pocket.

"That's okay." Pete reentered the elevator and closed the doors to start the elevator down.

Now that was taken care of, Emma moved to her assigned room, the one that belonged to Harvey. Jeremy was investigating Louis' room.

She went in and saw the room was similar to hers. The difference between the two was the clothes strewn about and food and trash lying around. *What a pigsty,* she thought. She turned to study the armoire. It was the best hiding spot in this place. She moved the chair to check the top. The edge was higher than her head, but her arms would reach. Her hands patted the top and she stopped suddenly when she felt something there. She tried to pull at it, but it wouldn't move. She climbed down and thought to go get Jeremy. *No, first I need to search the rest of the room.* The bed was first, covers, clothes, trash, old food, mattress, then under the bed. *Nothing.* She looked around the room and saw the desk. She hurried over and found it empty. She went to the hallway and called, "Jeremy!" He came out of Louis' room, but so did the two guys.

"What is it? Did you find something?"

"A bag in Harvey's room. I can't reach it."

Harvey laughed. "Sure, check it out."

Jeremy frowned at him and went to retrieve it. He brought it down and laid it on the bed. He glanced at Harvey. "Go ahead. I have nothing to hide," Harvey said.

He opened it quickly and found a pair of boots.

"I like to have an extra pair with me," Harvey explained.

"Did anyone find anything?" Emma asked the group.

"No," each man said.

"Well," said Harvey, "why was this on top of your armoire?" He held out a bag.

It was Teddy's bag. "Obviously, I wanted to keep it up there in case someone searched the room."

"Hmm." He took it and dumped it on his bed.

"We've looked at this over and over again," complained Emma.

"If none of us have the money, it must be here," he reasoned. They looked at everything again.

Suddenly, a scream interrupted them. It was Peggy! Emma ran toward her room, the men not far behind. She didn't know what to expect, but she found Peggy bent over on the side of the bed, holding her stomach. Once the pain had subsided, she held out her hand. Emma ran over to take it.

"Emma, it's the baby!"

"What do we do?" Emma asked, looking at Jeremy for help.

"Okay, everyone out," Jeremy directed.

Harvey and Louis started to leave. Harvey stopped at the door and looked at Jeremy. "What about you?"

"It's about to get messy. You want to stay and help?" he asked. Peggy let out another scream.

"Oh, no," Harvey said, backing out. "We'll wait outside."

"Yeah, yeah, outside," Louis agreed. They both backed out.

Once the door closed, Emma asked Peggy, "Would you like us to get you to the hospital?"

Peggy laughed suddenly.

"Wha-what's going on!" Jeremy stammered.

"Shh," Emma cautioned. "Did you fake your pain?"

"Unfortunately, no." Peggy saw their panic and assured them, "It's okay. I have time."

"We need to take you to the hospital," Jeremy said, beginning to panic.

"And notify Tony," she reminded them.

They started to pull her into a sitting position. "Wait," she said, stopping them for a moment to let out a loud scream.

"Are you in more pain?" Emma asked nervously. That scream had put her on edge.

"No, I wanted to keep up the charade. Wait, before we go, what's happening? Did one of those men kill my brother?"

Jeremy laid his hand on top of theirs and said, "It's possible, but right now we just don't have enough evidence."

"Please do what you can to find out who killed Teddy."

"We will," Emma promised.

Peggy grimaced; the pain was returning. Jeremy said, "I really don't want to deliver a baby here. Could we get moving?"

"The bag!" Emma exclaimed. "We need to get it."

"I have it. I gathered it up when Peggy screamed." Jeremy reached into his coat and handed it to her.

"Let me put this back," Emma said and threw it on the top of the armoire.

They each took an arm and put it over their shoulders to lift Peggy. "Peggy?" asked Emma.

"Yes," she replied, trying to breathe through the pain.

"This might be a bad time, but did your brother have any children?"

Peggy stopped abruptly. "I don't know. He was gone for such a long time. It's possible. Why? Is there someone who says they're related to Teddy?" she asked, raising her voice.

"Shh," said Emma. "Yes, we think so. Mystery girl. She has dark hair and looks to be about the right age."

"And she's also after the money," commented Jeremy.

Peggy was silent as they got to the door. They opened it and walked Peggy into the hallway.

"Hey!" called Harvey. "Where are you taking her?"

Emma and Jeremy ignored them and walked to the elevator; Jeremy pushed the button when they got to it. Harvey and Louis were yelling behind them, but they gave them no heed. Peggy and the baby were more important than any money.

Pete pushed open the door and saw who was waiting. He immediately went to help. They got Peggy on and, when the two men tried to get on with them, Jeremy started to move to stop them, but they were surprised when Pete stepped up.

"We're full, no more may board." The doors were pulled closed, and the gate engaged.

The two men stared at the closed door.

"Now what?" Louis asked.

"Stairs!" yelled Harvey. They ran toward the door and down the stairs. They reached the bottom just as the three exited toward a waiting carriage.

"Sisters of Charity Hospital, quick!" Jeremy called to the driver after the three of them were in place. The driver looked surprised at the request and called to the horses to move. They lurched off and the ride smoothed out.

The pain seemed to be coming faster. "Tony," Peggy said.

"I'll have the driver get him after we drop you off," Jeremy assured her. The carriage stopped abruptly.

"What happened?" asked Emma, holding Peggy's hand, which she gripped fiercely. The door swung open, and Jeremy readied for a fight. The person who stuck his head in was Tony!

"Tony!" cried Peggy. Jeremy and Emma moved across from them so that Tony could hold her close to him.

"How are you? Is it the baby?" he asked.

"Yes, I think so," she said, laying her head on his chest.

He sent a worried glance to Emma and Jeremy. "She'll be fine," said Emma. "The sisters will take care of her." Emma had had a medical emergency a few years ago and they had saved her life.

They fell silent as Peggy let out a real scream. They stopped and Emma looked out. "We're here."

Jeremy and Emma climbed out and Tony helped Peggy move to the door. Jeremy guided Emma and Peggy down to the ground. Tony wouldn't let her walk and picked her up to take her in.

"I'm too heavy," Peggy protested.

He shot her a don't be silly look and she shut up and laid her head on his shoulder. The pain was coming faster, but she knew she could do it now that her love was there with her. They entered the hospital and Sister Catherine and Sister Anne ran up to them. "Is it time?" Sister Catherine asked.

"I believe so," said Tony.

Peggy couldn't talk; she could only grimace in pain. The sisters directed him to the stairs to take her into a room. The sister at the desk asked, "Will you be waiting?"

"We'll wait," Emma replied.

"You may go upstairs."

They started up. Emma thought of something and went back to the desk. "Sister, two men may try to get into the hospital. They're after us."

The sister pulled herself up to an impressive height. "I'm Sister Bernadette," she said with an Irish brogue, "and they won't be getting past me."

Emma rejoined Jeremy and they headed upstairs. They heard Harvey and Louis enter and state loudly, "We're here with Miss Latimer." Sister Bernadette said something they couldn't hear and then a couple of loud thumps.

"That sounded nasty. Should we check?" asked Emma.

"Yeah, why not." Jeremy grinned. He was a little anxious to see the duo put in their place by the large sister.

They peered around the corner. Sister Bernadette had everything under control as she towered above both men and held Louis by the collar. She dragged them swiftly toward the door and out. They heard something or someone fall.

"Well, that's taken care of," said Jeremy. "I sure don't want to anger that woman."

"You and me both," Emma replied and started back up the staircase. They went to the door they were directed to and took the chairs opposite it. The screams coming from the room rang down the long hall. It all sounded very real.

"A new baby," Emma mused. She'd been there for Lottie's birth, and she knew it could be hard on a woman.

"She'll be okay," Jeremy said, wincing as he heard another scream. He hoped he was right.

The hours passed and the sun set as they waited for word.

Finally, a baby crying broke them out of their stupor. Tony came out with Sister Anne, carrying a baby. "It's a girl," he said, pulling the blanket away from her face.

They looked down at the new baby. "Isn't she beautiful?" she exclaimed.

Jeremy nodded and touched her hand. "So tiny," he murmured.

"They all start out that way," Sister Anne pointed out.

Emma dragged her eyes away from the baby to Tony's beaming face. "Congratulations, Tony. How's Peggy?"

"She was amazing," he said, his eyes bright with tears.

Sister Anne spoke up. "We need to take her back to her mother."

"Yes, of course."

"Congratulations, Papa," teased Emma with tears in her eyes.

"Yeah, I'm a papa now." He grinned and turned to accompany Sister Anne back to the room.

Emma and Jeremy sat back down for a moment, and he said, "Why don't we leave the happy couple? With us here, there's a chance Harvey and Louis are hanging around and planning all sorts of mischief."

"Oh, should we?" she said, disappointed. She really wanted to see the baby again.

"I'm pretty sure there's gonna be plenty of Marella's here soon enough." Tony had a very large, loving family, and he'd notified them of the impending birth.

She nodded, looking back toward the door that Tony went into. She took Jeremy's arm, and they started down the stairs. There was the sound of many footsteps rushing toward them. It sounded like a small army was coming up the stairs. Emma and Jeremy stopped, unsure of what was happening. The first person who turned the corner toward them was Michael Marella, Tony's father. Not so far behind him was Tony's mother, his brothers and their wives.

"Emma! Jeremy!" Michael exclaimed. "You're leaving?"

"Yes. We thought we'd leave so that family could visit," Emma replied, unsure of herself.

"Oh, hush," Tony's father said, pulling her into a bear hug. "You know you're family."

"Michael's right, we'd love you to stay," said Tony's mother Doris. She and Emma had trouble in the past over Tony's feelings for Emma, but they'd been on good terms for years.

"We got word the baby came," Marco called from the back of the group.

"It did."

"Well," he called, "what was it?"

Emma looked at Jeremy. He gave a nod, and she turned back to the group. "A girl."

There were whoops and grins all around. "Well, let's get going, I want to see my new granddaughter," Doris said.

Emma and Jeremy moved against the wall so the family could pass. "Tony's in with Peggy," she called. They moved further down the stairs and Emma hesitated for a moment. "Such a lovely family," she said.

"They are," agreed Jeremy. They pushed the door to the hospital entry open and made their way to the outside door.

Emma leaned on Jeremy. "You know what? I could use a nap."

"I'd like to eat first. All of the shenanigans with Pete and the guys and then the baby to top it all off, I'm starving."

Emma stayed by the stoop and Jeremy went to call a carriage; they weren't up for a long walk back. Harvey approached him. "Hey, um, how is she?" Harvey asked, squirming a bit.

"She's fine," Jeremy told him. "They had a little girl."

The man nodded. "I'm glad it went well. Um, I'm sorry if we had anything to do with her coming early."

Jeremy decided to give the guy a break and said, "I think it was her time."

Emma walked up to the duo. She looked around and asked, "Where's Louis?"

"He headed back to the hotel," said Harvey. The carriage pulled up next them and Jeremy helped Emma into it. "Where are you two headed now?" he asked suspiciously.

"Headed for some food. It's been a long day. See ya."

"See ya." He watched them climb in and depart. "I guess no invitation for me to join you," he muttered to himself as he walked back to the hotel disconsolately.

Louis entered the hotel. He had a limp from the fall he'd taken at the hospital when that nun had thrown them out. *Who would've thought a sister could be that strong?* He walked to the elevator. Pete was there and took him up to his floor.

Finally at his room, he took out his key, inserted it into the lock, but the door opened before he could turn it. He frowned at the knob and went into the room. He'd locked it before he left, hadn't he?

"Hello, Louis," a voice called from the bed. He squinted into the dark room, trying to see who was there. He didn't know many people in Chicago.

"Who are you and why are you in my room?" he asked, raising his voice.

"Come over here," the voice called softly.

Louis approached the bed slowly and the person standing next to it turned up the gas lamp. The light slowly illuminated the room and revealed the face of the person talking to him. He stopped and said in a shaky voice, "But, but you're dead!"

"You think so?" he asked as he pulled a knife and buried it in Louis' chest.

As Louis collapsed, holding his hand to the knife in his chest, he stuttered out with his dying breath, "Why'd you have to do that?"

The man didn't answer as he watched the life slowly drain out of the dying man. When he was sure Louis was dead, he went to his bag and pulled out a dark suit and a clerical collar and got to work.

CHAPTER 15

$\mathscr{E}$mma and Jeremy had stopped to eat close to the hotel and strolled back to the hotel together, "I hope Pete has that drawing for us," Emma said.

"He may not have gotten off shift yet," he reminded her.

She nodded. "You know, we still have to deal with Harvey and Louis and we still don't have any answers."

"And Winsten," he reminded her.

"We haven't seen him in a while."

"Doesn't mean he's not around."

"I know."

They entered the hotel. The elevator had a sign on it - CLOSED.

Emma sighed. "Ugh, I guess it'll be the stairs for us."

They walked up the stairs and to their rooms. Each entered their individual doors. She climbed to retrieve the bag from the armoire and, as Jeremy walked through the connecting door, she emptied it on the bed.

"It's here, Emma. We just don't see it. Otherwise, why would Teddy have it with him on the train when he was obviously running away?"

She pulled out the list of items studying it again and started, "If the painting is the clue, it might be…"

A sudden scream sounded. Emma and Jeremy jumped, not moving. "What now?" she asked as they went to the door. A maid was running down the hallway yelling, "He only wanted more towels!" She screamed again and ran down the stairs.

Jeremy looked at Emma. "That's a lot of noise for towels. Did you see whose room she ran out of?"

"Louis' I think."

They moved slowly down the hall and Jeremy put his hand on the knob to open the door. They were about to enter when Harvey stepped out of the stairwell. "Hey! What're you doing going into Louis' room?"

Emma frowned at him. "We're not sure, but we think he might be in trouble."

Harvey jogged over to them and said, "Let's go in."

The door was opened, and they entered. "Look at the bed," she said. They all approached slowly. The form on the bed was covered head to toe.

"Who's going to check?" asked Harvey nervously.

"I'll do it," said Jeremy. He moved the blanket down. It was Louis; he was dead and dressed as a priest.

"Damn it. Poor guy," Harvey lamented. He glared accusingly at Jeremy and Emma. "It has to be you two."

"Why us?" asked Jeremy.

"I wasn't here, and you both were."

"How do we know that you didn't do this and then go back downstairs?"

"I was with someone," the other man said shortly.

"Who?" Emma asked suspiciously. They hadn't seen him with anyone other than Eddie and Louis.

Before he could answer, the maid ran up behind him, dragging the hotel manager with her. "Another body!" yelled the manager, glaring at the three. The trio stepped back from the bed to give them a better view. "And another priest! You three, you're causing too much trouble!"

Loud footsteps came towards the room, with Cole leading the party. "Jones, take the men, seal off the hallway. Don't let anyone up or down."

Cole looked at the dead man. He turned to them and said, "Another body in a bed wearing a priest suit?"

"Looks like," Jeremy said.

"We'll need to question everyone again."

"Could we do it here?" asked Jeremy.

"We do have fewer people to talk to," Cole said, looking at the man on the bed. "We'll use your room," he said to Jeremy.

"It's down that way, the last one on the left."

"And we'll want to talk to everyone. You first." He pointed to the maid. She followed him meekly. After the door closed, Jones let the hotel manager go back downstairs.

Harvey, Emma, and Jeremy waited in the hallway for their turn. Jeremy's door opened and the crying maid was led out by an officer. "It'll be okay," he assured her.

"Why do they keep turning up when I go to clean the room? I don't want to go into another room!"

Cole came out shaking his head. He pointed to Harvey. "You next." He ignored Emma and Jeremy.

Harvey glared at Emma and Jeremy before he walked to Jeremy's room. Cole stepped in and Harvey followed closely behind. The door closed behind them.

"You think it was Harvey?" Emma asked.

"No, but I think Harvey might be next."

"There's no one left that was involved in the scam."

They sat quietly and waited.

Harvey exited and held up his hand to them. "It wasn't me."

They looked at him and waited for Cole to come to the door. When he appeared at the doorway, he growled at them, "You two, now."

They stood and walked down to Jeremy's room. Once there, they entered, and they took a seat on the bed. Cole took a chair and sat it in front of them. "I'm beginning to think this hasn't been a very successful plan. You were undercover to find out who killed one man and now we have two additional murders AND they're all dressed as priests."

"What did Harvey say, Pops?"

"He said he was meeting someone else."

"Who?" asked Emma.

"The young Mystery girl who's yet to be interviewed. He couldn't or wouldn't give us a name."

"Did he say why they were meeting?"

"He said she was looking for the same thing all of them are: the money."

Emma looked at Jeremy. "We did find out Pete was the artist."

"Does he have access to the painting?"

"I don't think so, but he did mention he could provide sketches for us to look at."

"We need those now," Cole said desperately. "This has gone on for far too long. Three murders..." He stood and threw his chair against the wall.

"Give us a little more time. We need to find out if Pete knows where the girl is," Emma pleaded.

"What happens when another body shows up?"

"We think Harvey's at risk. He's the only one from the original scam."

"If it isn't Harvey, then who?" muttered Cole.

"We only have Max Winsten left, the detective who has both motive and opportunity."

"I think it's time to pull him in for questioning. Where is he?" Cole asked.

"I have no idea," Emma admitted. "I haven't seen him since the murders started happening."

"We need to find a way to draw him out."

"If Winsten is doing this, then we need to keep an eye on Harvey," said Emma.

"Okay, get the sketches and let me know where they lead. Also…"

"Pops, relax. We'll stay attached to Harvey," Jeremy assured his father.

"I'll leave you here one more night, but I don't want another body showing up," Cole said, pointing his finger at them to emphasize his point.

"We should probably follow up with Tony and Peggy."

"Tony's probably still at the hospital," Jeremy reminded her.

Cole's eyebrows lifted at that bit of news.

"Peggy had her baby today," Emma explained. The two of them filled him in on what had occurred that day.

"These people, whoever they are and whatever they want, are getting desperate. I'll put officers on them at the hospital and at their house."

"Three dead men," Emma reminded him, "and I don't think it'll stop with Harvey. I think they'll go after anyone they perceive as a threat."

"We'll have to be on guard," said Cole. "It looks like all of you are at risk now,"

"Agreed," said Emma and Jeremy together.

"Even though," she said thoughtfully, "I don't think we'll end up in a priest outfit."

Jeremy and Cole sent her identical looks of surprise, and broke into laughter.

"We'll talk to Pete and go to his house this evening," Jeremy said.

"And Harvey?"

"We'll keep an eye on him."

Cole left them then and they decided to stay in for the evening. There was a knock on their door. She went to answer it and found Harvey standing there. He shifted his boots and scraped the floor with his boot toe. "I, ah, I wanted to make sure that you were still alive." He looked up and down the hallway. "It's getting harder and harder to stay alive around here."

"Do you know anything we don't, Harvey?" Emma asked, noting his unease.

He looked hesitant and asked, "Can I come in?"

Emma stepped back and let him into the small room. His eyes went to the open connecting door, but left it alone. He started, "Just the one thing, there were five of us involved in the con. Not four."

"I know," she said.

"How do you know?" asked Harvey, his brow lowered, and his mouth clenched. "Eddie and Louis didn't talk to you."

"No," said Emma. "There's a detective after you and the others. He wants the money."

"Detective? Why haven't I heard about this before?"

"I had no reason to mention it to you before," she said, folding her arms over her chest.

Jeremy looked at him and said, "We'd like to hear the story from you. What happened to him, that fifth man?"

Harvey grunted. "He died on that last job. That was the one meant to set us up with plenty of money."

"Go on," encouraged Jeremy. Emma continued to study the man.

"Mind if I sit?" Emma and Jeremy nodded. "We were working this one together; it was a diamond delivery in New York City. The city's best jewels were based in Maiden Lane. It's a very affluent area. The priest con allowed us into spaces where customers weren't normally allowed. We did some tests and the stores were receptive to our coming in to view the stones. But that final day, Teddy wanted to go big, four different stores at the same time."

"What happened?" Emma asked breathlessly; she'd been drawn into the story.

"Teddy was our watch, and all of the stores were within steps of one another. Things seemed to be going well. We completed our business and each of us left the stores."

"Was anyone following you?"

"I didn't think so at the time. We each took separate paths to the meet up. It was a local warehouse."

"Was everyone there?" asked Jeremy.

"Yeah, we walked in separately. Everyone was happy and laughing…" Harvey's voice trailed off. He was lost in his memories. He shook himself and started again. "All of a sudden, all these men started running in from all directions. Some even came in through the windows. It was crazy! There were guns going off and we were diving for cover. Even as I was crawling around the space, it seemed too pat. Too planned out. And then I got a good look at some of the men. They were guards from each of the jewelry stores."

"How did you recognize them?" asked Jeremy.

"Teddy and I had gone to each of the stores to scope out the locations and guards. We got a good view of each of them."

"How'd you get out?"

"On my hands and knees. I crawled out a hole in the wall and I kept going."

"The others?"

"Eddie, Louis, Teddy, and I met a few weeks later. We had an emergency meet up, in case something like this happened."

"Only the four of you?"

"Yeah, once we got there, it was just the four of us."

"And the final guy, what was his name?" Emma asked.

"Arthur Smith," he supplied.

"Was he dead?"

"I honestly don't know, but he didn't show up at the final meeting. We figured he was dead."

"Is there any way you think he might still be alive?"

"I don't know, but who else would be killing everyone? I don't think it's just about the money anymore. I think it's personal."

"Can you give me an idea of what this man looks like?" asked Emma.

"Arthur was a big man, oversized in every way; he never seemed to fit into the priest gear. It always bothered me. I always thought bringing him in was a bad idea."

Emma sucked in her breath.

"You think Winsten is this Smith?" Jeremy asked her.

"It might be. There aren't a lot of people who would fit those traits." *It must be him!* Emma moved on to another topic. "You spoke to Mystery girl. Did she tell you who she is?"

"She didn't have to. I recognized her. She's Teddy's daughter," Harvey said simply.

"Just like we thought," Emma replied.

Harvey sent Emma a long look and drawled, "She seems very sure that you aren't Peggy Latimer."

Emma's eyebrows raised and she moved to sit on the bed. She didn't comment.

"Why does she think that?" asked Jeremy.

"She's seen a painting of her."

"Hmm. That painting is also missing. We think she has it," Emma told him.

"We need to examine it, and we'll need Tony to take a look at it," said Jeremy.

"Who's that?" Harvey asked.

Emma decided to start being truthful to the man. "The actual Peggy, you met her earlier today. Her husband is Tony."

"That woman we brought in?" He laughed suddenly. "I didn't expect that." He waved his hand at Jeremy and Emma. "I assume you both know each other?"

Jeremy and Emma looked at each other and back at him. "We do."

"Who are you?" he asked.

"I'm August, Arthur Smith's brother, remember?" Jeremy smirked.

Emma swatted Jeremy's arm. "I'm Emma Evans and this is Jeremy Tilden. We're friends of Peggy and Tony," she said.

"We're also investigators with the Pinkerton's. And we want to solve the case, but only because we want to know who killed Teddy," said Jeremy.

"Wait," Harvey said, "Your name is Tilden and you're with the Pinkerton's?"

"Yep."

"The guy who questioned me and Louis, his name is Tilden."

"That's my pops."

"Now, that's interesting. Have you any leads on the money?"

"I would think that would be resolved as part of this," Emma said.

"Will you give it to me if we find it?" Harvey asked.

"I'm not sure," Emma replied honestly. "We'd need to confirm that the stores don't have a right to the money."

Harvey sighed. "Done in by the law. Do you know what the next step is to find the money?"

"We need Pete or Teddy's daughter or both, and we need to see either those sketches or the painting. I think Teddy requested clues be added to it."

"That Teddy could persuade a person to do anything," Harvey said admiringly.

"Like changing you from a priest to a con man?"

"You know about that also," he said. He pulled out a cigar and asked, "May I?"

"Go ahead." Emma liked the smell of a cigar. They watched as he lit it.

He exhaled the smoke. "I was young and full of big ideas to change the world when I became a priest. My father believed one of his sons should be given to the church. And that was me. I didn't fight it at first. I thought I could help and would be placed somewhere where that could happen." He tapped his cigar on the side table and continued. "It was okay in the beginning, but then I was placed with a corrupt priest. I didn't like it and when I reported him to the parish priest, they didn't do anything about him. I went to the bishop of the diocese. They just moved me to New York, and I was turned into an errand boy. That was when I ran into Teddy. I was sent to pick up some jewels for the bishop and he was there. Teddy followed me out and, next thing I knew, we were forming up plans to do the first job."

"You went along with no argument?" asked Emma.

"Yeah, by that point, I was pretty easy to convince."

"Were Eddie and Louis also priests?" Jeremy asked.

Harvey threw back his head and let out a loud guffaw. "Now, that would be a sight." He tapped his cigar, letting the ashes fall to the floor. "Naw, I was the only priest in on the scam." He stopped talking and examined the end of his cigar.

"What about Arthur, the one you left behind?" asked Jeremy.

"Ol' Arthur. He joined us much later. The scam had been going on for a while."

"Who brought him in?" Emma asked.

Harvey frowned remembering. "It was Teddy. We went on his recommendation. He seemed to know him from before."

"Before? Chicago or later?"

"I'm not sure. But their relationship wasn't good. They'd argue over everything, even the littlest thing, and it sometimes led to physical fights."

"You didn't hear what they argued about?" asked Jeremy.

"I didn't really care. Like I said, they were always arguing. Hey, why're we talking about Arthur? You really think he might be behind this?"

"Maybe," Emma allowed.

"Arthur. He killed everyone." He stood and began pacing the small space. They watched him silently.

"We aren't sure," Emma cautioned.

"We need to get sure," Harvey said. "Before I'm found in a priest suit."

Jeremy looked at his watch. "It's getting late. Do we want to talk to Pete tonight?"

"I think we should," Emma said and the three of them stood, walked to the door, and out. As they turned to the elevator, Harvey started to go with them. Emma looked at him and hesitated; she didn't want to leave Harvey alone, but she wasn't sure Pete would want him with them.

Jeremy saw her hesitation and stated, "He should come with us." He looked at Harvey. "It would be safer if we stay together."

"Yeah, I don't want to be left alone. I'd rather go with you two."

They walked to the elevator. Jeremy pushed the button and Harvey kept gazing up and down the hallway. Emma watched him, not offering any reassurances. The man was at risk, but that didn't make him a good guy. He *should* be worried.

The elevator ascended slowly to their floor. They waited as it arrived, and the doors were pushed open into the hallway. Pete was the operator; he reached up to his tie and pulled at it. He gulped at seeing the three of them together. "Going down?" he asked, his voice going up.

Emma, Jeremy, and Harvey stepped onto the elevator. "Lobby, please," she said. Pete turned away from them and turned the lever to return to the lobby. They moved slowly toward the bottom floor. Once there, Emma stopped him when he went to open the doors. "Pete, it's time to see the sketches."

He took off his cap and swallowed. "You can't," he stammered.

Emma stepped toward him, forcing him backward. "Pete, I've given you enough time. We need to see them now."

He held up his hands placatingly. "No, you don't understand. I don't have them!"

"But you said…" she started.

"I did but she burned them," he muttered miserably.

"Oh, for God's sake. Mystery girl. What's her name?" she asked, exasperated. When he hesitated, she barked at him, "Pete! Name! Now!"

"Hazel. Her name is Hazel," he admitted.

"Where's Hazel and, more importantly, where's that painting?"

"I don't know," he said.

Jeremy took pity on the boy. "You painted it right?"

"Yes."

"Can you sketch a copy for us?"

Pete raised his head and his eyes sparkled. "Yeah. Yeah, I can do that! I hadn't thought of it."

"Now," said Emma.

"Well, I'm on duty." She gave him a long look. "Uh, I can, uh, I can have Issac cover for me," he admitted.

Finally, Emma backed off and let him open the doors, and they exited into the lobby. Issac leaned on the lobby desk. He was there to help guest with their bags. "Issac," Pete called, "can you cover the elevator for me for a while?"

Issac looked at three surrounding Pete and asked, "Are you sure?"

Pete said firmly, "Yes, I'm sure."

Issac nodded slowly and walked to the elevator.

"Follow me," Pete said over his shoulder. They followed him to a door a short distance away from the desk. He opened it as he descended the stairs. "The manager lets me stay down here," he explained over his shoulder.

As they descended, Emma saw ropes attached to the wall

and numbers on the ceiling. She said, "Abbey mentioned this building used to be a theatre."

"Hmm," said Jeremy as he looked around. "I wonder what those numbers mean?"

She studied the ropes and the numbers. "I'd have to ask Savannah, but I think they might be trap doors, so that people on stage can appear and disappear."

Jeremy cast a long look toward them. "Something to keep in mind later."

She didn't answer; instead, she continued to study the ceiling.

Pete had moved ahead into a room to the right. He'd turned up the gas lamps and the small room was illuminated. They followed him and took in a small table, four chairs, and a bed. He moved to the table and sat down. His sketch pad and pencils were already there for him to get started. The pencil moved across the page as he sketched a rough outline of Peggy. They watched without comment.

He paid attention to her hand and the ring that they'd given to Peggy before this. "The ring," Emma said, "had you seen it before this?"

"It was described to me," he said and moved from the ring to start work on the details of her dress.

"Who described it to you? Teddy or Hazel?"

Pete looked up with his mouth agape. When he found his voice, he said, "Teddy did at first. He got with me and suggested some changes."

"And," Jeremy prompted.

"Hazel said I got the color wrong. I'm not sure when she would've seen it but …." His voice trailed off as he continued to sketch.

Emma noticed the background he was adding. "I thought she was sitting in a dark room."

"No, Teddy wanted the background to be very specific."

Jeremy looked closer. "Peggy isn't inside at all."

"Where is that?" asked Emma. "It looks familiar."

Jeremy studied the area. "It looks like the area where Henrietta lived." Jeremy had spent a lot of time in that area when he was working a case involving kids working in glass manufacturing.

"Yeah, that's it," Emma said. "Is that a stoop she's sitting on?"

"It is," Pete confirmed.

"How did you prevent Peggy from recognizing it?"

"I used color to distract the eye."

"The sketch doesn't have that," Emma agreed.

"It makes the clues easier to see," said Jeremy.

Pete continued to work on his sketch.

"What is that?" Emma pointed. He'd drawn lines from a rectangle above Peggy's head.

"Well, in the picture, it was an effect to give light to Peggy's hair," Pete told her.

"Was it your idea?" Jeremy asked him.

"No, Teddy recommended it."

"Did he give you an idea of what it was? Or what it represented?"

"No, I assumed it was an effect he wanted."

"But now?" Emma prompted.

"Now, I think it might be a clue," Pete said as he studied his sketch.

"What does this have to do with us?" complained Harvey.

Emma turned to him. "Right now, I'm not sure, but I think we should head back to our rooms. I also think Pete needs to get back to work."

Pete stood up and the chair he'd sat in fell on the floor. "Yes, yes, I do." He rolled up the sketch and started to put it away.

"Could you give that to me?" she asked. He hesitated and she reminded him gently, "It'll probably be safer with me than with you." He nodded; his mouth turned down as he remembered the loss of his sketches. "Please?" He handed it over to her. Emma took it and said, "Thanks, Pete."

"Pete, where's Hazel?" asked Jeremy.

He sat back down into his chair and sighed. "The last time I saw her, she said she'd find that painting no matter what."

Emma stated, "We know she's Teddy's daughter. Why did she take the painting?"

"I think those answers should come from her." He hadn't wanted to discuss Hazel before; they knew it was a dead-end conversation.

Emma was torn. This case was dragging on and this boy was their only connection to Hazel.

"Let's go," Jeremy prompted her.

She looked at Pete and back to Jeremy. "All right, but I'd like to talk again tomorrow."

"Okay," Pete said. He stood more slowly this time and followed them out.

The lobby was quiet, and Isaac waved and ran over. "Not much has gone on since you left."

"Thanks."

"Everything okay?" Issac asked, eyeing the three.

"It's fine. I need to get back to work now." Pete walked to the elevator and the trio followed him. The group remained silent all the way to their floor. Jeremy, Emma, and Harvey got off at their floor and went to Emma's room without a word to Pete.

The door to Emma's room closed and Harvey turned to them shaking his finger. "Why do you think that picture and Hazel are the clues to finding my money?"

Emma sat on the edge of the bed. "Teddy didn't leave us anything else and that bag that we keep going through is useless. I think it is a distraction."

Jeremy nodded. "What're the next steps?"

"We need to get with Peggy and ask her about the things we spotted in the painting."

"Why don't we go now?" Harvey demanded and started to the door.

Her next words stopped him. "Because she just had a baby, and she needs her rest. This can wait for tomorrow."

"Oh yeah, when you put it that way, I guess you're right." He started to the door again and didn't turn when he said, "You know, I was a pretty good priest. I did care about people then. I think I've forgotten how."

Emma's face softened and she said, "You might bolt your door and move the dresser in front of it."

This time, he did turn to them. "I don't plan on wearing a priest outfit tonight. I'll see you in the morning."

Maybe, she thought. She hoped so. This man seemed different from the other two.

He left and Jeremy moved to bolt the door. They shoved the dresser in front of it and walked to Jeremy's room to do the same thing there.

When they finished, she pulled out the drawing and laid it on the bed. While she studied it, Jeremy came up behind her and wrapped his hands around her waist. She leaned back and asked, "Will Peggy know what these clues mean?"

"I think it was meant for her. The clues appear to be related to her childhood."

"Then we see her."

"Tired?" he asked.

"Long day," she said, not moving from his embrace. He turned her and they kissed. "Well, maybe I'm not as tired as I thought."

He grinned and lay with her on the bed.

CHAPTER 16

The next morning, they were up early. Jeremy pulled on his shirt and asked, "Do you think Harvey survived last night?"

"I hope so. I'd hate to have to talk to Cole about another body."

"That's true. Pops wasn't happy with us and our progress on this case."

"I think we should check on Harvey."

"Not real sure I want to see a body this early in the morning." Jeremy rubbed his stomach; right now he was hungry.

"Let's get ready to go and we'll stop by there first."

After they got ready, they gave up the ruse of two rooms and exited hers together. The hallway was empty at the early morning hour. He held out his hand to her. "Ready?"

"Not really, but let's do it anyway." She took the hand he offered, and they walked slowly toward Harvey's room. Once there, they stood in front of it and knocked. They waited. No answer.

"What now?" he asked.

"Try the door," she suggested. He tried and found it locked.

He cocked an eyebrow at her. She looked around, kneeled, and pulled out her lock pick. She maneuvered it and the lock clicked. She stood and he pushed the door open. There was a pile on the bed that could be a man.

"Go look," Emma nudged Jeremy.

"Nothin' doing. You want to look, be my guest. I've seen enough dead bodies for a while."

"Chicken."

"Bawk, bawk."

Emma took a deep breath and walked slowly forward. "Harvey?" she whispered. There was no answer. She looked back at Jeremy.

"Go ahead."

Emma steeled herself and reached to pull the blanket back. "Harvey, please don't be dead. If you're not dead, please don't be naked." She started to pull the cover back.

"Hey, kids, find anyone in there?" came a long drawl from the doorway right behind Jeremy.

Jeremy screeched and jumped about a foot in the air. They both turned to find Harvey. "Glad to see you're still with us," said Jeremy shakily.

"Me, too," Harvey said, exhaling a smoke ring. They watched it float by. He continued. "Though I did have a visitor last night."

"What happened?" Emma asked.

"Someone tried the doorknob and tried to push the door open."

"What stopped him?" asked Jeremy.

"I did. I slept right here," he said, pointing to the floor in front of his door. "I slept against the dresser I moved in front of the door." He saw their raised eyebrows. "You bet I was scared. That happens when three of your friends are murdered. So, where to this morning?" he asked, nodding toward the drawing in Emma's hand.

"We plan to go to breakfast and after visit Peggy at the hospital."

"That's a good idea. I'm mighty hungry myself." He started to follow them out. Jeremy stopped him.

"You can come, but you can't go to Peggy's room."

"And if I insist?"

"Let's just say, I'll be unhappy," Jeremy replied and put his hand in his pocket.

"And if you want any information we find out, I'd listen to him," said Emma.

Harvey raised his eyebrows at this, but responded with, "Sounds like a plan. And you can pull your hand out of your pocket. I know you don't have a gun."

"Actually," Jeremy said, "you'd be wrong." He pulled out a small pistol.

Emma's eyes went wide at the gun, but she kept her mouth shut. He slipped it back into his pocket.

"Well, okay then," Harvey said and led the way out of his room.

"A gun," she murmured. "Why would you bring a gun?"

"I thought it might come in handy," he replied in the same tone.

"Yes, it's that."

Harvey turned back to him and mocked, "Say, sonny, that was quite a screech you gave out back there. Weren't scared, were you?"

"As a matter of fact, you scared the bejeezus out of me," Jeremy admitted.

"Aw, sorry about that." The man snickered. Jeremy rolled his eyes at him.

They walked from the hotel to the café and ordered breakfast. Afterward, they caught a carriage to the hospital. Once there, Emma turned to Harvey. "You can stay downstairs and wait for us."

He started to complain, but Jeremy tapped his pocket. He held up his hand. "Sure, sure. Whatever you say." They went in and Emma pointed to the chairs across from the nurse's station. Harvey nodded and went to sit down. Emma and Jeremy walked over to speak to the nurse.

"Good morning, Sister Agnes," Emma greeted her.

"Well, Emma and Jeremy! Good morning! Are you here to see Peggy and the baby?"

"We are. How is she?"

"She and the baby are well rested."

"And Tony?"

"He stayed the night, though I think that chair prevented any real rest."

"Can we go up?" asked Jeremy.

"She can have visitors; you may go up."

They nodded and started to head to the stairs. "What about him?" Sister Agnes called over and waved her hand in Harvey's direction.

"Oh, him. He'll be here while we're upstairs," Emma said, "and he shouldn't be allowed up. If he gives you any trouble, have Sister Bernadette talk to him."

"I think I can manage that," Sister Agnes replied, squinting at the man. Harvey stared back and didn't move.

Emma and Jeremy went up the stairs to the room. As they drew closer to the door, Mrs. Marella, Tony's mother, stepped out. "Emma! Jeremy! You're back again."

"Yes, we wanted to see how everyone's doing," Emma said and leaned in to hug the woman.

She squeezed her back. "They're good. I got here early so that Tony could go home and change."

"I'm back," called a voice from down the hall. They turned and saw Tony hurrying toward them.

"Did you get some rest?" his mom asked with a frown on her face.

"Not much," he admitted. "But a bath helped. Thanks, Mom." He leaned down to kiss her on the cheek. "Good morning, Emma, Jeremy."

"Good morning," they said together and laughed.

"We'd love to see Peggy. Can we go in?" Emma asked.

"Let me check." He opened the door and went in. He came out a moment later and said, "That's fine, you can come in."

Mrs. Marella said, "I'll head home now. Let us know when you are home so we can come by."

"Thanks Ma," said Tony and kissed her cheek. They watched her walk to the stairs.

Tony held open the door for them. Emma and Jeremy walked in and saw that Peggy was sitting up in the bed holding the baby.

"Hey, thanks for yesterday," Peggy said.

"We help family," Emma told her. Tony smiled. He was happy Emma still considered them family.

"May I see the baby?" Emma asked as she walked to the bed. Peggy pulled the blanket back to reveal the little body in the small shirt. "She's beautiful."

"Would you like to hold her?"

"Can I?" Emma asked with a bright smile.

"Of course."

Tony reached over and took the baby to give to Emma. Emma gathered her up and looked at the little face. She yawned and Emma laughed in delight. "She's so expressive already."

"She is," said Peggy softly.

"What's her name?" Jeremy asked as he looked at the baby over Emma's shoulder.

"Louise Michaela. She's named after Peggy's mom and my dad."

"That's wonderful," said Emma. She reluctantly gave the baby back to Tony.

Jeremy looked at Tony and Peggy. "We have a few questions, if you don't mind."

"Have you found anything out?" asked Tony as he rocked the baby back and forth.

"We have a couple of new things," Emma admitted, "but we do have some questions."

"Go ahead," Peggy told her.

Emma pulled out the sketches and laid them on the bed for everyone to view.

"Tony, it's my painting," Peggy exclaimed, looking closely at it.

Tony handed Peggy the baby. "Let me have a look." He traced the drawing and said, "This was the original artist. Did you find him?"

"You remember when we mentioned someone named Pete?" asked Jeremy.

"The elevator operator at the hotel?" Peggy asked him.

"That's him. When we confronted him, he admitted he is the artist," said Emma.

"Were these the original drawings?" Tony asked, still examining the details.

"No. Those were destroyed."

Tony looked at them, his eyes wide. "He destroyed original sketches? That's unusual."

"Not him," Emma replied.

"Then who?" Peggy asked.

"It was the Mystery girl," Jeremy said.

"The one you thought broke into our house?"

"The same one. Pete said she burned the originals."

"That means the painting does have something in it," said Peggy and looked closer at the drawings.

"We believe so," Emma confirmed.

"It's easier to see the details without the dark paint. Look here, Peggy," Tony said, pointing to the drawing. "It's clearer that you're sitting on stairs."

"Yes," Peggy murmured, following his finger on the sketch. "It looks like the stoop outside my childhood home. I hadn't noticed that before. There was so much pain there. I wonder why Teddy would ask him to paint that."

"Do you see anything else?" asked Emma. She didn't want to press her friend, but they needed answers.

"A tree."

"Was there a tree in front of your house?" This was a poor area, and the trees were unexpected.

"Yes. It was a weed that had sprung up and wouldn't die. Eventually, it became a tree."

Tony pointed to the object that had lines radiating from it. "In the original painting, I thought this was there to lighten Peggy's face."

"Pete mentioned it was one of the items that Teddy asked him to add."

"It's a mirror," murmured Peggy. "Teddy was always fascinated with them. He would hang them in the tree to catch the light."

"What does it mean?" muttered Tony, studying the drawing. "And what does it have to do with the ring?"

The baby started to fuss. "I need to feed her," Peggy said.

"We'll give you some privacy," said Emma. She bent to pick up the drawing and Tony asked, "Could you leave them with me? I want to take a closer look."

Emma looked at Jeremy and he nodded. "Sure, I can leave them. We'll come back later. Send us a note." They hurried to leave as the baby's cries got louder.

"We'll get out of your way," said Jeremy and ushered Emma quickly out of the room. The cries stopped almost immediately.

"That's a happy baby," Emma said with a grin.

"Yes indeed. Downstairs?"

"Yeah." She followed him to the stairs. As they descended, they could hear two raised voices. "Sounds like Sister Agnes," said Emma.

"And Harvey."

They exited expecting to see Harvey; instead, they saw Sister Agnes standing at the station, alone. "Where's Harvey?" Emma asked.

"Outside," the sister said shortly.

The man was in danger, and they'd hoped he'd stay put. "What caused the argument?"

"He lit a cigar in here. That's just not acceptable."

"Yeah, I guess it wouldn't be," murmured Jeremy. "Thank you, sister, for putting up with him as long as you did."

She nodded. "I don't like to lose my temper; it's something I continue to work on."

"Me, too," said Emma.

"Yeah, but you don't yell. You pull a knife," muttered Jeremy in her ear.

Emma grinned and said, "Like I said, I'm working on it. And the knife will come in handy once this case finally moves forward."

They waved goodbye and headed outside to locate Harvey. "How do we find him?" asked Jeremy.

"Follow the smoke rings," she said and saw them drifting up from a nearby stoop. They wandered over to him.

"Find anything?" he asked from his reclined position.

"Maybe," commented Emma.

"Going to tell me what?"

"No, I don't think so."

At that comment, his laziness disappeared, and he stood quickly, annoyed. "Now see here."

Emma stepped toward him. "Now, Harvey, isn't your goal the money?"

"Yeah," he admitted.

"Then let us investigate."

"As long as I get my fair share."

"And you'd like to stay alive," commented Jeremy, "and the best way to do that is let us follow the clues without interference."

"Now, that's motivation. Okay, group, what's our next step?" Harvey asked them.

"We have two choices," Emma said. "Mystery girl or Winsten."

"Let's go with Mystery girl," Harvey suggested. "It'll be less likely for me to be killed with her."

"So, how do we find her?" Emma asked.

"She's likely in the area," Jeremy responded.

"And very likely watching us," she commented.

"Gotta say that's a rather boring pastime," Harvey replied.

"Well, we're so sorry we're not keeping you entertained," Jeremy said with an eyeroll.

"Yeah, well, what can you do?"

"Have you spoken with Mystery girl again?" Emma asked Harvey.

"Hazel. Her name is Hazel," supplied Harvey, "and no."

At that moment, a bike whizzed by. "Look! There she is!" Emma exclaimed. She looked around frantically and grabbed the nearest bike. She jumped on it and started after her. It was time to get some answers from the girl about her role in this mess. Also, she needed to be aware that there was someone dangerous in the area and she could be at risk.

"Do we need to follow?" Harvey asked Jeremy.

He shook his head. "Nah, she has it under control."

Harvey looked over at him and said, "That's good. I don't think I could ride one of those things. Say, I don't suppose you'll tell me what that sketch tells us. Does it have clues for where the money is?"

"I believe it might, in due time."

"What do we do now?"

"Wait. Let's go there to the café."

"Sure, I could eat. Will Emma be able to find us?" he asked and looked in the direction Emma had gone.

"No worries, she's resourceful." They walked over to the café.

Emma continued her chase of the young girl. She increased her speed and weaved through traffic to keep up. The chase continued around horses, carriages, and people; they changed to the sidewalk and several ladies jumped out of their way. "Hey!" one screamed.

"Sorry!" Emma called back over her shoulder. She pedaled quickly and wondered if she'd run out of steam first. Mystery girl shot down an alley and Emma followed. They both came to a screeching halt when a large horse-drawn truck blocked them in.

"I need to talk to you!" Emma shouted.

"Talk," the girl scoffed. "Yeah, I don't think so."

"Wait. Are you Teddy Latimer's daughter?"

Hazel squinted at her. "If I am, then I'm the only one related to him who's here in this alley."

"You'd be right. I'm not Peggy, but I do know her. I'm a close friend of the family."

"So close that you pretend to be her? Does she know about this game, you stealing her identity?"

"I'm working for her, looking into Teddy's death. She lost her only brother, and she was going to have a baby. I didn't want her to put herself in jeopardy."

"Was?" Hazel asked. "Is Peggy okay? And the baby?" Her worry seemed genuine.

"Yes, both are okay."

"Good," she said and looked Emma over. "And what does that make you, a detective?" the girl jeered.

"Yes, it does," Emma replied. "I work as an investigator with the Pinkertons and on independent cases."

She looked at her closely. "They let women do that?"

"They didn't 'let' me do anything. I decided I wanted to be a detective and I did it. You make your own opportunities."

"Yeah, I've seen that. Women can't accept the limited opportunities that's offered to them. They have to make their own way if they want to be anything other than a wife and mother."

"Hazel, where's your mom?"

"Dead."

"When?"

"When I was born."

"Have you been with Teddy all this time?"

"No. At first, I was with him and then something happened, and he sent me to my grandmother. She died and I was alone again."

"Were you in contact with him during that time?"

"He'd occasionally drop in and there were letters."

"He didn't send for you when your grandmother died?"

"I asked why he wouldn't send for me in the letters, but Papa was worried we were being followed. He said that, once he found Peggy, he'd settle down and send for me."

"And…"

"He just never did. I kept waiting and waiting."

"How did you end up here?"

"I found him," Hazel said proudly.

"How?" Emma asked, curious.

"Through the letters. I was able to trace him through them. He always managed to send money to us. The last six months, the letters have come from the same place, here. I knew it was time to come here and try to be a family."

"Smart thinking, that's what I would've done. How did you get here?"

"I sold everything; the house, the furniture, everything, and made my way here."

Like father, like daughter, thought Emma. "Did you get here in time? Were you able to see your father?"

"I finally got here, and I got off a train only to find out he'd been tossed from another one," she said and wiped her eyes.

"I'm so sorry," Emma told the girl. Her papa had always been with them. Her mother had died when she was young, but her papa had always been the person she counted on. "You do have family here. Peggy."

"Yes," Hazel murmured. "I do."

"Why haven't you contacted Peggy?"

"I wasn't sure she'd believe me."

"Did you bring the letters from your father?"

"I have them. They're the only thing I have left from him."

Emma decided to ask the questions that tied Hazel to Harvey and the other two. "Were you in on the cons?"

"Occasionally," Hazel admitted, confirming what Emma knew. "Little orphan girl and priest was a great game to play." She chewed on her lip and blurted out, "Did Papa mention me to Peggy?"

She hated to tell her this, especially here. "Maybe we talk in another location."

"The answer is no."

"I'm sure he was planning to."

Hazel lowered her head. "I don't know. Maybe he meant to, but things changed."

"Harvey's the one who told us your name is Hazel. Did you also work with Harvey?"

"Occasionally, but I mostly worked with Papa. What's your name? I can't keep calling you Peggy."

"Emma."

"And that man who's always with you?"

"My friend Jeremy. Hazel, what're you after? Is it the

money?" *Everyone connected to this case is after the money, why not her?*

"No, I'm after my father's killer."

Emma had to ask, "Do you know what's happened at the hotel?"

"Pete mentioned Eddie and Louis," she admitted.

"Being murdered?" Emma filled in bluntly.

"Yes."

"Hazel, did you kill those men?"

"No, of course not," she said quickly.

Emma watched her closely. Hazel maintained eye contact and her hands were steady. That was a good sign she was telling the truth. "Good, we're trying to keep Harvey alive at this point."

"I'm glad."

"You believe he didn't kill Eddie and Louis?"

"I know him, and I don't think he'd do that. He and Papa were close."

Emma asked her, "Did you know about the fifth man?"

"The one who died on that last job?"

"Yes."

"Papa didn't tell me, but Harvey did."

"You didn't meet him either?"

"No. I was there, but as soon as he joined, Papa had me on the first train out of the area." She got off her bike and bent down to check the chain. "Have you found the money?" she asked tentatively.

"Before I answer that, why did you take the painting? And burn Pete's sketches?"

"It's mine; it was the only thing left. Everything else was gone."

I think Peggy might think differently, Emma thought.

"And I was angry," Hazel admitted.

"At your father?" asked Emma as she leaned forward on her handlebars.

"Among others," she muttered.

"Can you tell me who else?"

"Not now."

"Hopefully one of them isn't me," Emma teased her.

"No, you're working to bring Papa's killer to justice. I won't interfere with that."

"Do you have anyone you suspect?"

"There's one man," Hazel admitted. "He's been hanging around, in the shadows."

"What does he look like?" Emma asked, a frown on her face.

"He wears a heavy black coat, a carries cane, and a top hat."

Emma nodded. "Yeah, I noticed him. Don't know who chooses his clothes, though. He's kinda hard to miss."

"I think he's dangerous."

"What've you seen?" Emma asked.

"I saw him carrying bags into the hotel."

"When was this?"

"The same day as when Eddie and Louis were murdered."

"Did you follow him?"

"I started to, but Pete stopped me. He told me he might be dangerous."

"Pete's a good guy."

"Always has been."

Emma wanted to follow up on that statement but let it go until later. "Would you like to come back to the hospital with me and meet the real Peggy?"

"Yes, I would." Hazel started to climb on her bike.

Emma sat back on her seat and asked with a grin, "How about a race back?"

"I think I can beat you," the other girl said confidently, riding her bike swiftly toward the opening of the alley.

"You think so?" Emma murmured, pedaling hard after her.

They exited together and immediately had to dodge vendors and wagons. It slowed them a bit, but they cut through alleys, each overtaking the other. They were close to the hospital and went down a long alley to get there. Emma edged ahead and she said over her shoulder, "Ha. Got you," as she set to exit and win the race.

"No, I have you," said a voice. Both bikers were going too fast to avoid the figure. The bikes collided and both women fell to the ground.

Emma rolled in her fall and, once on her feet, she ran over to Hazel "Are you okay?"

"I think I'm okay."

Emma put out her hand to help her up. "Did you break anything?" she asked as she looked her over.

Hazel wasn't concerned about her health, though. "How are the bikes?" she asked.

"I think you should worry about yourselves and not the bikes," the figure said in a low voice.

Emma turned and said to him, "That was dangerous. You shouldn't have blocked us."

"I need to have a word with you," the man said. With the sun at his back, his face was shadowed. Emma couldn't make out who it was. As he took a step toward them and it came into focus, Emma finally got a good look at who it was.

"Hazel, are you able to run?" she asked in a low voice.

"Yes," Hazel responded, staring at the man blocking their path.

"Run, go to the hospital now! Ask for Tony!"

"But..." she started, continuing to stare at the man.

"Now!" Emma said, not turning her gaze from the man. "Don't try to stop her."

Hazel didn't question her and ran past the man. He moved slightly to his left.

"I won't interfere with her. She isn't involved in this," he said. "It's you I want."

Emma pushed her hair back and off her shoulder; it had fallen when she'd taken the tumble from her bike. "All right, Arthur, what do you want?"

The use of his name seemed to take the breath out of him. "Harvey has been talking about me?" he asked defensively.

"Yes, we are working together now."

"Hmm, then you should be aware I know you aren't Peggy."

"You knew? How?"

"I know people," Arthur said in a low voice. "Who are you and what're you doing here?"

"I'm Emma Evans. I'm Peggy's friend."

He frowned. "Where's Peggy? She missed Theodore's funeral."

"She didn't miss it."

"It was the other woman?" he asked, his voice sounding harsh. "Where is she now?"

"It won't do you any good to find her. She doesn't know anything."

"I won't ask you again. Where's the money?" he demanded, clearly losing his patience.

Instead of answering, she asked him, "Why did you kill Eddie and Louis?"

"Why?" he exploded. "Because they left me, Ms. Evans. They left me behind and took all the money. They knew I was still alive, but they left me there."

"How did you survive?"

"The men who were working security for the diamond businesses thought I would die there; they just left me. They kicked my head until I blacked out and I woke up at the home of a person who lived in the alley."

"How long were you convalescing?"

"Healing took time," Arthur admitted. "Once I could walk

again, I had a lead on Louis. He'd stayed in New York. He changed his name and ran a local grocery store. I kept track of him, and I found out he was headed to Chicago. I figured he found Theodore. Theodore set me up to die, may have killed me, but he left the other three alive when he stole from them. Sloppy."

She raised her eyebrows at him. "And when you got here?"

"I spoke calmly to each person about their part in my demise."

"Calmly?" she interrupted. "Was that just before killing them?"

"You're a cool one," Arthur said, reaching his hand into his pocket.

Gun or knife, she thought. Her hand was on her knife, and she watched him carefully.

"Why dress them as priests?" she continued to question him.

He shrugged. "I figured they should go out in style. They should be dressed appropriately when they meet their maker."

"And Harvey?"

"I'll get to him, don't worry."

"Oh, I won't," she murmured, fingering her knife.

He made a sudden move toward her. He was imposing, but she wouldn't back down! "I wouldn't do that," she said just as he was on her.

"Why? It would be so easy to just get rid of you."

"Then you wouldn't get the money."

That stopped him. "You're not even Peggy. Why would you have the money?"

"Oh, I have an idea of where it is," she said idly. "You haven't asked what I do for work."

"Why do I care? You're just a woman!"

"You should. I'm a detective."

He laughed at that. "Yeah, sure you are."

He lunged at her with a knife. She elbowed him in the neck,

stepped back and jump-kicked him in the stomach. He doubled up, coughing and dropped the knife. She kicked the blade away from him and ran out of the alley. She looked around and started toward the hospital. "Emma!" called Jeremy.

She looked over and saw him across the street at the café. She ran over to him.

Jeremy saw her torn clothes and her hair down. "What happened?"

"Too much," she said as she reached up and pulled her hair into a high ponytail. "Do you want to talk in the café?" Harvey looked uncomfortable and started to ease away from them. Emma turned her gaze on him. "Stop, Harvey. The person who waylaid me was Arthur, and he confessed to the murders."

"So, he didn't die?"

"And it turns out he's not happy about being left behind."

"Where was he?" asked Jeremy, flexing his fist.

"Over there," she commented, pointing toward the alley. "He was about to puke his guts out from me kicking him in the chest."

"Why don't we head back over and introduce ourselves?" Jeremy asked Harvey with a twisted smile.

Harvey looked over and said, "You know, I wouldn't mind seeing good ol' Arthur again."

"Harvey," she said, "be careful. He said he's going to kill you."

"Then we need to have us a reunion, don't we?" he stated and pulled his hat lower on his face.

The trio headed over to the alley. When they got there, the alley was empty, and the two bikes were still piled together to the right of the opening.

"You found Hazel?" Jeremy asked, looking at the bikes.

"I did."

"Where is she now?"

"When Arthur appeared, I told her to run and go to Tony."

"Then that's where we go next."

"Hold it." Harvey stopped them. "Does this get us closer to the money?"

"Maybe," she said, "and Harvey, I think it's safer to stay in a group from now on."

He looked down at his suit and said, "Well, I don't think that priest suit will look so good anymore. I'll stay with you."

They walked to the hospital and entered the door. Sister Bernadette was at the desk this time. "Hello, Emma, Jeremy, are you here to see the baby again?"

"We are," Jeremy replied.

"They're still upstairs. You remember the way?" They nodded and headed to the stairs. Suddenly, Sister Bernedette stopped them. "You!" she growled, pointing at Harvey, "I don't think you're family and you are not going up."

Harvey stayed behind Jeremy; he had a healthy fear of the sister.

Emma whispered to Jeremy, "Let me talk to her."

She went over. "Sister Bernadette, the situation has become more dangerous for this man, and we need him with us. Can you make an allowance just this once?"

She glared at Harvey and said, "For you, I will. But you're responsible for him."

"I'll take it seriously," Emma promised. They started toward the stairs again.

Sister Bernadette called, "I believe they're getting ready to go home."

Emma thought of something and stopped again. "Sister, did you see a young girl come in and ask for Tony?"

"Yes," she said, surprised. "She said she was his niece. Was that not true? Have I done the wrong thing?"

Emma smiled. "No, that's who she is." Though she thought Tony was probably surprised to see the girl. Emma nodded and they moved to the stairs. Once they were on the second floor, they went across the hall to Peggy's room. Emma looked at Harvey. "Stay out here."

"Hey, what about staying together?" he asked and looked around nervously. They knew who was after them now and it made things worse.

"Sister Bernadette can probably take him out if needed," she commented and knocked on the door. Tony's voice called them into the room. Jeremy chuckled and followed her in. They didn't know what to expect, but they were surprised to find Hazel sitting on the bed holding the baby!

"Well, I guess you've all met," Emma said drolly.

"Emma, come in," called Peggy. "Isn't it wonderful? And she looks like Teddy."

"She does," agreed Tony.

Jeremy saw their bags and asked, "We understand that you're ready to go home?"

"We are," confirmed Tony, "and with a new niece."

Hazel grinned. "They asked me to live with them."

"That's wonderful," Jeremy said. Emma frowned; Jeremy reached over and smoothed the lines. He said in her ear, "We'll protect them, and we'll keep an eye on her."

"What about the painting?" asked Emma in a low voice to Jeremy.

"We'll ask once everyone is settled at home." Jeremy turned to Tony and said, "We need to notify Cole and I think we need to have an escort for you to get home."

"Why?" asked Tony, casting his eyes to his family. "Has something changed?"

"The detective involved in the case is hanging around the hospital," explained Jeremy.

"Wasn't he always around?"

"Yes, but now we know that he was the one who murdered Teddy," Emma told them.

"And Eddie and Louis," stated Jeremy.

Peggy's face went white and Tony gripped her hand tightly. "Breathe. At least we know who killed him."

"But why would he be after us? Wouldn't he just still be after you?" asked Peggy worriedly.

"About that. I also disclosed that I wasn't Peggy," Emma confessed.

"Why? Why would you do that?" Tony asked, his voice deep and rough. "This was all supposed to be about protecting Peggy. How does your telling him the truth do that?"

"Tony, he already knew," said Emma.

"Who would've told him?" Peggy asked.

"I'm not sure. I saw an opening and confronted him; he admitted to being the murderer of Teddy and Eddie and Louis."

Hazel handed the baby to Peggy and said, "That man in the alley, he killed my papa?"

Emma looked at her and recognized the look; she'd had the same one many times. "You're not to get involved in this anymore," Emma told the girl sharply.

"Who, me?" she asked, eyes wide and hands held out.

"Tony, you recognize that look on her face? Keep her with you and Peggy," Emma said in a firm voice.

Tony got her meaning and said, "Hazel, we need to leave this to the professionals."

The girl looked like she wanted to argue, but changed her mind when she looked at Peggy and the baby. They were more important to her than getting revenge. "For now, at least, I won't get involved."

"Good," said Peggy. "I'll want to get to know you."

"Can I help with the baby?" Hazel asked hopefully.

"Yes, I'd love that."

"Hazel, where have you been staying all this time?" Emma asked her.

"Papa's apartment," Hazel said.

"I thought it'd been sold."

"It has, but the new owners haven't moved in yet."

"But," protested Peggy, "there's no furniture."

"I've been sleeping on the floor," she admitted.

"Well, not anymore. You'll have your own bedroom in our house," said Tony.

"I will?"

"You will," Peggy said firmly.

"How are we going to get out without creating a scene?" Tony asked with a frown on his face and a tight fist.

Jeremy stepped forward. "I have an idea on that. I need to contact Pops. Can you give me a little time?"

"As long as you need. I want my family to be safe."

Jeremy nodded and left the room. It was a short time later that the door opened again. Jeremy was there, a bit out of breath. "Cole's getting organized. He'll have a distraction in the front, and we'll leave by carriage from the back. He'll send someone to let us know when it's safe to head out."

There was a knock on the door. Jeremy went to open it and saw Harvey standing there. "What's going on? You ran by me without a word."

He stared at him and said, with a grimace, "We forgot about you."

The whole room studied him silently.

Harvey's eyes went wide. "Hey, I don't want to be left behind!"

Emma looked at Tony. "Would you mind if we take him with us?"

"To our home?" Peggy said faintly, gripping the baby tightly to her. She started to fuss. Tony reached over to take the baby from her to rock her back and forth. He didn't comment on her question.

"I'll keep him in line," Emma assured them and turned her eyes back to Harvey.

"How?" Hazel asked.

"Yeah, how're you going to do that?" said Harvey with a raised eyebrow.

That made Tony laugh. "Oh, don't worry, Emma can manage you."

"For now, I won't cause any trouble."

Hazel continued to study Emma. There was so much she wanted to find out about this lady detective.

Harvey looked over at Hazel. "Hey, Hazel."

"Hey back. Didn't expect to see you again so soon."

"Yeah. I get that a lot."

"You know each other?" Tony asked as he continued to rock the baby.

Harvey said, "Yeah, we go way back. She helped out on some of the cons. She was pretty good at it."

"What did you do?" asked Peggy. She was fascinated by this side of her niece.

"I was sometimes an orphan, sometimes a child from a poor family."

"Your father was okay with this?" Peggy asked.

"It was his idea, and I was able to stay with him," she explained.

"It couldn't have been an easy life," said Tony.

"We moved a lot," she admitted. "We'd meet up with the team at various times."

"Yeah," Harvey added, "it was early days and things were going smoothly."

"Until that man showed up," she griped.

Emma asked, "Arthur?"

Harvey answered for her. "Yeah, he was trouble from the beginning."

Hazel wrapped her arms around herself and said, "I was sent away after he joined us. That man was not a nice man."

"What did he do? Did he threaten you?" asked Jeremy.

"Papa wouldn't let him near me. He didn't like him."

"No, he didn't," Harvey agreed, "and I didn't understand why he was on the team."

"I know Papa didn't trust him to work the con. Arthur was always angry."

"Why was he still around? Teddy was still your leader at that time?" asked Emma.

"Teddy was always in charge. But Arthur seemed to have some kind of hold over him," commented Harvey as he reached for the cigar in his pocket.

A hard look from Emma stopped him. "How so?"

Harvey frowned. "I don't know. They fought constantly. It could get violent."

"He broke Papa's arm," said Hazel bitterly. "I was sent away after that."

Harvey continued, "And when she left, any joy Teddy had was gone. It was just a job after that."

"What was Arthur's hold on Teddy?" Emma asked the group. No one answered. "Why didn't Teddy get rid of him?"

"Arthur tried to take over and started telling people what to do," Harvey said.

"He wanted all of Papa's money. I heard him after he broke Papa's arm. He said he'd hurt me if he didn't give him the money."

"I didn't know that," Harvey said quietly. "We just knew you were gone right after that."

"Papa wanted to keep it quiet. He told me he'd deal with Arthur and come for me after that."

"And after that?" prompted Jeremy.

"We did other jobs, but Teddy started planning a big one, the last one," Harvey explained.

"Was leaving Arthur behind planned?"

"Not outright, but since none of us liked him, we weren't too keen to risk ourselves to go back for him."

Emma asked Hazel abruptly, "Arthur was the man in the alley."

Hazel's eyes were narrowed. "He's evil."

"And very dangerous," confirmed Emma.

Hazel took the opportunity and charged toward the door. Emma grabbed her and the girl struggled against her, yelling, "Let me go! That man needs to pay! He took my papa from me not once but two times."

Emma held her tightly. "He will but we need to make sure you're safe."

Peggy called from the bed. "Hazel, I need you with me. They'll make him pay."

She stopped struggling and said, "You sound like my papa. He said something similar before he sent me away."

Emma slowly loosened her hold. "Can I trust you not to run?"

"Yeah." She sighed as she was released. "I'll stay with Peggy and Tony."

Emma would've liked to continue questioning Hazel and Harvey, but she didn't want to upset Tony and Peggy any more than they had already.

The time passed slowly, and it was more than an hour later when Jeremy got a note at the door. He left and was gone for a few moments. He entered the room quickly and looked around. "Everybody ready to go home?" he asked.

"What's the plan?" Emma asked.

Jeremy looked at the group of people. "It's all worked out. Tony, Cole says your carriage at the front entrance."

"Okay," said Tony, "but how is that not creating a scene?"

"We'll be moving some of the sisters into that carriage while we move you to the back with your family in several small black carriages. It won't be as comfortable as you normally have, but I think we can get you home safely. Emma and I will be with you."

"Who'll be with the sisters?" asked Tony.

"Cole will manage the front."

"Will it work?" asked Peggy. She looked at Tony and their baby girl; they were her whole life.

"Hey, it's me," Jeremy said smugly. "Of course it will."

"Let's get moving then," Harvey said. He was just as eager to get away from Arthur as anyone else in the room.

Emma and Jeremy led the group to the back stairs; she saw Cole talking in a low voice to several sisters with blankets over their heads. One also appeared to be carrying something.

"What is that?" Tony asked.

Jeremy glanced over and said, "They need to look like they're carrying a baby."

"Do we need to worry about the sisters?" asked Emma. Ever since she'd worked on a case for them and they'd provided her medical care that saved her life, they held a special place in her heart.

Jeremy looked back. "Are you kidding? They volunteered; they love the adventure. And Pops will stay with them the whole time."

Emma laughed suddenly. "I can't wait to hear how that goes."

They moved to the first floor and Jeremy edged out around the corner to check the area. Once it was clear, they walked out back to the waiting carriages. Tony called up to the driver, "Take it easy, please."

The driver was Jones. "I will," he promised. "Don't worry, I'll get you home."

They moved out slowly and away from the back of the hospital. The plan was to take a circuitous route back to Tony and Peggy's house. It would be a longer path, but it was safer than going straight home.

***

At the front of the hospital, Cole pulled down his hat and

said to the sister with him, "Sweetheart, move slowly so we don't wake the baby."

"Yes, darling," Sister Mary Faith teased back.

Cole hid his grin and held her to him. He lifted her into the carriage and, once settled, he told the driver to move on. He expected them to be followed. The path he told the officer to take was to the park and around town, then back to the hospital.

Sister Mary Faith, sitting next to Cole, pulled the cover down from her face. "Do you think it worked?"

"I do," he said. "I believe we're being followed."

"What'll he do when we don't go to a house, but we come back to the hospital instead?"

"The man's murdered three men, so we can't guess what he'll do. But we're ready for him." Cole had Pinkerton men and Chicago police officers surrounding the hospital.

They'd completed their trip and the carriage stopped back at the hospital and Cole said, "I'll help you down." He opened the carriage door, stepped down, and the sister had pulled the cover over her head again and held the bundle to her. He assisted her down.

When she stepped down to the ground, she deliberately let the bundle roll out revealing nothing but towels. She lowered her blanket revealing her habit.

At that moment, they heard a yell and breaking glass. "Good," he said to his officer at the door, "After him!" The office took off running, others quickly joining him. "This way!" they yelled, heading down the long alley alongside the hospital.

"Do you think we gave them the time to get home?" Sister Mary Faith asked.

"I think it worked perfectly." Cole studied the broken window. "I'll get someone over here to fix that today."

"Thank you."

"It's the least we can do. Thanks for your help. I'll leave some men here in case he comes back."

"That would be fine. We also have Sister Bernadette here today."

He knew her well and teased, "So, I should only send one man."

"Well, several might be helpful, in case she's busy."

The carriages pulled up slowly to Peggy and Tony's home. Tony opened the door to descend and found Jones there waiting. He assisted them out. "Careful," Peggy said as she handed Tony the baby.

"Always," he said, his eyes shining as he looked down at the baby. He turned the same eyes and love onto his wife.

Jeremy and Emma had exited the second carriage and Jeremy called, "I think we need to get everyone inside."

They nodded and approached the house. Carmichael opened the door and stepped back to let them in. Once inside, he called, "Sir, shall I take care of the drivers?"

Jeremy answered for him. "They won't need payment. I told them to go on their way."

The butler nodded and moved to Peggy's side.

"Carmichael, would you like to see her?" she asked.

His face transformed with a wide smile. "Please." She took the baby from Tony and pulled back the blanket, revealing her face. "Miss Peggy, she is beautiful."

"Thank you," she said and held the baby close.

"First, let's get Peggy and the baby settled," Tony directed.

Carmichael noticed Hazel. Tony said, "This is Hazel. She's Peggy's niece."

"Is this Mr. Teddy's daughter?"

"She is and she's going to stay with us. Please make sure a room is made up."

The butler nodded and directed the maids upstairs to get the rooms ready.

Peggy started to move upstairs, and Tony said, "Hold it." He looked over and saw Hazel. "Can you come up with us?"

"I'd love to," the girl replied, running over to them.

"Take the baby," he said. Peggy looked torn; she didn't want to give her up just yet. Tony saw her expression and assured her, "Just until we get upstairs."

"Okay," she said and handed the baby to Hazel. When she saw that Hazel held her carefully, she turned to go upstairs. Tony took it from there and picked her up in his arms.

"I can walk," she protested.

"No, you can't. The doctor said you need rest, and that's what you'll get."

"I want the baby with us in our room."

"I already asked for the cradle to be moved to our room. I don't want to be away from her either."

"I love you," she murmured into his ear.

He turned red and grinned. "I love you, too."

They moved up the stairs, with Hazel coming up behind them with the baby. The housemen followed with their bags.

The butler turned back to the group that stood in the foyer. They were a motley crew; he cocked his head and looked at each one. "And what do we have here?"

"I don't know about them, but I plan to stay for a while," drawled Harvey as he looked around the spacious home.

Carmichael walked over to the man, looking down at him from an impressive height. "And who said that was going to happen?"

"I did," called Tony.

"Sir?" Carmichael asked, not tearing his gaze from Harvey.

"He's at risk. We're going to help," Tony said from the second floor.

The butler's eyes narrowed at the man. He didn't look trustworthy. He watched disapprovingly as Harvey pulled out a cigar. "Sir, we do not smoke in the house. The rule has been put in place since Mrs. Peggy would get sick at the smell."

"Well, I do smoke," Harvey said and reached for his matches.

Before they came to blows, Jeremy asked, "Can he smoke out back?"

The butler didn't want to help this man, but he said begrudgingly, "That would be fine."

Harvey said with exasperation, "Well, can I at least sit down?"

Carmichael's mouth twisted. He could read the man and knew he was not to be trusted. "You'll move to that room." He pointed to the sitting room. He turned to Emma and Jeremy. "And you two will watch him."

Jeremy cleared his throat as Emma wiped a smile from her face. "Anything you say."

"Hey, he can't talk to me that way," Harvey protested.

Emma and Jeremy disregarded him, and each took an arm and pulled him up toward the indicated room. Once there, they walked him to a chair and sat him down. He snatched his arms out of their grasp and groused, "I don't know why I'm being treated this way."

Emma shook her head as she moved to a chair near him. Jeremy moved and sat next to her. He murmured, "How did we end up with him on our team?"

"Seemed like the only way to keep him alive," she murmured back.

"Hey, I'm right here," Harvey groused, folding his arms over his chest.

"We know. We just weren't talking to you," Emma replied sardonically.

"Hmmf," he said and sat back. "Can't smoke, can't walk by myself."

"What next?" Jeremy asked, ignoring the man's muttering.

"The painting," said Emma. "We need to identify the location."

"Painting?" Harvey asked and sat up straight. "Speaking of paintings, any of these belong to Teddy? Should we take these and sell them?" He ran up to one. "Is this one? Or is it this one?"

Emma sat back. "Calm down, those are valuable, but they belong to Tony and Peggy."

"All of these look valuable."

"They are," Tony said from the doorway. "But they didn't belong to Teddy."

"You're sure?" Harvey asked wistfully.

He ignored the man. "Lunch will be ready soon. Peggy wants to lie down for a bit and then we'll discuss the sketches."

"It would be nice to review the actual painting," said Emma.

"We'll need Hazel for that."

"Where is she now?" Jeremy asked.

"She's with Peggy and the baby."

"They seem to be getting along," said Emma.

"Yes, I think Hazel is good for Peggy."

"Keep an eye on her," she warned. "You don't know her. And she's already stolen from you."

"I know, and we will," said Tony. "But Peggy's already attached to her. You know, Hazel will say it was her painting and she was just taking it back."

"Yes, I get that," said Emma.

Carmichael entered and said, "Lunch is served."

"We might as well tie the feed bag on," Harvey said. He pulled himself to his feet, daring Emma and Jeremy to stop him. When they didn't, he followed the butler into the dining room.

"Are we now hosting him also?" Tony asked. The house was getting full.

"Until we find out where the money is," she confirmed.

"Shall we go to the dining room?" asked Tony. They walked together into the dining room.

"Say, man," started Harvey when he saw Tony.

"Tony," he supplied with a sideways look at him.

"Yeah, yeah," Harvey said as he sat forward and started to fill his plate from the platters on the table. "Tony," he started again, "the art and things around here, was any of this given to you by Teddy?" He wanted to make sure nothing here belonged to him.

"Those belong to Peggy," Tony responded shortly.

"How was she able to do this on her own? You're sure Teddy wasn't sending money to her?"

Tony brought his fist down on the table, causing the platters to bounce. "I'll say this once more, nothing in this house is up for grabs without my or Peggy's express permission. And if you take anything or make overtures to Peggy, we'll put you out. We won't care if there is a murderer trying to get you. Is that clear?"

Harvey knew he'd pushed too far. He nodded and stuffed his mouth with food. He was here at their discretion.

Emma and Jeremy watched the interaction and didn't interfere with Tony. This was his home, and he had every right to protect it.

Tony called over to the butler, "Please take up a tray for Hazel and Peggy." Carmichael nodded and walked to the kitchen to carry through the instructions.

Lunch was completed in silence. Tony put down his napkin and glared at Harvey before he said, "I'm going to go check on Peggy and the baby."

"Would you mind if I come up and check on Hazel?" Emma asked.

"Sure." They walked up together.

Jeremy stayed at the table with Harvey. Harvey saw his gaze and said, "I don't plan to start taking things."

Jeremy raised his eyebrows. "I'd appreciate that."

They finished eating and Harvey leaned back, reaching for his cigar. "Though I could get used to this."

"Don't," Jeremy warned. "They're serious about the cigar. *And* once we resolve this, we don't want them bothered again."

Harvey narrowed his eyes but didn't comment. What he did was slip the cigar back into his pocket. Jeremy watched him closely.

Upstairs, Emma and Tony stopped at Peggy's room. "Wait here while I check with Peggy."

She stopped him with her hand. "Congratulations, Tony. You have a beautiful family."

"Thank you," he said and leaned to kiss her on the cheek. He took her hands in his and said, "And I am glad you have Jeremy and Hen."

"Thank you Tony." He released her hand and went into the room. She stayed here she was in the hallway, looking at the paintings hanging on the walls.

"Are you looking for a particular painting?" Hazel asked.

Emma continued to study the paintings and said casually, "No, not really. I know where the painting is that I want to look at." She turned her attention to her. Hazel stood across from her. "Do you like your room?"

"I do." Hazel looked around and down the stairs. "I can't believe they invited me to live here."

"They're your family."

"Yes…" She let the word hang.

Emma started, "Hazel, where…"

At that moment, Tony came out. "Peggy said you can come in now."

Emma looked to where Hazel had stood and saw that she'd disappeared. She wondered about that but followed Tony inside. Peggy was dressed in a dark blue dressing gown and reclining on a large four poster bed. The baby lay in a cradle beside her.

"Come over," she beckoned. Emma went over. "Sit, please,"

Peggy said and patted the bed beside her. Emma sat and Peggy asked, "What's next?"

"The painting," guessed Tony.

She turned her head toward him and flashed him a grin. "Exactly." He was part of her extended team and knew how she thought. She turned back to Peggy. "This seems to hinge on the clues in that painting."

Peggy looked down and picked at the bed clothes.

"Peggy, what's wrong?" Tony asked.

She turned her eyes to him, tears gleaming. "It's just that that's the last thing he gave me and I'd like to have it back."

Emma took her hand. "He gave it to you because he trusted you. We'll talk to Hazel about getting it back."

She took a deep breath. "Okay."

"Would you mind going over the sketches again with me?" asked Emma.

"It's time," said Tony, he retrieved them from the side table and laid them on the bed.

Peggy touched them and said, "Teddy always had dreams of doing something in the art world, but we were too poor. He'd haunt the museums when he wasn't working."

"Like Tony," said Emma.

"Yes, he reminded me of my brother. I felt drawn to him." Tony smiled and continued to study the sketch.

The room was quiet as each studied the sketches. Emma finally cleared her throat and said, "I think we need everyone for this part. Peggy, can you move downstairs?"

"I can."

"She can but she won't," stated Tony firmly.

"What? Why not?" Emma asked, surprised.

"I'll carry her down."

Peggy blushed prettily at his words. He wrapped the cover around her. "But the baby," she protested, not wanting to leave her.

"We have a nurse," he reminded her. He called, "Nurse Baxter." An older woman entered briskly.

"Don't you worry. I'll be here and notify you if she needs anything."

"Thank you," said Peggy.

Emma moved toward the door with the sketches; Tony picked up Peggy and followed her. They walked out of the room and headed downstairs.

Emma stopped and said, "Hazel should be with us. I'd like to view the painting with these."

Tony had his hands full and asked, "You think she has it here?"

"I think she would want it close."

"Can you go up?"

"I can." She carried the sketches with her up the stairs. They were bulky, but she didn't want them out of her sight.

When she reached the floor, she saw Hazel sitting on the floor with her back against the spindles. "Hey, we're ready to start the evaluation and we'd like the painting you took," she said boldly.

"Know about that, do you?"

"We do," she confirmed.

"What gave me away?"

"Mostly your size. Nobody else involved in this could've gotten through that window."

"What's that you have there?" the girl asked and pointed at the sketches.

"These? Pete drew some new sketches for us when his own just happened to get burned."

Hazel's head dropped. "I didn't want to do that."

"Then why did you?"

Hazel lifted her head and looked Emma in the eyes. "I kept thinking there might be something in it, something that might lead the murder to the money."

"Can you get the painting for us to look at?"

She turned her head away and ran her hand on the spindles. "Has everyone else seen the sketches?"

"Yes, Jeremy, Peggy, and Tony. Can you get the painting? Is it here with you?" Emma pushed.

"Yes."

Emma frowned. "Where have you kept it?" She hoped it wasn't damaged.

"When I took it, I hid it in the attic."

"So, you never took it out of the house?"

"I thought it was safer here."

"Okay, let's go get it."

"We can't," Hazel confessed.

"And why not?" Emma said, letting exasperation show.

"The door's locked," she said simply. "I tried it earlier."

"Oh, is that all? Let's go."

She squinted at her and finally pulled herself up and moved toward the stairs. As they ascended, Emma said, "You know, that the money wasn't Teddy's, Harvey's, or yours. It's stolen money and must be returned."

"Isn't there some kind of time limit on that stuff? I think it's called the statute of limitations from 1830."

"Done your research? Are you a lawyer now?" asked Emma dryly.

"Papa did."

"Was that the reason for the delay in handing out the money?"

"He had it planned and, when he felt it was finally safe, he settled here."

"Well, we'll have to check those rules out. I clerk for a lawyer and there may still be some restitution and the police will still be involved."

"You think so?" she muttered.

"I do."

They stopped in front of the door. Hazel tried it and turned to Emma. "It's still locked. I can get Tony." She tried to move past her.

Emma stopped her. "No need." She knelt in front of the lock and pulled out her lock pick set. She pulled out the right pick and quickly inserted it into the lock. The click of the lock disengaging could be heard. She pushed the door open. "After you."

"You've gotta show me how you do that," Hazel said in amazement.

"I might."

"What else can you do?"

"We can talk later. For now, show me the painting."

Hazel moved quickly into the room and headed toward the far wall. She opened a desk and pulled out a rolled up painting.

"Can I have it?" asked Emma.

Hazel pulled it to herself. "I'd prefer to carry it."

Emma studied her and finally said, "Fair enough, you can carry it, but we'll be examining it as a group."

They walked downstairs together. Once they started down the last step, Carmichael walked up to them. "They're in the study," he directed.

Hazel and Emma followed him to the room. Tony met them at the door and took the sketches and the painting from them. He didn't ask how or why Hazel had the painting. It was moved to the long table in front of the couch. Peggy was sitting on there with her feet up.

"Hazel," she called, "come sit with me."

The girl looked torn. She wanted to be near the picture in case they tried to destroy it.

Emma noted her reluctance. "Hazel, we'll let you know before we do anything with it."

She nodded and moved to sit with Peggy, who took her hand, and Hazel laid her head on her shoulder.

The group sat on the floor, around the table. "How does this tell us where my money is?" Harvey asked. No one responded to that question. Emma, Jeremy, and Tony studied the painting and the sketches.

Emma didn't look up from the painting and asked, "Harvey, is there anything you recognize?"

He joined them and frowned while he looked hard at all parts of the painting. "I'll be damned."

"What is it?" Emma asked, trying to see what he saw.

"He used the jewels."

"Tony, does Peggy own these jewels?"

He looked at each piece. "No. I haven't seen those before this."

"Why are these jewels familiar to you?" Emma asked Harvey.

"Because they're from our stash. That ruby bracelet came from New York, a small job, and the necklace was another case."

"And the ring?"

"Not from a case," said Harvey. "At least, not one I worked."

"Is it an opal?" Hazel asked suddenly.

"It is. Is that important?" asked Jeremy.

"Hazel," prompted Peggy.

"It was my mama's ring. I was supposed to have it."

Emma documented that in her notebook.

"Tony, can you get that box for me?" Peggy asked.

"Are you sure?"

"Yes, it's the right thing."

He walked to the desk, took out a key, and removed the box and carried it to her. Hazel didn't say anything, but her eyes weren't moving from that box as it was passed from Tony to Peggy. She took it and opened it slowly and turned the open box toward Hazel.

"Is that the ring you mentioned?"

"You have it," she said shakily and reached out a hand toward it.

"I do," Peggy said kindly. She moved Hazel's extended hand to the ring.

"But how?"

"An old friend was holding it for me."

"Pete said he never saw the jewels that were in the picture. He went off the description Papa gave him," Hazel said.

Emma spoke up. "We confirmed that with Pete when he did the sketches for us."

"May I try it on?" asked Hazel. She could not tear her eyes away from it.

"Of course, it's yours," Peggy replied and watched as Hazel slipped it on her finger.

Tony wanted to protest; he knew how much that ring meant to her. Was the ring entrusted to Peggy for Hazel? They'd never know.

Emma cautioned them, "I'd leave it in a secure place."

"Can I hold it for now?" asked Hazel.

"Yes," Tony said, "but I think Emma's right and it should be secured until this is over."

Jeremy had been studying the sketches and the painting. "Let's move this over to Peggy. I'd like to know what else she might see."

"You really think the clues about the money are in the painting?" asked Peggy.

"We do," said Emma.

"Does that mean you don't have to destroy it?" Hazel asked, the hope clear in her voice.

Jeremy answered. "We must look at all angles. It looks like the painting itself is the clue. And the sketches."

They handed the painting to Peggy. She went quiet, studying it. "What do you see?" asked Tony.

"Well, I think it's related to our childhood," she murmured as she reached out to touch the painting and then the sketch.

In the picture, Peggy was sitting on steps; it was easier to see once the sketch was reviewed. "In the sketches, I can see the little house we lived in, there in the back, behind me. We lived there with our father. He wasn't a nice man; he was mean all of the time. There was rarely any food and we had to work all of the time."

"Your mother?" asked Emma gently.

"Died during childbirth, when I was born. Which is why we wanted Louise to be born in the hospital."

"We didn't want to take any chances," murmured Tony.

"What else do you see?" Jeremy asked.

"The tree," she murmured. "In the painting, it was swirling around me; in the sketch, you can make out limbs."

"I see it now. Was it special?" asked Tony.

"Yes. It was having some green in the city. We'd work all day and at night, that's where Teddy would hide. He'd go out and climb up in that tree."

The silence settled as she moved through her memories.

Harvey wasn't there for memories, and when he'd had enough, he said, "This is sweet and all, but that tree must be there. We should check it out."

Emma studied the painting and ignored him. "Peggy, have you been back since you were a child?"

"No, no," she said, shaking her head. "I married to get out of that life. I never looked back." She turned to Hazel and said, "Your papa had left years before I did."

"Can you tell me the general location of the house?" Jeremy asked.

Peggy described the area to them.

"Jeremy," said Emma, "Papa worked that area. A lot of it was torn down after the fire."

He thought about that. "We need to get with Ellis and mark a map up to work this out."

Peggy finally looked away from the painting and reached her hand toward Tony. He took it and squeezed. "Do you think he's put the money somewhere where our home used to be?"

"I do and I think he wanted you to find it," Emma told her.

Hazel tried to take it all in and finally burst out, "You're all about the money. What about Arthur? Why aren't we focusing on the murderer?"

"Hazel, we are. The money is what he's also after. Once we find it, he'll show himself," Emma assured her.

"Also, he's unstable and dangerous. We have to approach this cautiously," said Jeremy.

"We need you to do what they ask," said Peggy. "We'd like to know you're safe."

Hazel took a shaky breath and said, "I'll try."

Peggy pulled her close and stroked her hair.

"Well, not me," Harvey protested. "It's my money. Everyone else is gone."

"Not everyone. Hazel was also part of the events and deserves Teddy's share."

When Emma went to stand, Hazel grabbed her hand and implored, "Please let me know when you find out anything." She looked at Tony and Peggy; they nodded in agreement.

"We'll make sure you're included," Emma promised.

"Thank you." Hazel released her hand and her gaze lowered to her hands.

Emma moved to Jeremy's side and said, "We need to get with Papa."

"We'll go now." He stood and pulled her up with him. They started to move out and Harvey was at their heels.

Emma stopped and Harvey ran into her. She sighed and looked back at him. "What do we do about him?" she asked Jeremy.

"We might as well let him come," he suggested, ignoring Harvey. "Can't hurt, and he might see something we don't."

"Hey, I'm right here."

Emma turned to study him and begrudgingly nodded. "Fine. But you'll stay with us at all times. We don't need any surprises."

"Don't worry, I want to live through this. I'll be right by your side," he said.

Tony ran over and said, "Let us know what the next step is."

"We will."

Tony nodded at Carmichael to open the door. "A hired carriage would be best," said Emma.

"Let's go over a few streets to find one," suggested Jeremy. The three walked four blocks and hailed a carriage. Jeremy gave him the address to Ellis' home.

Once inside, Harvey asked, "How can your papa help us out?"

"He's an engineer and knows the area pretty well. He was involved in the rebuilding of the areas after the fire of '71."

Harvey nodded and sat back, watching them. "So, what is it with you two? Are you married?"

"We're a team," said Emma and took Jeremy's hand.

"Okay." He was puzzled by her non answer but didn't comment. His experience as a priest told him marriage was the ultimate commitment. He'd have to watch these two.

The driver pulled up and stopped in front of Ellis' home. They paid the driver and gave him extra to forget that he drove them there.

"Will it work?" she asked, watching the man leave.

"I think it will," Jeremy said. "It's highly unlikely that Arthur will pick that one carriage out of the hundreds in the city." They started toward the house; they hadn't told Harvey who also shared a house with the man they were visiting.

They knocked and, after a few moments, the door was opened by Abbey.

"Emma! Jeremy! We didn't expect you so soon."

"Hi, Mom," he said and leaned forward to kiss her on the cheek. "We're here to see Ellis."

"Is Henrietta here?" Emma asked as she peered over her shoulder.

"She's in school. Are you here to pick her up? Is it over already?"

"Not yet, but getting closer," said Jeremy.

"Oh?" She looked over at the man standing behind them. "Well, come in." They stepped into the foyer. "And you are?" she inquired.

"Harvey Simms, ma'am," he said, giving her an appreciative look and tilting his hat back on his head.

"I'm Abbey Evans," she said, reaching up to pat her hair.

"Abbey, is Papa here?" asked Emma.

"Oh," she said, pulling her eyes from Harvey. "Yes, he's downstairs." The trio moved toward the basement and Abbey's next words stopped them. "Cole's here also."

"Where is he?" asked Jeremy, turning toward her.

"He's upstairs in his room."

Emma said, "I'll go down to see Papa."

"I want to talk to Pops," Jeremy said. "I'll meet you down there."

Harvey looked at both of them and followed Emma to the basement.

Jeremy went upstairs quickly and knocked on his father's bedroom door.

"Come in."

He went in and found his pops tying his tie.

"Hey, Pops!"

"Hey back. Has something happened?"

"We're currently at a point where we need input from Ellis."

"Well, catch me up."

Jeremy reviewed the sketches and painting and the information Peggy provided.

"The Mystery girl..." Cole started.

"Hazel," he supplied.

"Hazel, what's her role in this?"

"We aren't sure right now. We do know that she's Teddy's daughter. She did steal the painting, though she seems more focused on the murderer than the money."

"Was she involved in the con with Teddy and the other men?"

"When she was much younger," he confirmed. "The last few years, she lived with her grandmother."

"Where's the grandmother now?"

"She passed away. Hazel said that once Teddy was settled, he was going to send for her."

"But something changed to cause him to run."

"It could have been several things. He might have gotten word Arthur was looking for him." Jeremy had briefed him when they organized Peggy and Tony's transportation home.

"Or any one of the other men."

"We will never know," said Jeremy.

"We were able to draw Arthur out today. The men chased but we were unable to apprehend him."

"A murderer on the loose and a case still in the air," pondered Jeremy. "Have you got the surveillance teams set up?"

"Yes, around the hotel. That seems to be the location he gravitates to."

"Yeah, it has become his personal murder house."

"We need that to stop now. So, you're here to follow up on the clues in the painting?"

"Yeah, we need to pinpoint the area Peggy lived in at that time."

"Didn't she give you the address?"

"She said the area has changed too much. I think she blocked out that time of her life." He raised his eyebrow at him. "The father sounds like he was abusive to them," Jeremy explained.

"That's too bad."

"Yeah."

Cole pulled on his suit jacket and said, "Okay, let's go down and see what Ellis has to say."

Jeremy stopped him. "Uh, I didn't mention it, but we have Harvey with us."

Cole frowned. "Is that a good idea?"

"It was the only way we could think to keep him alive. And we didn't want to leave him with Tony and Peggy."

Cole nodded as they continued their way downstairs. They moved through the hallway to the basement, waving as they passed Abbey.

They could hear Emma talking to Ellis as they descended the stairs. Once there, they saw all three of them bent over a large map on a slanted table.

"Would it be here?" Emma asked and pointed to something in front of her.

"Did you find it?" asked Jeremy from the bottom of the stairs.

Emma put her hand as a place marker on the map and turned to him. "We have some options."

Harvey turned toward Jeremy and noticeably jumped when he saw Cole. "You rat, you turned me in?" He looked around for a possible exit.

"Calm down, Harvey, he's working with us," said Emma. She'd turned back to the map.

"You jackass," Jeremy scolded the man. "I told you earlier this is my dad."

"Oh, yeah." He pushed back his hat and rubbed his face. "Lot's been happening."

"Harvey, we're all working to find the money. That's something you want, right?" Jeremy said.

Dropping his hand from his face, the man muttered, "Yeah, but now I guess it'll have to be given back."

"We can work that out later," Cole said. Harvey looked hopeful at that statement.

Ellis ignored the conversation and said, "I think Peggy might be wrong."

"You don't think the house is gone?" asked Emma.

"No, that neighborhood has improved since she lived there. New generations of people have adopted the existing housing stock and improved it. The new residents want the amenities, convenience, and charm of these neighborhoods. This area is under construction."

"Do you think the tree might still be there?" asked Emma, her voice going higher with hope.

"Well, there's only one way to find out," stated Ellis as he rolled up his drawings. "I rather suspect that that house is still there and is under construction."

"Why?"

"How else would Teddy have been able to hide anything there?" supplied Jeremy.

"True," said Emma.

"Let's go," said Ellis.

"Go where?" asked Harvey. This group spoke in shorthand, and he was having trouble keeping up.

"The house, of course," Jeremy and Emma said at the same time.

Emma started out of the basement.

"Hold off on that," Cole stated as he stopped the parade of people to the stairs. They all turned to him and waited.

"We may not be the only ones to figure this out."

"Smith," supplied Emma.

"Yes." He smiled slightly. "I'd like to set up men in the area for surveillance."

"And," Jeremy said, "we shouldn't show up en masse."

"Agreed. I'll get the information to the men." Cole left ahead of them and got a messenger to the Pinkerton office. He had men waiting for instructions. The rest followed him up and into the hallway.

Abbey came up to Ellis and took his arm. "Would you like some tea while you wait?" she asked the group.

"That would be nice, thank you," said Emma.

Harvey's eyes darted to the door. "Don't do it," Jeremy advised him. "You have nowhere to go that we won't find you."

"Why don't we move into the sitting room," suggested Abbey.

Harvey nodded and followed them into the room. He dropped down onto the settee and waited with them. The tea and cakes were brought out and he enjoyed them more than he thought he could.

It was more than an hour later that the front door opened and slammed shut. Cole walked quickly into the room. "The men are set," he said and took a cup of tea from Abbey. "Thank you." He drank it quickly. "We have carriages set up."

Emma drummed her fingers on her lips and said, "We need to be dropped off at a distance."

"Yeah, that'll work," confirmed Cole. "The men are expecting us, but they'll keep out of sight until they're needed."

The carriage was waiting behind the house. They climbed in. Emma, Jeremy, and Ellis on one side and Cole and Harvey in the other. Harvey hadn't appreciated Cole accompanying them, but they left him little choice.

They had the carriage drop them off a few blocks away from the house. Emma, Jeremy, and Ellis through the neighborhood. Harvey and Cole hung back. Cole didn't want Harvey spotted if Smith was in the area. The man was a target, and he didn't want anyone put into jeopardy.

"Peggy didn't know that the area's has been improving," murmured Emma.

"I think she didn't want to think about it. She hadn't returned, even as an adult."

"I wonder why Teddy would put the money where there were so many bad memories for Peggy."

"The tree, that's what he connects with. It was a safe place."

"We were lucky," she said.

Jeremy didn't have to ask what she was talking about and replied, "We were. Not everyone gets parents like ours."

That comment made Emma's mind shift to Henrietta and her life before moving into their home. She reached over and took Jeremy's hand. He squeezed it, knowing that they were thinking the same thing.

"We're close now," said Ellis. He inclined his head toward the area in front of them.

They followed his gaze. The houses were still there, under various states of construction. The one thing that stood out was a large tree.

"Is that…" Emma wondered.

"Peggy's tree?" Ellis asked. He checked his map and looked back at it. "Yes, I think so."

"Why not remove it?" she asked as they strolled toward it.

"The new owners might have seen the value," said Jeremy.

"What would that be?" she asked.

"Shade in the summer. See how the limbs extended over the house?"

Emma looked at the house located behind the tree. She could picture a small boy climbing out of the window and into the tree. She wiped a tear quickly and struggled not to turn away from the house.

Jeremy walked ahead of them; he did a quick circle around the areas of the tree.

Ellis and Emma followed him. "Anything?" she asked.

"Maybe, it's hard to tell if the area's been disturbed now or earlier," he replied, walking around the tree again.

"There's spots where the soil is exposed," said Emma as she kicked at the dirt with her boot.

"It could be children digging," he suggested. "Not necessarily Teddy burying something."

"Could it be elsewhere?" asked Emma, looking around. "Are we sure this the right place?"

"The house matches the picture," Jeremy pointed out.

"It's the right place," Ellis said firmly.

"I hope it is," she said, looking around. All of it was being changed and rebuilt; people were finding value in the old neighborhoods. "When would he have put it here?" she asked, eyeing the different carpenters working on the home they stood in front of.

"And," added Ellis, "there's the chance of someone digging it up."

"The chances of being seen are high," Emma agreed.

"What else was in the picture?" asked Ellis. He hadn't reviewed the painting or the sketches.

"Some jewels from the thefts," Emma replied.

"The ring," Jeremy reminded her.

"Yes, an opal. It meant something special to Hazel."

"It was her mother's."

"I think it meant more than that. The opal, does that also mean a change in color?" Emma recalled.

"Among other things," said Ellis.

"Changing colors," she mulled and looked up at the tree, drumming her fingers on her lips. "There must be a way to work this out." A flash of something caused her to walk closer to the tree trunk. *Is there something up there?* The sun hit the object again and she slapped her hands together. "Got it!"

"What do you see?" asked Jeremy, his gaze following hers.

She pointed. "Up there, you can see it sparking in the light."

"A mirror maybe?" he asked.

"That's what I'm thinking. Remember what Peggy said when she saw the sketch? The bright light that illuminated her hair?"

Ellis listened to their description and studied the tree and said, "He used the mirror for direction? Pointing to the right spot."

She moved quickly to the tree and started to climb.

"Emma," said Jeremy, "maybe we don't do this in the daylight."

Ellis suggested, "We come back tonight, when no one is here."

Jeremy noticed they were getting attention from nearby workers pointing their way. "We might want to head back to the carriages."

Emma and Ellis followed him back down the street. The carriages had been moved to the alley. There, they found Harvey and Cole. "Harvey," Emma started, "did Teddy use mirrors in his jobs?"

Harvey dropped his cigar down and smashed it with his shoe. "Yeah, Teddy had a thing for mirrors. He used them to signal if something went wrong with the job. That last day, we didn't get a signal that something was wrong…" He tapered off, thinking about that day.

Cole said, "We need to get moving." The group was silent as they climbed into their carriage. Emma and Jeremy sat next to Harvey and across from them were Ellis and Cole.

Jeremy mentioned, "We need to send word to Tony and Peggy to let them know the plans."

"I agree," Cole said. "It's important that they're aware of the steps we're taking."

"We can drop you off at their house," Ellis suggested.

"Yes, let's do that," said Emma. She studied Harvey out of the corner of her eye. *He is quiet, too quiet.*

Ellis asked, "What time do you want to meet this evening?"

Jeremy said, "It has to be good and dark. Shall we meet at your house?"

"That would be best," he said absentmindedly, thinking of how to use the mirror at night.

"That will give us a chance to see Henrietta," Emma commented.

Jeremy smiled. "That'll be nice. I miss her."

"Me, too," she said softly.

The carriage pulled to a stop in the back of Tony and Peggy's home. Jeremy and Emma descended first; he twirled her to the ground and stepped back as Harvey descended. Cole leaned out and shook his hand at Harvey. "Consider yourself in their custody."

Harvey nodded. "Understood."

The three watched the carriage pull away. Jeremy started to go inside, and Emma said, "Wait." She turned to Harvey. "Have you figured out what bothered you about that last day, that last job?"

He reached for the cigar in his pocket, then stopped. "Almost, I need to think on it a bit more."

Emma nodded and the three walked to the back door and knocked. The cook opened it and stepped back as soon as she saw who was there.

They moved through the room and into the long hallway. The cook moved with them and called, "Carmichael!"

The Butler entered at the far end of the hall. "Mr. Tilden, Miss Evans, this way." He acknowledged them and ignored Harvey as he guided them into the sitting room.

"I will tell Mr. Tony that you are here. He's up with Miss Peggy, attending to the baby."

"Thank you, Carmichael," said Emma graciously.

"Would you like some tea and cakes?" he asked them.

Jeremy answered for the group. "Thank you. We'd like that." Carmichael nodded and left the room to communicate the company to Tony. They heard feet running down the stairs. Jeremy looked over at Emma and teased, "Sounds like someone I know."

Emma was well known for running up and down the boarding house stairs. She'd noticed similarities between herself and this Hazel. That was also the reason she thought the girl was still hiding something from them. If she was in her place, she wouldn't be sharing all of the story either.

Their guess on who was on the stairs was answered when Hazel appeared abruptly in the doorway. She demanded, "Well? Was he there?"

Emma sat back and said casually, "Why don't you join us?"

Hazel frowned at them as she begrudgingly took her seat. She didn't settle back but instead stayed on the edge and tapped her foot. "Well?" she asked again.

At that moment, the footman, followed by the butler, entered with two trays, one with filled teacups and another filled with assorted cakes. The three ignored Hazel and moved to retrieve teacups and cake. "Hazel," Emma began, anticipating another outburst, "take some cake and settle down. We'll want to share the information with Tony and Peggy."

"Peggy has gone back to her room to rest," said Tony from the doorway. He rubbed his hand on his neck and said, "I thought babies slept."

Emma laughed. "They do eventually, give it some time. Would you like some tea?"

He nodded and joined them. Tony took a long sip of tea and sighed. "What did you find out? Was the money there?"

"Finally," muttered Hazel.

Emma didn't spare her a glance and replied to Tony, "No money yet, but we think we have the location."

"Was the house still there?" he asked. Peggy hadn't wanted to talk about that part of her life, and they hadn't gone to the area since he'd known her.

"Papa confirmed the area has changed and looks to be still in transition."

"I'd expect the area to eventually be part of the bigger city," Jeremy added, thinking of the expansions that The World's Fair would bring.

"Was the tree still there?" Hazel asked impatiently.

Emma turned to Hazel. "It was, and we found something in it."

"What was it?" the girl asked. She'd calmed now that she knew more of what they'd discovered.

"A mirror," supplied Harvey. He hadn't contributed to the conversation up until that moment.

"Papa carried a small one with him all the time."

"You remember that?" he asked, surprised.

She frowned. "Yes, he used them on jobs when he was signaling you."

"Harvey, have you thought about why the mirror and that last job bothered you?" Emma asked again.

He stood and walked to the fireplace, absently pulling out a cigar. Tony commented, "Harvey, don't."

He looked up in almost in surprise and said, "It's a habit. I didn't mean to light it." He put it back into his pocket. "That last day, we had several jobs going at the same time. Teddy had picked stores in the same general area. He was the lookout, and he was managing it with the mirror. He would use the sun to flash the light to us, so we knew if we needed to get out quickly."

"Did you normally do more than one job at a time?" Emma asked.

"Sometimes, but this was different. It was supposed to be our last big scam. We'd walked the area in our plain clothes, scouting out the locations for the next day. I was cautious about him being the only watch and the rest of us on the job. We were in the diamond district; this would allow us to hit multiple stores at one time."

"Was there anything else odd about the setup?"

"Yes," he said slowly. "We were each working alone."

"But Papa always said a team was better!" Hazel protested.

Harvey looked at her. "I know. I thought it was odd. There didn't seem to be enough people or time. And Arthur's job seemed a little far away from our location. When I brought it up, Teddy assured me that he'd make sure Arthur got what was coming to him."

Jeremy sat forward and asked, "Did you take that to mean Teddy wanted to get rid of Arthur?"

"I didn't think too hard about it; we had a job to do."

"Did Arthur question it?" asked Emma.

"No. That score was supposed to be big with four different places being hit. Arthur was focused on the money; he was *always* focused on the money."

"What happened next?" asked Jeremy.

"We dressed as priests and moved to our locations; Teddy was outside with his mirror. Each of us concluded our business and the plan was to meet in a vacant building a few blocks away."

"What went wrong?" Emma asked.

"At first, nothing. When I arrived, Teddy was already there. Eddie and Louis arrived next. It was when Arthur entered that we were surrounded by men with guns."

"How did you make it out?"

"We dropped to the floor and crawled."

"And Arthur?"

"Funny thing about that. Teddy threw a bag his way and ol' Arthur, he jumped up to catch it. I guess he thought it was the diamonds. All the guns were pointing at him, in the commotion, we got out."

"So, you all left him to die and now he's holding a grudge."

"Sounds about right."

"A setup?" Emma murmured. *What was between the two men? Why the animosity?*

"It seems Teddy felt there was no other way to get rid of Arthur," mused Jeremy.

"Now we know why he's so intent on killing everyone

involved. And Harvey is the last one he plans to settle his revenge," said Emma.

Harvey shrugged.

"What're the plans for tonight?" Tony asked.

"We go back to the tree and look again," Jeremy responded.

"A mirror at night? How's that going to work?" asked Tony.

Jeremy raised his eyebrows at Emma.

"My portable lamp," she explained.

"Will it be strong enough?" Jeremy asked.

Emma frowned and said, "Papa may have an idea."

Harvey asked, "What about Arthur? Do we know where he is?"

"Pops is managing that. We'll get an update tonight," Jeremy responded.

"I don't like that he's out there," said Emma.

"There are agents in the neighborhood and staff have been notified to not let any strangers into the house," assured Tony.

"When will you go?" asked Hazel.

"Later tonight. We don't want to be seen," Jeremy replied.

"And that what happens then?" she asked.

"We dig up the money and decide on our next moves," Emma told her.

Hazel sat back and began tapping her shoe again. Emma watched her, wondering at her reaction.

"Will you stay here until the meeting?" asked Tony.

"If you don't mind. We'll meet when it is time at Ellis' house," Jeremy commented.

"I'll let Carmichael know you'll be here for dinner." Tony left the room.

Emma looked at Hazel. "Hazel, you still seem upset about something."

"No, I just want this to be over," she said, moving her hands restlessly in her lap.

Which part? Emma thought. *Finding the money or the killer?*

Tony came back. "We have everything settled. I also asked for some rooms to be made up for you, if you want to rest."

Emma said, "Thank you. I think we could all use that."

"I could go for a nap," Jeremy said.

Hazel excused herself. "I'm tired, I'm going to lie down for a while. Can you let me know when dinner is ready?" she asked Tony.

"Of course. Get some rest. It's been a trying day," he said.

She walked to the stairs and out of their sight.

Emma stood and went to the doorway and watched as she ascended. "What's bothering you?" asked Jeremy.

She tapped her fingers on her folded arms. "I'm not sure. I keep thinking we don't know her all that well."

Tony interrupted. "But she is family. We need to take care of her."

"Yeah," murmured Emma as she moved back into the study and sat on the sofa. "I hope she stays put."

Tony cast a worried gaze at her. "Do you think she might hurt Peggy or the baby?"

Emma thought about how careful Hazel was with the baby and how close she already seemed to Peggy. "No. I just have my suspicions."

Jeremy grinned. "You wouldn't be Emma without them."

Tony laughed.

Emma grinned back at them. They both knew her so well.

"Sir," Carmichael said from the doorway. "The bedrooms are ready."

"Good," said Jeremy. "You might wake Harvey; I don't think he slept much last night."

Tony and Emma looked toward Harvey; he'd fallen asleep leaning against a wall. Tony looked at Carmichael. "Can you and Daniels help him to his room?"

"Yes, sir. Of course."

He disappeared for a moment and then reappeared with the footman. They walked to Harvey and started to take his arms.

"You might not want to do that abruptly," she cautioned. She walked over and put a hand on his arm. "Harvey."

He jumped violently and his hands reached toward her, his eyes still closed. Jeremy strode over and yelled, "Harvey, wake up!"

The man's eyes opened, and he dropped his hands from Emma's shoulders. "What?" he mumbled and rubbed a hand on his face. "What is it?"

Emma shook her head at Jeremy and said to Harvey, "Nothing. These two men want to help you to your room. You should get some sleep; it should be a long night."

"Yeah, I guess so." He stood, still looking a bit unsteady. Carmichael took one arm and Daniels the other. They moved with him to the staircase and upstairs to his room.

"I think we should also go up," Jeremy said to Emma.

"I think so, too," she agreed. "Where have you put us, Tony?"

"Third floor. The first and second room on the left."

They nodded. It was best to keep up the charade of the separate rooms, even though Tony knew of their relationship. They moved up to the rooms and met at the connecting door.

"These doors are convenient," stated Jeremy, pulling at his tie and unbuttoning the top of his white shirt. Emma removed the pins from her hair. The long braid dropped down her back. She reached up and started to undo it. They quickly undressed and climbed into the large four poster bed. Jeremy pulled her to him, and they went to sleep.

Time passed quickly and they were woken by a knock at the door. "Madam, dinner will be served in thirty minutes."

"Thank you!" she called as she yawned and raised her arms above her head to stretch. She looked over and saw Jeremy was still asleep.

She reached over and touched his face. "Sleepy head, it's time to wake up."

"Hmm," he responded, pulling her down to him and keeping his eyes shut.

"Enough of that now," said Emma briskly. "We need to get up and get dressed to go down to dinner."

He released her and reluctantly opened his eyes. "We need to plan a vacation and take Henrietta with us." They had a beach house in South Carolina that they used to relax between cases.

"I think she might like that," she said. The ocean had a calming effect on them during a stressful case. "We'll have to wait for a long school break."

"That's true. School means a lot to her. We can discuss it after this case."

Emma moved to the side of the bed and reached for her combination chemise and drawers. She slipped on her top and bottom before adding on the corset. Jeremy came up and helped pull her laces and secured them. Her petticoat and dress came next.

While she buttoned up her blouse, Jeremy dressed quickly. He ran his fingers through his hair.

Emma sat down and re-braided her hair before pulling it up into a bun on her head. Boots were pulled on and they separated to enter the hallway. They continued together to the sitting room to join Tony. Carmicheal stepped out of the dining room and announced that dinner had been served.

Tony said, "We need to let Hazel know."

"I can go up," suggested Emma.

The men nodded and Tony said, "We'll be in the dining room."

Emma went up and knocked on Hazel's door. She heard a thump and moved to put her ear against the door. "Come in," called Hazel.

Emma turned the knob. It opened easily, and she went in. Hazel lay in the bed.

"Did something fall?" Emma asked as she approached her.

Hazel moved her head on her pillow. "No, I don't think so."

"Time to get up, dinner is being served."

"Okay," Hazel said and stayed where she was.

Emma frowned and moved closer to her side. "I'll wait for you, and we can walk down together."

It became a contest of wills with Emma and Hazel not moving. Finally, Hazel pushed back the covers and got out of bed. She was still in her clothes.

"You didn't take the time to change?" Emma asked.

Hazel looked down. "I don't have anything else here with me."

"Where are your bags?"

"Still at Papa's apartment."

"We'll have to make arrangements to get them for you."

"That would be nice, thank you." Hazel patted her hair, and they went down the stairs together. The smell of dinner pulled them into the room.

"It smells wonderful," said Emma.

"It does," agreed Hazel.

They entered and found Tony, Harvey, and Jeremy waiting. They sat, prayers were said, and dinner served. Hazel waited until after dinner to say, "I'd like to stay here. I don't want to go to the site with you."

"Are you sure? We want to include you," Emma said.

"I want to stay here," Hazel said firmly.

Emma squinted at the girl. "If that's what you want."

They finished dinner and moved to the sitting room to wait.

"I'm going to go upstairs and lie down," Hazel announced.

Tony stood and asked, "Are you feeling okay? Do we need to call a doctor?"

"No, I'm just tired."

They watched as she walked upstairs. Emma whispered in Jeremy's ear, "I bet we'll have company tonight."

"Yeah, I'm not taking that bet," he whispered back.

Before he could respond, Carmichael appeared. "Sir, the wagon has arrived and is in the back."

Emma, Jeremy, and Harvey moved to the back door. "Ready?" Cole asked. They climbed into the back of the wagon and rolled out slowly to pick up Ellis. Once they arrived, Jeremy helped Emma down and Harvey followed them to the door. They knocked and quickly found themselves face to face with Henrietta.

"Emma! Jeremy!" She squealed and hugged them quickly. "Come in." She saw Harvey enter but didn't question his presence. It was a full house as Lottie and Patrick joined them in the foyer to greet them.

"Busy night," Emma observed as she leaned down to kiss Patrick and Lottie on the head.

Abbey joined them. Her hair had come loose, and she appeared to be out of breath. "I'm having a wonderful time. Come into the sitting room." There, they found Ellis surrounded by books, games, cards, and toys.

"I thought Harvey was going to accompany you," he said.

"What?" Emma exclaimed, looking around behind them.

"Don't worry," Jeremy told her. "Pops hasn't let him out of his sight." His father removed Harvey when they were talking to the children in the foyer.

They stayed for a while longer, listening to everyone talk about their plans for the night. "Hen," said Jeremy, putting an arm over her shoulder. "How's school going?"

She looked up at him. "Good, I have several projects I'm working on."

"*We*," Ellis corrected. "That one is keeping me on my toes."

Jeremy smiled. "I'm glad." He ruffled her hair. "Are you enjoying your time here?"

"I am." She leaned toward him and whispered, "But I'm looking forward to all of us being at home."

"Us, too," he whispered back.

"Jeremy," said Emma and she nudged him. He looked to where she was gesturing and saw Cole wave at them.

"Time to get organized," she said. They moved to the doorway to follow Cole to the study.

They entered the room together. Harvey brightened when he saw them; the plans were coming together. "Almost time to go get my money."

Cole looked at his watch and said to the group, "I think it's time to go." They started out the front and he said, "Back door. We moved everything to the back."

They filed out to the wagons. Cole mentioned as everyone loaded in, "I have Pinkerton guards set up around the perimeter. Just in case of trouble."

Harvey sat with Emma in the back of the second wagon. "You think Arthur'll be there?" he asked, his voice cracking.

"I'm counting on it. We aren't just on a mission to find the money; we're also trying to capture a murderer."

The group had worked it out that, when they found the money, they'd return to the hotel. That way, if they were being followed, the hotel would provide a smaller location to corner Arthur.

The wagons moved through town, the darkness covering their path. They arrived at Peggy's old neighborhood and went directly to the house. Emma, Jeremy, and Harvey jumped down and moved toward the tree. There was no reason to hide their wagons; the area was empty at night.

Emma pulled out her portable kerosene lantern. "Little girl," called Ellis.

"Yes, Papa," she said and walked over to him.

"I have something with a bit more shine to it." He showed her what he was carrying. It was a larger version of her lantern.

This one was not only bigger, but it had a reflector to help guide the light.

"Perfect," she said. Once lit, she shined it toward the mirror in the tree. It reflected a beam back down to ground. She hit the ground with her boot, making a dent, and said, "I think this is it."

The soil was quite loose; Jeremy and Cole moved in with shovels. It was a matter of minutes before they hit something metal. They knelt and worked to clear the dirt from the box and off the sides to allow it to be reached. It was heavy. Harvey and Jeremy reached down to lift it out.

Breathing hard, Harvey said, "Well, open it."

Emma nodded to them, and Jeremy used the shovel to knock the lock off. He knelt and pulled open the lid.

"Wow!"

The others got a good look at what was inside. There was a piece of paper in the very empty box. Harvey reached in a shaking hand and took out the paper. He unfolded it slowly. "Why, it's only a name! Where's the damn money?" He clenched the paper tightly.

"Harvey," said Emma, "can I see it?"

He slowly unclenched his hand and gave it to her. Emmy smoothed out the note. Jeremy raised his eyebrows in surprise. There was a name on the paper—Nathan Lombard, their new accountant!

Jeremy took the paper and moved it to his pocket. Emma continued to examine the dark box. "Wait," she said, "there's something here."

They all stood still as she reached in and pulled out a cloth bag. She opened it and poured the contents into her hand. Jewels flowed into her hand; one of them was the bracelet shown in the painting.

Harvey seemed stunned as he reached out to touch the bracelet. "He kept it."

"What's the significance of the bracelet?"

He looked down and back to her. "It was the first thing we went after, when it was just the two of us."

"Put it back," Cole said. "We'll need it for the next part of the plan. This is what I think we should do next."

Jeremy and Emma listened and nodded. They huddled up to discuss the plan but didn't include Harvey.

"Agreed," Emma said. "We deal with Nathan later, but this first."

The items secured and the box closed, they made their way to the wagons.

"Harvey, you haven't run away," observed Emma.

"Why haven't I run? Well, initially, I was afraid I'd be murdered."

"And now?"

"Now, I want to see how this is going to play out."

As Jeremy and Emma started to climb into the wagon, Emma stopped him and said, "I think Peggy and Hazel will want something." She moved to the tree and grabbed the bottom limb to pull herself up.

Jeremy shook his head and walked over and took her by the waist. "I think I can do that for you. I assume you're after that piece of mirror?"

"I am."

He grabbed the first limb and used it to climb into the tree. Navigating the large limbs, he reached the mirror tied to the tree with a wool string.

"Careful," she called.

He didn't comment; instead, he pocketed the mirror and climbed to the ground. He handed it to her. "Happy now?"

"Very," she said. "I want Peggy to remember her brother, not the man he became."

They walked back to the wagon and were transported to the hotel. A block away, the wagons stopped. Jeremy and Harvey jumped down, each carrying one side of the box. Emma accompanied them and the wagons moved on.

"Time for the next step," Jeremy said.

Emma nodded her head. "People who've been in the shadows in this case need to be brought into the light."

When they entered the hotel, they didn't try to hide the box. They wanted to be seen. They walked through the lobby, making their way to the elevator.

"Is that what I think it is?" Pete asked, looking at the large box.

"It is indeed. The thing that everyone's been looking for," she said without explaining further.

Pete pulled the lever and the elevator started up.

Once they reached their floor, all three exited. Emma stood next to Jeremy as he opened the door to her room. "Is he still there?" asked Emma, looking at the door.

Jeremy said, "Yes, and watching us closely."

Emma turned to Pete and said, "I don't think we need anything else, thank you."

"Oh, I might wait for a few minutes in case I'm needed," he said innocently.

They looked at him, then entered the room. Harvey and Jeremy put the box on top of the small desk.

Emma sat down on the bed. "Now…" she began.

A knock sounded and Jeremy started to answer it. Emma stopped him. "I've got it." At the door, she called, "Who is it?"

"Tony."

Emma hurriedly opened the door and, when she saw him, she grabbed him by the coat and pulled him in. "Hey!" he exclaimed. She locked the door behind him.

Tony looked around the room and spotted the box. "You found the money?"

"We found what Teddy wanted us to find," said Emma noncommittally.

"Did the mirror work?"

"We were able to use it to reflect the light and locate the box," Jeremy confirmed.

"Wow."

"We also kept the mirror for Peggy," Emma told him.

"She'll like that," he said. "It will remind her of him as a boy, experimenting with light."

"Tony," Emma asked, "what're you doing here?"

"It's Hazel. She's gone. Peggy's worried and asked me to find her."

Emma looked at Jeremy. "Pay up, sucker."

"If you'll remember, I didn't take that bet," he commented.

"What do you know?" Tony asked, his voice higher with his stress. "Do you think she was taken? Should we be looking for her?"

Emma halted his excited statements. "Tony, I don't think she was taken."

"Why not?"

"Because I think she's more involved in this than we thought."

Harvey laughed suddenly. "Her papa was like that. One minute your best friend and the next stealing you blind. The apple didn't fall far from that tree."

"She's part of this? But she's so young," Tony remarked, reaching up to rub his neck.

"We think that she has help," Emma said simply.

"But who could it be?"

"Pete."

"The guy that did the painting. How does he know Hazel?"

"Did you see the young guy running the elevator?" Jeremy asked him.

"Him? You think he has Hazel?" he asked and headed to the door. "I want to talk to him."

Jeremy grabbed his arm. "He doesn't have her. But we think

they're working together. We can't rush out there without a plan." He looked over at Emma.

"I'll go," she said. "We need that young man to talk."

She opened the door and headed to the elevator. The doors opened and she murmured, "Perfect timing." He must have been waiting for her with the doors closed.

"Need a ride?" he asked innocently, holding the cage door open for her.

"Hmm," she said and walked into the small space with him.

"So, you have the money now. Is it over?" he asked, keeping his back to her as he operated the lever.

When she didn't answer, he turned toward her. Emma was holding her long knife, examining its long edge. "What are you doing with that?" he shouted. He pulled the lever, and the elevator abruptly came to a stop between floors. The sudden stop caused both to stumble, the knife coming dangerously close to Pete's throat. "Hey, watch out!"

"Not to worry," Emma said, stepping back, though she still held the knife in her hand. "I won't cut you." He started to look relieved. "Unless you don't answer my questions."

"Questions?" Pete swallowed, following her knife with his eyes.

"Hazel. Where is she? I know there's something more going on with you two than you've shared." Pete's mouth tightened and he stayed silent. *He's protecting Hazel,* she thought. She chose another tactic. "Pete, I want to help Hazel. Her family wants to know where she is. They're worried about her."

The elevator suddenly started to move down slowly. "What?" he exclaimed. "I'm not doing that."

"I wonder," Emma said and looked around. "Pete, I think it's time that we get out of here."

"But how?"

She sheathed her knife back into her pocket and said, "Up, and we need to hurry." She looked at him. "Pete, I need a boost."

He looked conflicted but didn't want to know who was going to be there when the doors opened. He made his decision quickly and immediately cupped his hands. He lifted Emma to the ceiling, and she pushed on the panel there. It popped open and he pushed her higher. Once she was on top, she reached back down and held out her hands for him. He backed up and took two steps forward to jump. She got a good grip on his hand and pulled him up.

They were on top of the slowly moving elevator. She grabbed onto the ladder attached to the wall. They climbed to the closed doors one floor up. Emma reached for her knife and used it to wedge the doors open. Pete climbed up behind her and they both pried the doors open. They made their way out into the hallway. "Shut the doors," she ordered.

He closed them. "What now? He's going to know we aren't there."

"Up the stairs and back to my room," she said, turning toward the stairway.

"No! I need to go to Hazel. She's at risk from him."

"Him?"

"Arthur. You told her that he killed her father."

Emma sighed. *Damn it, I knew this would happen.* "Pete, what did she do?"

He looked shamefaced and hung his head low. "She told him you would be bringing the money here."

"Why?"

"She wanted him exposed."

"We need to find her. Where did you see her last?"

"Downstairs in the lobby."

"First, we get Jeremy." They ran up the stairs and went to her door. She knocked and waited. Jeremy answered and saw that she and Pete stood there. She briefed him quickly and looked at Harvey. "Stay here with that box." He nodded and sat back down. "Tony, come with us."

The four ran quickly down the stairs and, as they exited into the lobby, they heard a girl scream. "It must be Hazel!" Pete cried. The scream came again from the ballroom. They started to run toward it.

"Wait," Emma said. She thought about what was under the floor. Pete tried to pull her toward the ballroom when Hazel screamed again.

"We have to go help her!" he said desperately.

"We will," she said. "I have a plan." They listened to her intently.

"Yeah, that's a good idea," agreed Jeremy. He looked over at the desperate young man. "Pete, come with me."

"But why? I don't understand!"

"You will. Follow me."

He looked conflicted but followed Jeremy and Tony to the basement.

Emma ran to the ballroom and tried the door. It was locked. She was too angry to take the time to pick the lock, so she reared back and kicked at the doors to force it open. They hit the wall with a bang and Emma stepped into the room. A scream sounded in the large space. "Let her go!" Emma shouted to the man's back.

The man whirled around, taking his captive with him.

Emma's eyes went wide, and she saw it wasn't Hazel, but Peggy!

Peggy bit the man's large hand and, when he jerked it away, Peggy yelled, "It's Papa, Emma. He killed Teddy!"

Emma strolled slowly toward a round table surrounded by chairs. "So, you're their father. We've heard quite a bit about you."

The man's brows lowered, and he growled. "Was it you?" he asked his daughter.

"No Father, not me."

"I'm not the bad guy here. Theodore tried to kill me! Me, his own father! He's the reason I almost died. I had to pull myself out of that building and find someone to help me. It was a long time until I was able to walk again."

"And when you did?"

"I searched for the little snot. Oh, I was patient. I waited; I planned. I knew he'd come here. To her," he jeered. He pointed at Emma. "Now, you'll give me the money and you can also hand over Harvey. He and I have some things to discuss before I'm finished with him."

"So, let me get this straight," Emma asked. "First, I give you the money, and I turn over Harvey so that you can kill him?"

"Yes," he said triumphantly. "That's exactly it."

"Oh, I don't think so." Emma grabbed a chair and threw it toward him.

"What the hell are you doing?" he demanded, moving back, dragging his cane with one hand and Peggy with the other.

Emma needed to get close to Peggy. "I have an idea. Why don't you let Peggy go and I'll get the money and Harvey for you."

"No! I want them here or I won't let her go!"

"Now, Arthur—it is Arthur Smith, isn't it? Or is it Max Winsten, master detective?" she taunted.

"It's neither. I'm Aloysius Latimer, father of these two ungrateful brats."

"Very well, Aloysius, why would I leave Peggy with you? I can't trust that you won't hurt her while I'm gone. Why don't you let her sit down? If you do that, I'll make the arrangements."

He tightened his arm around Peggy's neck, and she screamed again. "Fine, fine. She's hurting my ears anyway. Such a screamer, that one." He shoved her away. Emma held out her hand and Peggy took it. Emma led her to a chair.

She needed him to move that club leg and cane. She distanced herself from Peggy and decided to bait him. "By all accounts, you were a bastard of a father, putting your kids to work when they were too young to know any different. Plus, all the beatings and belittling you did to them. Heh, I gotta tell you, you deserved everything Teddy did to you."

"You have no right to say anything like that to me!"

"Oh, really? How about if I tell you Teddy didn't leave any money? The box we found? It was empty."

"NO! That's not true. Theodore lived in an expensive apartment; he had art, expensive furnishings. I know there was money! There must be money. You..." he stammered. "You're lying. And I'll make you give it to me." He lifted his cane to pound it into the floor; Emma waited for the signal.

At that moment, she heard a voice behind her, and Emma watched the man freeze.

"Really, Grandfather," Hazel said.

Emma turned and saw Hazel there with a gun trained on him. She sighed. *Damn it, I was so close.* "Hazel, put the gun down."

"No, I don't think so." She turned her attention to her grandfather. "Papa wanted you dead and I think I should make that happen for him."

"You? You're my granddaughter?" Latimer scoffed. "Figures he'd have a useless girl."

"I'll show you how useless I am." She cocked the gun and pointed it at him with a steady hand.

"See here, young woman! I will not have this." He pounded the floor with a cane.

Suddenly, he disappeared from view. Peggy, Emma, and Hazel stared at the blank space left by the man. They walked carefully over to the hole in the floor and glanced down. Jeremy, Tony, and Pete stood with the collapsed man. Peggy asked, "Is he dead?"

Jeremy looked up. "If he's not, he's going to need a lot of bandages. Again."

"Jeremy, honestly," Emma scolded him.

Pete kneeled and checked Latimer for breathing. "Dead, finally."

Tony looked up. "Peggy! How did you get here?"

Emma answered for her, "That's a long story. Come up."

Peggy sighed and reached out her hand to Emma. Emma immediately put her arm around her waist and guided her back to her chair. "What happened? Why are you here?" Emma asked her.

She didn't answer that question. Instead, she looked around and said, "Emma! Hazel's gone again."

Emma whipped around. "Where is she?"

"I don't know. Family's hard to manage."

"Yes, it can be. How did he find you?"

"We were at home. Tony had gone to check on you at the hotel. I had Carmichael and our men and felt protected. He just showed up at the door." She shook her head. "Emma, I just couldn't believe what I was seeing. Father! It was the last thing I expected."

"How did he get you to go with him?"

"He had a gun on Carmichael. I told them I'd go. I knew you'd be here to help us."

"You know this could've gone badly."

"I couldn't let my father hurt anyone else. I just couldn't."

Cole rushed into the room. "Basement," Emma directed him.

"Do you need anything here?" Cole asked them as he directed his men to the basement.

"Emma, could you find Tony?" Peggy inquired. "I'd like to get home to the baby."

At that moment, Tony rushed to her side. She started to cry when she saw him.

Cole said, "Come on, we'll get you both home."

Jeremy joined her in the now empty ballroom. "Where is everyone?"

"Tony headed home with Peggy. She's worn out."

"Who contacted Cole for help?"

"I did, I sent a message over with one of the bellman," Harvey said from the door.

"I thought I told you to stay put," she said.

"Yeah, well, I thought I could help."

"You did," murmured Emma.

"So, let me get this straight," Harvey said. "Arthur was the detective Winsten, but he was also Teddy's father? And Teddy set up the last job just to off his old man? Now he comes back to start killing us off because of that?"

"Yep," Emma confirmed.

"Huh. And I thought my family had problems."

"Hey, where's Hazel?" Jeremy asked.

"I don't know. She disappeared after Latimer died."

He continued to look around. "Poor kid."

"She's a strong kid. She'd planned to kill him; she had a gun. I don't know what would've happened if the floor hadn't dropped out."

"Where's Pete?" asked Jeremy.

"Probably with Hazel," Harvey said.

"Basement!" they all said together.

The three headed down, walking past Cole and the men retrieving the body. Jake was taking pictures and didn't acknowledge them as they passed. They hurried down the hallway and to Pete's room. They tried the door. When it wouldn't open, Emma called, "We want to talk to you both. Open the door, please." When it still didn't open, Emma leaned on it and said, "Hazel, you know I don't need a key."

The door eased open, and Pete stood there. He moved back to allow entry.

Hazel sat on the bed; she'd been crying. She looked at Emma. "I would've killed him."

"I know," said Emma, sitting on the bed next to her. It was said without judgment.

Hazel frowned. "You aren't shocked."

"Should I be? You lost your father to that monster."

Hazel fell back on the bed.

Emma looked between Pete and Hazel; this was the first time she'd seen them in the same room. Her gaze moved to Pete's hand gripping Hazel's. It was the first time she had seen him without gloves; he had rather large hands. The morgue flashed into her mind. Teddy's hands were an unusual size. The hands that had gripped Peggy had been similar to Teddy's and now Pete's. "Are you two related?" she asked.

Jeremy looked startled. "You're married?"

"Eww. No," Hazel said, and she and Pete started laughing.

"You mutton head," Emma said. "I think they're brother and sister."

Hazel and Pete turned shocked eyes on Emma. "How did you know?"

"Your hands, your grandfather and father have the same hands."

Pete looked at his. "Yes, I kept them in gloves and tried not to call attention to them."

"We're actually twins," Hazel said.

"Hazel was sent to our grandmother," Pete said.

"And Pete was sent to live with an artist friend in Paris."

Harvey spoke up. "Teddy wanted them safe, but he'd always planned to bring them back together as a family. What he hadn't expected was that Pete and Hazel would be in contact and start to look for him."

Emma grinned. "Tony has an artist in the family. Won't they be surprised?"

CHAPTER 17

arvey, Hazel, Pete, Tony, Cole, Emma, and Jeremy exited the elevator into Nathan's office. It was a large office with many desks. They walked toward the main door at the far end of the room. It opened suddenly, and Nathan came out. "Jeremy, Emma, Cole, welcome." When he saw their serious faces, he stopped and asked, "Has something happened?"

Rather than answering, Cole asked, "Can we talk?"

"Of course. Let's move into my office." He frowned as Harvey, Hazel, and Tony joined them. After they sat at a round table, he asked, "What's this about?"

Cole nodded to Emma to start.

"Did you know Teddy Latimer?" she asked.

"I did," he said slowly.

"In what way?" asked Jeremy.

"I managed some accounts for him and other private matters."

"Since when?"

"When he moved to Chicago, I met him at a function at the museum. We got to talking and he wanted to meet me for some investment advice."

"Did you help him sell some diamonds?" asked Emma.

Nathan didn't say anything. Instead, he walked to his desk, opened his drawer, and pulled out a small black bag. He walked back to them and sat. What he did next stunned them; he opened it and let the diamonds drop onto the table. They spilled across the surface and fell to the floor.

"Hey!" Harvey exclaimed and tried to grab them.

Nathan made no move to stop them. "The diamonds aren't worth anything. They're extremely poor quality."

"What!" Harvey said as he stopped trying to gather them up. "What do you mean? We got these from dealers!"

"You did," Nathan agreed, "but Teddy had that planned."

"Planned?"

"Teddy worked with the store owners to get the bad stones he wanted out. He thought that would end it."

"Then what was the last job for?"

Emma supplied, "To get rid of his father."

"That's what he said all right. He couldn't get away from the man and thought this was the only way." He looked lost. "So, there was never any money. He didn't meet with us because he had nothing to share from that last job." Harvey dropped his head to the table; he'd lost three friends and the money.

Hazel sighed. It wasn't her focus, but she'd hoped there would be something for her and Pete.

"Oh, there's money," Nathan said.

Harvey's head raised immediately. "What're you talking about? You said these were worthless."

"Those are. He had other money from investments that he made when he got here. He also held on to his share of the jewelry over the years."

So, still no money for me, thought Harvey. He shrugged. *That's the way it is, I guess.* Drawing a line through his thoughts for the future, he stood abruptly, and the chair dropped to the ground behind him. He left it there and said, "I guess I'm out now?"

"Wait, Mr. Simms," Nathan said.

Harvey hesitated.

"The money is for you, Peggy, Pete, and Hazel."

"Just a minute," Cole said. "Any money needs to go to restitution of the thefts."

"No, I don't think so," Nathan said. He saw their confused looks. "No, I don't mean I'd bypass the law." He winked at Emma. "At least, not this time." He looked at the group. "Teddy has been working on paying back all of the stores that had been robbed. I helped him with that and documented the transactions."

"Can I review those?" Cole asked.

"Of course, I think you'll find all is in order."

"How much is left for us?" Pete asked.

He wrote a number and handed it to Pete. His eyes goggled and he shared the number with the group.

"All right then, we share that?" Harvey asked gleefully as he rubbed his hands together. Things were looking up.

"No," Nathan replied. Their faces dropped. He hastened to assure them. "That's the amount *each* of you will get. And since there was money set aside for Eddie and Louis, their shares will be divided among you also."

The stunned group learned how their money would be distributed.

As they left, Tony took Pete and Hazel with him. Peggy was excited about her family living with her. Tony wasn't as sure, but he wanted Peggy to be happy, so he'd do anything for her.

Harvey looked more lost with the money than without. He looked down at his hands.

"What's the matter, big guy?" asked Emma. "You finally got your money."

"I don't know," he said and held out his hands. "I didn't plan on what would happen after the money was found. Teddy really did care about me."

"He cared about all three of you—you were all listed," Nathen reminded him.

"I know."

"Harvey, you said that you didn't like being a priest because you weren't able to help the people you wanted to help," Emma said.

"That's right, though it feels like a lifetime ago now. I'm probably unredeemable."

"Oh, I don't know about that," she said, drumming her fingers on her lips.

Jeremy followed her train of thought and asked, "Would Claire mind?"

"Why would she mind? She redeemed herself. I think he could definitely help and probably guide support to other areas of the community."

"You think you can include me in the planning for my future?" Harvey asked dryly.

"Yes. We run a charity," Emma began.

"Hey, I don't take charity," he protested.

"You're not taking charity but giving. I'm thinking you could work with our charity director and extend some to the community here and later into other cities where we operate."

"Helping people, me?" Harvey asked, more to himself than to them.

Emma answered anyway. "Yeah, I think this can work. Harvey, would you like a room in our boarding house?"

Great, another specialist, an ex-priest con man, Jeremy thought. *This oughta be fun.* He followed Emma and Harvey out as Emma was telling the man about her plans for him.

EPILOGUE

*E*mma and Harvey stood on the steps of the Holy Name Cathedral, looking at the building.

"Are you going back to the priesthood?" she asked.

"No. Maybe. I don't know. I just know I need to cleanse my soul," he replied.

"Want me to go in with you?"

"No. I need to do this on my own."

"Good luck." Emma stood on her toes and kissed his cheek. "I'll see you at home."

Harvey watched her walk away and then moved up the steps into the cathedral. He headed to a confession booth, found one empty, went in, and sat down. The screen opposite him opened and Harvey made the sign of the cross.

"Bless me, Father, for I have sinned."

HISTORICAL NOTES

The Priest scam also called the 'Man of the Cloth' dates back to 1890 in New Castle, PA. A man, disguised as Father McGurk visited a jewelry store and asked to see gifts for the cardinal, he was given an assortment of diamonds to review. He took off with them, never to be seen again.

Skipper and the Chicago World's Fair. Turn's out Emma and Ethan were wrong about Skipper. His story was an actual civil suit. The city tried many times to evict him but his maintained his hold on the land and resisted all evictions efforts. Eventually the area became known as Streeterville, named for George. His legacy survives to this day, Streeterville is a vibrant part of Chicago.

Notebook Mysteries

Books
1-2-3

KIMBERLY
MULLINS

ABOUT THE AUTHOR

Kimberly Mullins is the author of series of books titled "Notebook Mysteries". Her stories are based on historical events occurring in 1871-1890's Chicago. She holds a BS in Biology and a MBA in Business. She lives in Texas with her husband and son. When she is not writing she is working as a Process Safety Engineer at a large chemical company. You can connect with her on her website www.kimberlymullinsauthor.com.

Photo Credit: Blessings of Faith Photography

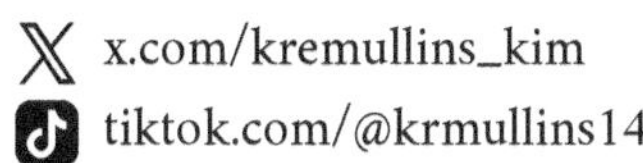

www.ingramcontent.com/pod-product-compliance
Lightning Source LLC
Chambersburg PA
CBHW070449300726
48975CB00007B/2092